About the Author

Keith Cornwell studied both engineering and philosophy as an undergraduate student in London. Engineering led to his gainful employment as a researcher, teacher, Professor, Dean and such things in Edinburgh and latterly in the Middle East. Philosophy led to wondering what it is all about.

His writing has been largely scientific non-fiction and this is his first venture into the realms of fiction. Here on Mars he has the freedom to probe accepted earthbound ideas of the meaning of life.

Dedication

This book is dedicated to my wife, Sheila and family, Robert and Tessa for their encouragement and forbearance.

Keith Cornwell

OUR MAN ON MARS

AUSTIN MACAULEY PUBLISHERS™

LONDON • CAMBRIDGE • NEW YORK • SHARJAH

A CIP catalogue record for this title is available from the British Library.

ISBN 9781528993180 (Paperback)
ISBN 9781528993197 (ePub e-book)

www. austinmacauley. com

First Published (2021)
Austin Macauley Publishers Ltd
25 Canada Square
Canary Wharf
London
E14 5LQ

Tell all the truth but tell it slant
    Success in circuit lies.
Too bright for our infirm delight
    The truth's superb surprise.
As lightning to the children eased
    With explanation kind,
The truth must dazzle gradually
    Or every man be blind.

EMILY DICKINSON

1

The Consultation

STEVE McKAY SHOULD have felt on top of the world that morning sitting in his chaplaincy study with his first cup of coffee. The fact that he did not was due to it being Mars and not the world and to a tinge of discomfort with his lot. In spite of all the excitement of leaving the green pastures of Scotland to travel to another planet and the challenge of serving as chaplain in the most remote parish in the universe, he had become a trifle bored. There was plenty to do on a day by day basis, it was not that sort of boredom but rather the sheer weariness of being in a position where he was programmed to act out an expected role. In this role, he was perceived by the residents as somewhat aloof and distant and that was not really him.

The UN Interplanetary Committee had discerned that major impediments to the survival of the first colony on Mars would not be technical alone. There were medical matters which were addressed by shipping out plenty of medics but there were also potential human hazards in the areas of physiology, sociology, psychology and half a dozen other ologies not to mention spiritual matters. The armed forces across the world had appointed chaplains to deal with these issues and, if that was fine for Earth, it should be fine for Mars. How Steve McKay came to be that chaplain is a strange story for later but this morning here he was, sitting in his wee office in the chaplaincy under the vast Central Dome of the Mars village, feeling somewhat misunderstood.

It was not that his colleagues were dismissive of his role or unsupportive; in fact, if anything that was part of the problem, they treated him with kid gloves, with an air of distant respect. When they came to consult with him on a person to person basis, it had overtones of patient to doctor or confessor to priest which he found uncomfortable and not the role he wanted. If he went to the Mars Bar for a half-pint of beer (the allowance , brewed from hops in the greenhouse tunnels) he felt the folk adopting more formal language than normal or holding back on ribald stories in deference to his presence. Perhaps they thought he had some special knowledge and insight, even on Mars. It contributed to his growing sense of remoteness and isolation. However, all that was due to change over the next few months and it started with a knock on his door which brought him down to Earth, sorry Mars, with a bang.

He abandoned his musing and opened the door. She had jet-black hair, long enough to reach the shoulders of her light blue Mars village Gilet and big smiling brown eyes that completely disarmed him. He stared at her for a few seconds before his normal politeness prevailed and he wished her a good Mars day and offered her a chair by his desk.

"I had difficulty finding your room because I've only been in the Central Dome a few times, they encourage us to stay in our residential domes, you know."

He then remembered that a Dr Jo Thanawala had been referred to him by John Abraham, the head of the Biology Section because it was thought she might be suffering from some form of depression.

"Yes I'd noticed that too," he observed. "I know we need these massive domes to protect us against the high radiation and to create a suitable environment but they do rather segregate folk. Which dome are you housed in?"

"Dome D, which I'm told is meant to signify Dubai."

"That's right. Apparently, the United Arab Emirates did much of the groundwork on living in a gigantic dome because it suited them as they already had the experience of air-conditioning large spaces in the desert. The temperatures there can reach 50 degrees in the summer you know."

He realised he was slipping into an agreeable discourse with his client rather addressing the reason for her being there.

"So why have you been asked to venture from Dome D to the chaplaincy this morning? While your name was placed on my consultation listing, no reason was given for the consultation at this unearthly hour."

"It's sure unearthly!" she commented, but he just looked at her so she carried on, "Well, it's slightly embarrassing but essentially, I was 15 minutes late at my workstation."

"And they've sent you here for that alone?"

"Well, not quite alone, I was late three or four times running actually. I explained to my head of Section that I did set my cabin alarm but had vivid dreams as I woke up and could not break out of them into the real world—well real Mars."

Steve stroked his beard thoughtfully. His was the only beard allowed among the residents, a concession that he had fought hard to achieve. He explained to her, as he had to several folk before, "You are probably suffering from Celestial Depression (CD) which is a common response of the human system to the shock of finding, on waking

11

in the morning, that it is on a remote planet; it will pass with time. Meanwhile, I would recommend you take the special medication developed by the authorities for this condition. It's a sedative which gives an adrenaline boost on waking and it's available from the Medical Centre."

"But you must know this," he added, "it would have been part of your training before you came to Mars?"

"Yes, I read about CD," she admitted, "although I'm a space biologist, not a medic. There are so many of these odd things we're meant to recognise, all with important-sounding acronyms that merge into a meaningless jumble. I had thought CD would be like waking up after a bad night but it's really weird and disorientating. What I really hate is not being able to get up and just walk outside into the fresh air. There's nowhere on earth where you can't do that."

"Actually, that's not the case," said Steve, "As it happens, I was in Dubai a few years ago and in the Summer, the temperature and humidity were so high that if you went outside for 10 minutes you were ringing with sweat; it was pouring down your legs, dripping off your nose, your eyes itched and you had to retreat back into the air-conditioned space indoors. If you were bald and went out without head covering you would end up in a dermatology unit having your cranium examined; folk just stayed in their air-conditioned homes. If you wanted to walk it had to be round and round the Malls until lured by the Arabic coffee aroma into a café. Eventually, you get used to it; there's no evidence that the people in Dubai suffer, in fact, they rate pretty well on the happiness scales. So, on that note, I'll tick the CD box on your assessment record."

"But you are not bald," she observed.

"I said *if you were* bald," he responded a little irritability as he realised the point he was making had been completely lost owing to her circumspection with some physical feature of his.

"OK, I see, so that's me with a tick in my CD box and appropriately ticked off. You psycho-analysing people think you've solved issues once you've categorised them with a neat acronym."

"I don't see that as my role here at all and remember, you were referred to me by the Council for being late for work several times, a *deviation from the norm which may signify some deeper issue,* they said. Was there anything else that you wished to raise?"

"You mean any *other* deviations?" she volunteered with a smile.

"Well, just anything relevant to include in my record," he said, realising that the word *deviation* did sound a little pejorative.

"Nothing apart from being pregnant."

He just looked at her for a minute in horror.

"Pregnant! Pregnant, you can't be, it's not allowed, you've only recently arrived on Mars and they screen you for all that sort of thing before you come here and—Oh dear, it'll cause a major rumpus; you'll have to terminate you know, and you cannot get back to earth for nearly a year. Oh, dear."

"I'm JOKING, just joking," she said, turning to laughter, "but you sounded so robotic I just couldn't resist; although it's *very* interesting to know what your reaction would be!"

He recognised he'd been a little pompous but she immediately diffused his awkwardness by asking politely about his role as a chaplain on Mars and what it involved. He explained how he was expected to offer similar services to the population on Mars that he would have done in a parish on Earth, that is to be their local Vicar, Priest, Pastor, Imran, Rabbi or, as in Scotland, their local Minister. He was expected to offer care and support and perform ceremonial duties such as funerals and give advice and comfort to those in crisis.

"And guidance to people like me when the authorities think I need it," she ventured.

"Yes, that too and with the growing community on Mars with all their different cultural backgrounds, it merges into care in the widest sense together with the performance of civic and religious functions."

"That's quite a responsibility with the diverse lot here in mind from what I've seen," she said, "I suppose, the authorities thought it would be a calming influence on the community—stop us killing one and other when the remoteness sunk in. Out of all the people who might be asked to perform this duty, how did *you* come to be selected for this odd position?"

Steve was beginning to feel uncomfortable at the drift of the conversation with his new client.

"That is a long and involved story for another time," he said vacantly staring into the distance. Then, focusing back on the matter in hand, he gave her a quick look and added, "Meanwhile, can you appease the Council and earn yourself some credit points by demonstrating that you can be punctual for work, perhaps by taking the medication and setting your alarm half an hour earlier. That way, you can enjoy the luxury of your waking thoughts and still be at your workstation on time."

"Maybe," she admitted, "and that gives you a credit point too as another case resolved."

"Yes, something like that."

"OK," she said, smiling and rising to leave. "Sometime, I would like to hear more about how you came to be doing this job, but that can wait until it's not early morning and we don't have a hundred more immediate and boring things to attend to."

As Jo walked back from the Central Dome through the link tunnel to Dome D, she wondered whether she should have said *boring things*. Mention of boredom was not politically correct on Mars and the groovy Mars drum band had even written a *risqué* song about it called BYPO (Boring your Pants Off) which had been played late one Saturday night in the Mars Bar. Boredom was recognised as a serious problem and a disincentive to potential recruits for the Mars programme. If he had ticked that Box on her assessment form it might be a pity.

Steve was also wondering about something. Her question about him being the chaplain on Mars and why he had accepted such a position had recently been bothering him too, now that he had been there for six months and the novelty was wearing off. Many would ask why at this time in the mid-2030s he had given up a cushy life among the lush green parishes of Scotland, to literally reach for the skies. There would, of course, have been challenges especially as the Church was in crisis with so few ministers and so few folk attending but at least it was a well-worn route. What had caused him to take the path less trodden? He needed to think it through and be ready with a plausible explanation as he was sure to be asked time and time again.

2

The Green Green Grass of Home

BOREDOM WAS INDEED an occupational hazard on Mars and it occasioned much research at top universities. Academics from around the world held Boring Conferences at exotic locations and published their findings in JOBS, the Journal of Boring Studies (which also advertised vacancies in the field). It was generally argued that boredom led to severe introspection and the Authorities were keen to prevent this so they devised hundreds of minor duties to keep the folk on Mars busy. While Steve, as we saw, found his role as chaplain somewhat uncomfortable, it at least had the advantage of protecting him from some of the more irksome of these duties and therefore time to think. Jo had phased him a little by raising the question of why he had left the Earth and he fell to contemplating how he had become the Church's Man on Mars.

He had been born at the turn of the Millennium into a homely middle-class family in North Berwick, a pleasant harbour town near Edinburgh. He went to the local primary school at the bottom of the Law, that extinct volcanic hill just to the South the town, now completely surrounded by houses. On Sundays, he attended one of the Town's Sunday Schools at the insistence of his Church-going parents. At the age of ten, his father found a new job in Harwell, Berkshire at the Atomic Energy Authority so they moved South to England. Stephen, their only child, progressed well but in no distinguished way at the local School and obtained a place on a *Space Engineering* course at Middlesex University. At the time, the competition to attract school leavers into engineering was intense leading to the non-research orientated universities struggling and having to brush up their courses with sexy titles. The course was almost entirely self-study of conventional engineering enlivened by a few retired astronauts who had been enlisted to give guest lectures. Steve obtained a B-level honours but by then, he had become disillusioned with the sheer complication of engineering and the obsessive degree of assessment his course entailed. His secondary or liberal subject had been sociology which seemed to be more fun and a little easier, so on completion, he kept his eye open for something which involved people rather than purely engineering.

In the event, he undertook a contract job which, while it was in engineering, was also associated with the social aspects of space exploration. It involved the design of residential domes for Mars and was being undertaken by the United Arab Emirates government. Being based in Dubai was an attraction and the job was a little more exciting than those offered to his fellow students. The contract was for three years and he learnt how life could be lived in an artificial environment consisting of a Dome of 500 metres diameter stuck out in a desert. The Dome contained housing quarters, community centres (gym, café, bar etc) and a so-called *outdoors*, an area under glass and attached to the Dome but with gardens and vegetable allotments. This was the UAE's contribution to the international space programme and was staffed by people from many countries. Steve spent the first couple of years in Dubai working on the thermodynamics of the air-conditioning system and the last year actually in the Dome in the desert reporting on operational matters such as the effects of temperature and humidity on the residents. At the end of the contract, he was at a loose end and returned to his parent's home in Berkshire. After a week there, wallowing in home comforts, he yearned to start some new project in a completely different area.

Late that summer, he visited an aunt back in North Berwick, lured by the offer of a week or two of free food and accommodation and the chance to go to the Edinburgh Festival Fringe. Being only 25 miles from Edinburgh city centre and serviced by a good rail connection, North Berwick provided an excellent base. His aunt, his mother's sister, was a lively busy widow whose husband had died many years before of some cancer (now curable he understood) and whose only son lived in Australia. She was good fun, highly demanding and a superb cook and she took it upon herself to find him a proper job by scouring the job listings on the Internet. Come the first Sunday morning she insisted he came to the local Kirk with her.

"If you're going to laze around and eat me out of house and home you can at least come to the Kirk with me," which he grudgingly agreed to do *just once*. He had discerned that she wanted to show him off to her church folk and he went along with it as the price one pays for a free holiday. However, his aunt was unwittingly responsible for the next stage of his life on two counts.

Firstly, she drew his attention to a job advert on the Edinburgh page of the Local News App for a traveller care manager with Calrail the Scottish train company. Following a couple of interviews, where his *engineer-*

ing with sociology degree came in useful, and where his UAE experience created an interesting talking point, he was accepted for the post. After subsequent training, he settled well into the job with its smart office in Waverley Station and free travel. Secondly, one of the 'church ladies' whom he ended up chatting to over coffee after his duty trip to Kirk was actually a young single mother named Margo who homed in on this new arrival with all her charms. He got to know her well over the next few weeks having extended his stay (to give his parents a break, he told his aunt). He was also a real hit with her five-year-old son Bobby. When he later started his new job, the three became an item, eventually living together in Margo's flat in North Berwick. For appearance's sake and to appease his aunt and parents more than Margo, they got married using the new fast-track wedding service and had a party to celebrate. They became immersed in their jobs, hers being with an estate agent, and in the local life of North Berwick. This included joining the Opera group and helping with their annual productions (his idea), the local church (her idea) and the primary-level kids swimming pool competitions (Bobby's idea).

For two years, life flowed along amicably enough but then it all started falling apart. Calrail merged the Traveller Care Centre at Edinburgh with the one in Glasgow and as a result, Steve became second in command and had to travel to Glasgow. This was not to his liking and he foolishly resigned before ensuring his next job was in the bag. After floating around for several months and desperate for some meaningful vocation in life, he noticed an advert for a scholarship on a theology course at New College in Edinburgh, funded by the Church of Scotland who had plenty of money but no ministers. In this, he surprised his friends who, though aware he was a deep thinker , had not thought of him as being particularly devout. However, as he explained to them, it enabled him to be a student again and stay in Edinburgh which he loved. This was somewhat ingenious because he had always had an incipient belief embedded well within him but he did not explain that to his friends. Being raised in a church-going family meant he was well acquainted with the basics of Christianity and his period in the Middle East had given him plenty of time to contemplate such issues. There was no born-again moment or anything like that, just an abiding conviction that there was more to life than purely the material things.

It also surprised Margo who was hoping he would be the family breadwinner and thus enable her to live a life of comfort and security in her beloved North Berwick. While being associated with the church and involved in activities there, she certainly did not see her church role as being anything more than this. The possibility of ending up as the wife of a parish minister expected to offer support services to all and sundry was not to her liking and she spent many weeks trying to dissuade him. Attending and helping out at services and meetings was one thing, a lifetime of being linked to a church run by lots of committees who monitored your every step, expected you to be always on call, forced you to live in a tied house and paid you an abysmal salary by professional standards was another. Her work on conveyancing of properties at the local estate agency was fairly mundane and not too well paid but did provide enough for her and Bobby to survive. Coupling up with Steve had created possibilities for the future that were now dashed if he was to be a mature student and then a probationer and then after all this study, a minister, possibly ending up in some god-forsaken parish in the wilds. It led to some rather lively domestic infighting which became increasingly frequent and vocal and even led to the neighbours downstairs complaining on one occasion.

There was also an incident which sealed the fate of their marriage. Margo had been offered the lead role of Liza Doolittle in the local operatic society's rendition of My Fair Lady and Professor Higgins was played by the Town's heart throb, a certain highly attractive guy several years older than her with a mop of black hair and an arrogant casualness about him. Six months of working with him on rehearsals and the excitement of the performance nights led to a little more intimacy than strictly necessary for the acting roles. This, coinciding with tensions at home and a romantic incident while Steve was away on a course somewhere, had resulted in further deepening of her attachment to Heart Throb Higgins. When Steve returned, she felt obliged to tell him and, after a loud discussion which again disturbed the neighbours downstairs, he left in a pre-emptive fashion and found a studio flat on North Berwick seafront two days later. She thought he seemed more upset at leaving Bobby, by then a lively 8-year old, than her.

Two and a half years later, having immersed himself in college and Edinburgh life (but still retaining the flat in North Berwick) he graduated with an A-grade Honours Batchelor of Theology in Edinburgh University's McEwan Hall. He was totally separated from Margo by then but she was happy for him to see Bobby on occasions and he sometimes took him out for a day visiting places or watching Hearts play football. The newly-graduated Steve had no fixed idea of what he should do about his career which seemed to be in a mess. His upbringing together with the influence of the more pious lecturers on his theology course had instilled the need for prayer in

22

such a crisis but this yielded no results, at least that's what he thought at the time.

During the later stages of his course, he realised that he was less than enthusiastic about being a parish minister. Ministers had become a very rare breed, partly for the reasons that Margo, bless her, had discerned and partly because the job in his view had changed. Maybe he had just not had the *call* that one or two of his fellow students prominently claimed to have experienced. His tutor for the final year thesis was a kindly old Professor named Green. Professor Green was somewhat rotund with a mop of tight curly white hair (students called him cabbage green) and a rather aloof other-worldly style. He invited his final-year thesis students and others to his home and generally took an interest in them and Steve came to confide in him. When the Church of Scotland decreed at one of their annual General Assemblies that henceforth ministers would operate from Hubs and that the country would be divided into 32 such hubs within which each constituent church would be visited at least once per month, Steve became totally disillusioned about undertaking parish ministry. As he explained to Prof Green, he would have enjoyed the care and spiritual aspects of the work but saw it becoming a constant grind of administrative functions overlaid with scrutinising committees. Prof Green suggested he just kept his eyes open and awaited a call that he could not resist. That was all very well Steve thought but he had to find a job as soon as possible to keep his flat in North Berwick going now that his grant was finished. He started to search for a university or armed forces chaplaincy position; he could not avoid noticing that these jobs attracted salaries that were more aligned with other professions. There was also a deeper reason why he declined to follow the well-worn path of parish ministry. His association with space engineering and his time in Dubai had left him with a wanderlust after something beyond a cosy existence among friendly folk in familiar surroundings.

Looking back now from his viewpoint on Mars, he realised it was a *flat earth* time of his life, a *two-dimensional period* when the complications of other dimensions were unrecognised, a time when life was bounded by the *Green Grass* of home. (This had associations which went beyond what he meant but it would have to do. Those in the West may think of the colour Green as homely and may hear the distant strains of Tom Jones singing his 1984 hit. However, to the Canadian from the far North, it may be walking in the crisp *white* snow outside his log cabin and to the Omani villager, it may be walking in the soft *yellow* sand outside his white-washed wind tower.) For Steve, it simply denoted a halcyon period when everything seemed homely, familiar and straightforward. But then he discovered with great disappointment that it was fake and nothing was straightforward.

For example, if he arose one sunny morning, grabbed his compass and went for a walk South for 5 miles, then East for 5 miles then North for 5 miles he would end up somewhat tired and exactly 5 miles East of his starting point having gone around three sides of a square. A straightforward uncomplicated journey where everything is what it seems. Steve could spend his life in two dimensions, happily believing this, as indeed did early man for thousands of years because civilisations developed near the equator where this would most nearly be true. However, had Steve been an Inuit at the Magnetic North Pole and gone for the same walk using his compass, then he would not have ended up 5 miles away but *back where he started*. His life would be less simple and clear because

24

he had come up against other things such as curvature and magnetism; he would have encountered a three-dimensional reality and would have to think more deeply about it. Indeed, had Steve then started to wonder why, with the same rate of walking and in the same time and level of tiredness he could end up either where he started or with further walking to do to get back, then he might start wondering about Time as a fixed dimension. And well he might wonder because, in the mathematics of the universe, time has no reality other than in our minds as it's actually a consequence of curvature in space. And had he been a photon doing it at the speed of light there may be a few more dimensions to worry about because in the end of the day reality itself is relative. In fact, it's all very confusing and maybe best not to think about it at all but go along with the deception.

That's why there is still a Flat Earth Society with a wide membership. He would never have joined but it is a most interesting example of fake news and belief being used to shore up a simplistic view of life. The Society's current view is that the earth is a disc with edges so that the sea does not fall off. Aeroplanes fly around in a flat atmospheric layer above the disc. As a good Texan member points out in his blog, he has been driving around the United States for 50 years, and always it's flat and when he goes up in his helicopter and hovers in one place the world is most certainly not rotating under him. The Society has many members from all walks of life including some who are well-known. Some also deny that men have visited the Moon and argue that the TV coverage was an elaborate deception to confuse the masses. Fake news is not a new phenomenon. We were introduced to it at a young age (in the form a well-known Christmas character with a white beard) and it soon became an acceptable way of life. He found it disappointing that a quarter of the population of the USA, mainly religious evangelicals, are reported to deny the concept of evolution and believe that the world, flat or otherwise, was created in recent times, indeed to be precise in 4004 BC, as calculated by Bishop James Ussher in 1654.

He felt, at the end of the day, that the question was whether life should be optimised for happiness or truth because the two are not necessarily compatible. The Texan flat-earth supporter may be a most honest and helpful person living a good life and adding much to his local community but having just one peccadillo, an aversion to a spherical earth. *Truth is often sacrificed on the altar of congeniality.* No amount of logical argument was ever going to prise him away from his happy band of flat-earth adherents. *Life, liberty and the pursuit of happiness* are inalienable rights and nobody has the right to take them away in favour of truth. The last thing Steve wanted to do was to upset folk who were totally content with a simple life unadulterated by the need to venture into other dimensions. Indeed, for a time, he was satisfied with this himself but after a while, he found it insufficient and he needed to know more, to go beyond comfort beliefs and the confines of two dimensions. He accepted that ending up on Mars was perhaps more than he bargained for but that's the way it goes.

3

The Job Interview

WHEN PROF GREEN had sent him an email, with no comment but just a link to a rather odd advert on the Church of Scotland website, he was intrigued. It called for a young and fit (were they still allowed to say that?) person to undertake a special role leading to a mission and care position in a remote location. Deciding that he qualified on these two criteria, being surely still young in his 30s and having just run the Edinburgh marathon, he was intrigued to find out more and filled in the attached form out of curiosity rather than any expectation. Following several weeks during which he heard nothing, there arrived on his iPad 22 a request to complete a much more expansive form. This amounted in places to a critical self-analysis which asked all sorts of impertinent questions about his background, family, health, interests, marital position and even theological views on liberalisation, the literal reliability of the Gospels, evangelical extremism and other current in-house issues in the church. He very nearly abandoned the application especially as he had, in his view, little to offer but as he'd got this far and had plenty of time to whittle away, he persevered. Again, nothing was heard for a while until he got an invitation to *discuss a special mission in a remote area* with the church authorities. He was asked to present himself at the newly built Church of Scotland *Outer Centre* (surely an oxymoron) in the Gyle on the West of the City rather than at the old building in George Street.

Steve caught an earlier train than he need have done from North Berwick to Edinburgh just in case there was a holdup; he needed not to be late. It was the autumn of 2034 following a difficult three years in which both his home life and his career had more or less collapsed. He very much hoped that this interview might auger a change in his fortunes. There was something cathartic about trundling along a familiar old railway line and he preserved the relaxed feeling by treating himself to a taxi from the station rather than taking another train out to the Gyle. Quite why the invitation was couched in such odd terms he had no idea but the Church of Scotland usually kept its cards close to its chest. The building was a modern glass-fronted block of the type popular a few years ago but now falling out of fashion. The receptionists gave him a security tag on a light blue ribbon (the church had to be so careful about intruders it seemed), took him to an imposing room and asked him to take a seat at the oval directors' table (meaning he assumed the shape of the table). He did not sit down but wandered around looking at the guilt-framed paintings of previous moderators of the church (most were indeed oval) when in came the big guns including the chairmen of two Central Committees, the current moderator no less and finally to his surprise, Professor Green. The chair of the Appointments Committee, a wizened, bespectacled, gentleman with precision and exactitude oozing from every pore, bid them all be seated and explained why they were assembled. Steve was totally amazed by what he heard.

Apparently, as *Spectacles* explained to them, NASA and Space Co, a key private company had become concerned about the performance of some staff on their joint Mars

Programme. In particular, while CD (whatever that was) and some other symptoms were well recognised and could be treated, there remained a worrying tendency among colonists after a few months on Mars to exhibit odd psychological and social characteristics. Analogy to the armed forces under conflict conditions had high-lighted the long tradition of appointing a chaplain to administer to the spiritual and care needs of those at the fighting front. After much discussion (and an element of derision from the more macho NASA top brass), it had been decided to seek out a chaplain who had the necessary technical and personal background to perform such a role and who could also contribute to the Mars programme in other ways to justify his keep. It was agreed that a Chris-tian Chaplain should be appointed but with an all-faith remit. This was based on the preponderance of Chris-tians among those at NASA who admitted to any religion at all, and a perception that Islam and indeed most other religions except for Buddhism were less inclined towards all-faith concepts. The cost of sending a chaplain was to be covered by the UN Mars Committee Administrative Fund but with a token 5% covered by the chaplain's own church organisation.

Spectacles further explained, enjoying the undivided attention he was eliciting, that national churches had been approached both in the USA, Europe, Africa and the Far East. Some had not replied at all after 6 months and some, including the Catholics and the Episcopalians, had declined on the basis that they would need much longer than 6 months to fully consider the ramifications on communion arrangements and the Eucharist. The Amer-ican Baptists and various other evangelical groupings espoused the evils of going to Mars at all when there was so much to be addressed here on Earth and some more extreme sects foretold eternal damnation would fall on the whole project, pointing out, *God so loved the World*, and that meant the world alone. But it just so happened that the Korean Christian Church, where a more pragmatic understanding of Christianity had developed and the Church of Scotland who happened to have a moderator with a scientific background, responded positively, or at least in an enquiring manner.

The moderator took over at this stage and, buoyed up by the positive reference to his background, explained that he had a degree in Aeronautical Engineering from way back as well as his theological PhD and as such had encouraged the Church of Scotland to be less dismissive of scientific achievements than in times past. In fact, he also boasted that he was the only moderator who could fly his own aeroplane. Some of his *protégés* reckoned it was his preferred way of being closer to God. Be that as it may, he was certainly flightier than most of his forebears and to his credit, he took a chance on the church offering a candidate for the Mars mission. Again, it must have been meant to be that in chatting to his friend Professor Green about it a week or two before, the Prof had suggested that a student of his who had difficulty aligning with the expected parish role might be a worthy candidate. No other names had been offered and so it came to be that Stephen McKay was being considered as the Church of Scotland's nominee for the new post of chaplain on Mars.

In the event, that was jumping the gun a little because there were several constitutional and administrative difficulties to be overcome before the church could formally offer a candidate to NASA. The forthcoming assembly of the church would need much persuasion, in view of the very limited number of ministers emerging successfully from the heavy training required, to allow one of them to escape to Mars. The moderator felt that in this case, allowing this slightly turbulent conscript with some doubtful views and a divorce to boot, (Margo had insisted) might be more acceptable as he was unlikely to be an ideal establishment-orientated minister. However, that was down the line and the business in hand for today was to assess the suitability of Stephen McKay for the assignment.

Steve began to wonder, since these two on the panel had been explaining their positions for over 15 minutes, whether he would be required to contribute at all—a not unusual position on interview panels where members are more concerned with their peers' views than the applicant's. However, the third member, Professor Green, proffered no view of his own and started to probe Steve's reaction to the disclosure that the Church of Scotland had in mind nominating him for this Mars role.

"Reverend McKay," he enquired, giving him a title he did not have yet, "did you really have no idea what the mission referred to in our correspondence was about?"

Steve felt slightly exposed as if he had not done the expected homework.

"Er, no I did not, although I do follow the Mars missions closely and am amazed at the rapid development of the colony to over 100 people already. I do not understand why, of all the possible churches and other organisations that could be asked, the Church of Scotland has been selected to offer a candidate."

The moderator chimed in quickly, "And why not; many others were asked but have not responded and Scotland is seen worldwide as a small but significant country with a long record of emigration over the past few hundred years. Indeed, if you go into any country in

31

the world the chance of finding a Scottish presence is way above that predicted by our size."

Yes, thought Steve but not on Mars but he decided to keep quiet. Professor Green then asked, "Is the idea of you undertaking this mission on behalf of NASA at all appealing? We should inform you that all the current suitably-trained ministers have been screened and you are the only one with appropriate technical background, of the right age and fitness and not in line for a parish position."

Obviously, they had done their homework and his liberal views and a divorce had made him an oddball but sending him off to Mars was surely a bit extreme. He ventured slightly frivolously that this was not the other-worldly experience he had been trained for, but they just stared at him and he realised with something of a shock that they were deadly serious.

Spectacles then came in with:

"The wider church as you will be aware has been undergoing a crisis of confidence and perception, not only in Scotland but everywhere else for that matter and having a high profile involvement in an exciting venture watched by the whole world would do wonders for us all. Furthermore, you are relatively free and unattached and it need not be for more than a few years."

"A few years," echoed Steve, "Do you mean I should leave all I have here and just go off like some nineteenth-century missionary to another country to be eaten alive by—"

"Yes, more or less," said the moderator with a smile, hoping to diffuse Steve's obvious irritation at spectacles suggestion, "Only in this case, it's another world and there are no natives but a band of brave and frightened scientists and engineers who have ended up there and need the temporal and spiritual help that somebody like you could offer."

Steve paused to reflect. They had spent much time and research on identifying him as the one to go; he should at least give it serious consideration, even if he was inclined to turn it down.

"Alright, I would obviously need to study what is involved and speak with folk and satisfy myself that this is what God would wish me to do before I give an answer as it's quite a commitment. How long do I have?"

"Until the end of the week," said the moderator, "but bear in mind that there still may be other submissions from elsewhere and that NASA and the private companies involved could reject any candidate. Also, the Church of Scotland General Assembly could dis-allow it, so you would not necessarily be totally committing yourself for some months."

Professor Green added, smiling, "And NASA's Mars Committee also undertake their own assessments based on psycho-analysis and blood groups and perverse habits etc so there's a fair chance they might still reject you." This raised a laugh all round.

Steve later wondered what perverse habits they were referring to but decided that his mentor and friend had merely been trying to lighten the mood. And it had worked because they then went for coffee in Costa (which had opened a minibar within the new church building based on analysis showing that Church folk were generally coffeeholics).

In the event, over the next few months, the only other serious submission from the Korean Christian Church fell away (the Americans still had hang-ups about Korea from way back) and NASA and others were happy with Steve as a fit and well-balanced submission for the position. The only issue was the General Assembly which the moderator thought he could persuade with ease. It only met once a year, in May, and was underpinned by scores of committees who saw it as their remit to continue the status quo come what may. The ministerial placement committee (ministers were no longer allowed to apply for advertised Parish vacancies) was very short of new recruits because, in the words of the past-moderator, 'so few of the new generation receive the call to ministry'. It was, of course, nothing to do with the poor pay (good remuneration might attract the wrong type) nor the tied house (which relieved the incumbent of temporal worry about housing) nor the increasing use of parish ministers by the councils for every conceivable social care support. Unfortunately, the placement committee, when approached, stoutly refused to allow one of their few recruits to be flitted away to Mars when the good parishes of Scotland needed them so badly.

The wily moderator circumnavigated the issue a few days before the Assembly by convincing the chair of the committee that Rev Steve McKay was something of a maverick and was also divorced at his own instigation and for no acceptable reason (not quite true, but excusable in the interests of the wider good) so would, therefore, be an embarrassment to the committee when it came to placement. It was unheard of that a parish church declined an allocated minister and he did not want to seed the possibility. The Finance Committee for Special Projects approved the spending as they had a lot of money and no projects to spend it on. This did not stop them pontificating and adding riders to the conditions until the last moment. However, one way or another Steve was accepted as the first chaplain *for* Mars but not yet chaplain *on* Mars as he was not there yet and as we shall see, actually getting there was quite an ordeal.

Steve had some difficulty in coming to terms with the fact that the Church of Scotland of all churches should agree to place itself at the forefront of scientific progress. While he had long argued that it was time the church instigated a truce in the traditional battle with the scientific community, he never saw it happening in his time. He reflected that in early antiquity, religion sat alongside philosophy and science as part of the overall learning of the age. It was known for example that the Earth was spherical by the Greek philosophers and Eratosthenes worked out the diameter to within 10% in 240 BC. By the time of Jesus, the well-informed in every land and not least the Hebrews who were highly educated accepted that the world was a sphere and Jesus himself would have known this from the age of 12 when he conversed with the Scribes in the Temple. Indeed it was seen as no big deal until the Christian Church of the early Middle Ages insisted it was flat, largely based on an overly literal interpretation of the Scriptures and depictions by contemporary artists. The Catholic Church was traditionally blamed for this but the Reformed Church of whom the Church of Scotland was a prominent member, was even more opposed. Martin Luther ended his rant about science and Nicholas Copernicus in particular by stating:

> *The fool wants to turn the whole art of astronomy upside-down. However, as Holy Scripture tells us, so did Joshua bid the sun to stand still and not the earth.*

Strong stuff for the 1540s; even his religious opponents were not deemed to be fools. Maybe it is unfair to restrict it to the religious establishment; the Establishment in whatever form will always be reactive to advancements that challenge the way things are. Some would argue that this is due to corporate self-interest but in fairness, most of the authorities, societies, clubs, charities, institutions and government organisations that constitute the Establishment are well-meaning and sincere in their endeavours. Steve felt it was because the status quo yields a certain stability and comfort, the cosy happiness, the green, green grass of home. Also, close friendships, so important to human beings, are usually based on a convergence of view and as he'd concluded earlier, congeniality is a great barrier to progress. After all, it was hardly congenial of him to leave all his family and friends and go to Mars.

4

Why did Steve Go?

FOLLOWING THE INTERVIEW, Steve chatted to his mum and dad and his friends about the possibility of him serving on Mars. His parents, now submersed in local Berkshire life, were so pleased that he had, at last, a proper job (contract jobs were still too temporary to rate as proper in their eyes) but were astonished and incredulous when they heard where it was and obviously disappointed although they tried not to show it. Friends were supportive after a short period of disbelief but in some cases, he wondered whether this was encouraged by the fact that they would get street credit from having a friend in high places, literally. The universal question he had to face was *why would he want, or even be persuaded, to go to Mars?* And closely coupled to this was the question *would he ever come back?* Satisfying his wanderlust, as we have seen, was probably the most important motivation but also the most difficult to explain. In seeking an answer to give them, he firstly homed on precedents; had mankind taken such giant steps before and how had it turned out?

A little searching showed that not only had it occurred before but quite frequently over the centuries. Perhaps it was only in modern times that mankind's naturally inquisitive spirit had faded or perhaps world-wide communication and social media had dulled the mind-shattering excitement of venturing into the unknown. In early times there was the initial spread of Homo Sapiens from Africa and the great migrations of antiquity and later the spread of Europeans to America and to Australia. On a minor scale, Steve was well acquainted with the trek of the Israelites to and from Egypt. While that was different from going to Mars, it was actually in its time very adventuresome.

Take the case of North America. Leaving aside the exploratory ventures of Leif Erikson from Iceland around 920 AD and the rediscovery by Christopher Columbus and others in the late 1400s, the advent of serious numbers venturing to America commenced with the well-known voyage of the Mayflower. It set forth from Plymouth in 1620 with some 130 souls on board but the conditions for those early immigrants were appalling; only 43 were to survive the first year. However, it was the forerunner of hundreds of ships crossing the Atlantic and by 1650 some 20,000 had made the trip. It had to be remembered that very few of these adventurers ever made it back to Europe (even if they had wanted to) so this became a one-way trip with no expectations of return. It took three to four months of physical hardship being tossed about on the deck or in the bowels of a doubtfully-sea-going vessel often written off from active service. There was a strong likelihood of catching scurvy or some dreadful bug from the inferior food and if you made it alive (the only way as they buried the dead at sea) there was no chance of any sympathetic reception on arrival. You entered the unknown with no clear plan of what to do and where to go and in the sure knowledge that those there before would take advantage of you. It took roughly the same time as going to Mars and the initial numbers involved were similar at around 100. The discomforts of the travel were greater then, but while Mars has no air to breathe, a big negative, it had, on the other hand, no potentially unfriendly inhabitants.

The adaptability of Homo-Sapiens is amazing. In the physical domain, we can accommodate wide ranges of temperature and humidity and even shortfalls in oxygen percentage and pressure. It is recorded for example that we can live for extended periods at a third of the air pressure on earth. Furthermore, our minds can adapt to adverse surroundings and accommodate long periods of extreme conditions; examples are numerous. In the mental domain, there is no great difference in the cognitive ability between races nor even between generations. Steve remembered once staying in a harbour hotel in Lerwick, the capital town of the Shetland Islands off Scotland. The waitress was from Greenland and working in the Summer to help with her fees at a Danish University. She was fluent in six languages yet her grandfather was illiterate and had lived his whole life in igloos on barren ice fields. On that same trip, he had visited the prehistoric settlement of Jarlshof near Sumburgh Airport which in its own way is as much a marvel of ingenuity and intelligence as the pyramids, built at the same time but about 4000 miles away. Ancient folk from different races across the earth were not that different to us now.

Steve reckoned the core ingenuity, both physically and mentally, was there in abundance and some explorations of the past were just as mind-bogglingly adventuresome and attracted the same fearful apprehension as going to Mars today. In fact, it could be argued that, with the greater respect for the value of life and with modern communications and extensive support, a Mars trip is less dangerous. So, one reason for going to Mars was to satisfy his inherent curiosity and his dissatisfaction with inadequate two-dimensional explanations, as we saw earlier. Another reason was the sheer adrenaline-pumping exhilaration of being an explorer, of being counted among those who are determined to see a new country or a new world before they die. It's a mix of excitement, pioneering spirit and achievement. It's the need to leave a footprint; the desire to be remembered in an otherwise humdrum existence.

All this applies to individuals. If the same question is put to trading companies or governments, then the answer is more prosaic; it's money and power. Mars has an abundance of heavy elements on the surface, largely from asteroids that have crash-landed over the last few billion years. The atmosphere on Mars is weak and the asteroids or large meteorites do not burn up as they do on earth. Some are rare on Earth partly because the cooling process led to heavier elements being sucked to the centre by gravity rendering them unobtainable. Retrieval of these elements from the surface of Mars and taking them back to earth would be a costly exercise but possibly competitive as the availability on earth decreases and the needs of the electronic industry continue to expand. Alternative possibilities have included using them for manufacture in situ on Mars and shipping back the micro-electronic parts, but that would be much further ahead. Either way, the dictates of economics will determine the outcome. There is also the use of Mars as a stepping stone to wider exploration into space, the potential for enhanced communication and the possibilities for national security by having an extra-terrestrial outpost on a nearby planet rather than using satellites alone.

Lastly, there is the propaganda war. Long after conventional military combat has been relegated to history books like the trench warfare of previous centuries and bows and arrows before that, there remains the need for a stage on which international tensions can be played out. The rise of the Internet and social media late in the last century paved the way for electronic warfare which had seen cyberattacks on Governments around the world. This coupled with the build-up of chemical weapons and the prospect of biological warfare has transformed the international scene. While NATO endeavours to reach an agreement between the USA, Russia and other countries, China may be going it alone and claiming parts of Mars as its own. The international accord established way back in 1967 to treat all Mars as common territory is beginning to creak and needs to be re-established. So another reason to go to Mars is national identity, each country wanting a slice of the action. All these things combine to ensure the importance of going to Mars. To agonise over the logic of going there is simply not accepting the way things are and how the minds of individuals and the collective views of commerce and governments work. It's the status, the fashion and the contemporaneousness that matter at the end of the day.

Did Steve expect to come back; that was the second question they would ask him. Yes, he did; perhaps not to stay back but at least for an extended visit. In many ways, it was no different from those going to America or Australia from Europe or India 100 years ago. They worked remotely and came back seldom but with the thought that one day they might retire to their home country. In practice, after many years away and long-established local friends and possibly family, they would stay where they were until too old and entrenched and maybe too content to ever go back. Their country of birth became a nostalgic dream discussed on long evenings with old friends. Some of the newer countries have only recently allowed 'retirement visas' for folk who have been there for many years and have a pension to spend in the local economy.

Steve knew that for Mars, this was an important issue. The cost of a ticket back was expensive and, although the Mars council which employs most of the village population includes it in their contracts, it assumed many would not return. The exception here was the so-called *terminauts*, being those who wished to make the Mars trip their last cruise and were not given this option in their contracts. The fuel per kilogram of lift when leaving Mars is much less than that leaving from the Earth due to the much lower gravity. However, this is more than compensated by the high cost of fuel on Mars owing to its production by local extraction of hydrogen, oxygen and carbon being in its infancy. Since the early 2030s, Mars had become a highly commercial enterprise and absence on a long trip home was risky in a buoyant local job market. Steve well understood that where he was concerned, being relatively unattached socially and with a varied career to date, he was viewed by the authorities as an ideal person to go.

5

What Should Steve Take?

TRAVELLING TO MARS at the right time when it
is near the Earth involves about four months living in
cramped conditions in a spacecraft with zero gravity.
Once there, Steve would once again experience gravity
albeit only about a third of that on Earth and have to live
in large domes with a pressurised atmosphere.

"Don't forget to pack your toothbrush," his Mum had
said in a valiant attempt to show some humour in spite
of her real concerns. In fact, as Steve had learnt on the
NASA preparatory course for Mars, cleaning your teeth
was very difficult in the zero-gravity of a spacecraft. They
were told that the foam stuck around your mouth or in
bubbles nearby and you had to be very tidy and method-
ical in order to achieve any success. In fact, the same
applied to all normal personal activities with the result
that everything from cutting your toenails (bits everywhere) to toiletry activities (don't even think about it)
took at least three times longer than on earth. Apparently,
once on Mars with some gravity, things were more tolerable so in some ways, the journey in the spacecraft was
good preparation for immigrants.

He had flown to Los Angeles for the NASA preparatory course following exhaustive medical examination
undertaken on their behalf at the Royal Infirmary in
Edinburgh which he surprised himself by passing with

flying colours. The psycho-assessment was also positive although they had ticked a box marked PFM which on persistent questioning they admitted indicated a propensity for melancholy but nothing to worry about, they said, as it was quite common. On the course, he made his first acquaintance with a few of the others who were scheduled for trips to Mars over the 2036-37 period. They were called paranauts by the Mars council as para-astronauts was a bit of a mouthful. It correctly implied that all passengers on the spacecraft were expected to support the astronaut crew in various ways and they were trained to do this prior to the voyage. The paranauts were from a wide range of countries but had a narrow range of ages being typically late 20s to early 40s He also had his first encounter with the older terminauts who, although they paid handsomely for the privilege of going to Mars, still had to undergo much of the training and preparation. There were more men than women although the council had been studiously gender-neutral and there was a preponderance of people from the Northern Hemisphere, particularly Northern America, Europe, Russia, the Middle East, China and India. There were virtually none for example from Australasia (some said they had plenty of space around them on earth) or Africa.

Then there was the long period until the final stage of preparation when the core activities and safety procedures were drummed home by a series of trial runs and further assessments. Finally, as the time approached, they were no longer allowed to leave the care of NASA. This restriction had been instigated after several incidents when folk had panicked and retracted at the last moment, in one case delaying a take-off and putting others at risk. Well prior to the final period, those departing were expected to ready themselves for leaving Earth by saying goodbye to their loved ones and putting their arrangements in order. It became a replay of times a hundred years ago with emigrants from Europe to say Australia and however positively it was portrayed, there was an overarching gloominess about it. Once embarked, the chance of getting to Australia safely was about 99% while safely landing on Mars was still a few percentages below this. Consequently, the goodbyes were fraught with apprehension and concern.

When the time came, Steve's mum was surprisingly stoic and he wondered if this was because she could hide her feelings better than his dad who was really cut up and could not hide his grief and misgivings so well. They had after all been through crises before in their lives and his poor grandfather had died of the dreaded COVID-19 pandemic of the early 20's so they well knew how precarious life could be. Margo thought he was off his rocker and continued to say so, whatever she really thought, but Bobby was *over the moon* with excitement at having his dad going to Mars. (Actually, it was dad number two but he thought of him as his true dad rather than his new dad, number three, with whom he did not really bond.) As a teenager, this gave him bragging rights at North Berwick High School beyond his wildest imagination and Steve did promise to give a talk to the school on his return. Others simply wished him all the best on a *see you when you get back basis* and got on with their lives which made it easier for him. He left the managing and letting of his flat to a North Berwick Solicitor who also drafted his will and placed his personal papers into long term storage.

Then, there only remained the passport and the emigration papers, surely a straightforward process since the British Government had been so insistent that the UK had a major role to play in Space exploration. Unfortunately, the relationship between the Government and the Passport Centre (changed from office which sounded too administrative) had been difficult for some time. It had deteriorated markedly over the last decade since the full implications of what was then called Brexit had played out. Entry visas were required from some European countries and not others, there were several types of visas depending on status (student, business, tourist, accredited employee, etc) and renewal was only granted by attendance at approved centres owing to a major hacking of the software. There was a big issue about the procedure for stamping passports on Mars which led to several brainstorming sessions until it came to the attention of a rebel parliamentary backbencher who then fumed about valuable time being wasted when there were only eight UK nationals expected to go in the first three years. Even this held no sway but it was quietly dropped when they discovered that previous British astronauts from way back such as Helen Sharman and Tim Peake were not asked to comply; precedent it seems is everything. Steve made several visits to London to sort it all out (not Edinburgh as inter-planetary matters were deemed beyond the remit of the Scottish Parliament) and was eventually issued with a special purple passport for extra-terrestrial travel. In the end though, he was not allowed to take it with him to Mars because NASA, who had to account for every gramme taken into space, disallowed it.

What therefore could Steve take with him to space? NASA's policy since the early days of space travel had been strictly limiting on personal effects but often this was honoured in the breach by astronauts. One notable occasion was back in 1965 before the launch of Gemini 3 when American astronaut John Young nipped into a takeaway and picked up a corned beef sandwich which he secreted in his spacesuit pocket in direct defiance of regulations. He produced it as an introductory gourmet offering for his fellow travellers a few hours after lift-off. However, encapsulated food was less developed then and on opening, it burst into bread and beef micro-crumbs in the low gravity environment and floated around the spacecraft for days. He received a reprimand from NASA but they used the event to make a case for more research funding on congealed food. The Russians had been similarly venturesome but had had the insight to take a highly compacted gourmet sausage from Siberia which did not crumble but, according to the Americans, tasted horrible.

This is not to mention the case of interest to Steve involving 300 samples of microfiche bibles being carried aboard by Apollo moonwalker Edgar Mitchell as a favour to NASA chaplain John Stout in 1971. (Yes, NASA had always had a chaplain and the Russians had their spacecraft sprinkled with holy water by a Coptic priest.) NASA turned a blind eye to this in view of the heavy support received for the space programme by Republicans of the Bible-belt States but it became quite an issue later when a lucrative after-market trade developed for items that had been to space and Astronauts were subsequently more severely restricted. As a matter of interest, the so-called Lunar Bibles found their way to senior politicians as well as Apollo staff and ownership has been the subject of legal battles ever since. This did not stop one being sold for $56,250 at Sotheby's back in 2012 so Steve decided to keep his eyes open for a souvenir.

Nor is it to mention the case of an unnamed Muslim astronaut who sneaked aboard a small HARD COPY of the Koran on a more recent flight to the International Space Station (ISS) according to Scott Kelly. On the ratio of regulation infringement versus volume, this beats the microfiche bibles by a substantial margin as the whole of the King James Bible occupied only a 2.5mm square and even 300 were only a sugar lump in size. It is interesting to note the lengths even astronauts go to preserve the manifestations of their faith under dire conditions. And perhaps the *even* here is unwarranted as there is no reason to assume they would be any less aware of an overarching spirituality in the universe than anybody else, but more of that later. Where Steve was concerned, he insisted on taking one hard copy Bible under the official *Tools of your Trade* allowances as he was after all a Christian Chaplain although he was happy to include the Quran in electronic form. He argued that the legal systems in the USA and some other countries still preferred witnesses to swear on the Bible and that this should be equally the case on Mars. He also made a case (why did everything need a case being made) for the inclusion of ample chocolate limes in cellophane wrapping. These had helped him through the most bizarre and stressful occasions in his life since the age of three and while leading him to being ejected from an exam on one occasion, the soothing discovery of the soft chocolate in the centre after a period of hard suck was more cathartic than any of the new-fangled anti-stress fidget gadgets available.

Hence it was that on the appointed day of departure, our new chaplain found himself, with 47 astronauts, paranauts and terminauts, a hard copy Bible, lots of chocolate limes and a few other things on the inside of a very expensive elongated cylinder of metal with seats, windows and tons of electronic gear. He had a momentary flip-back to the school bus outings of 25 years before. There was the same air of excitement and anticipation and, as they were each strapped in and finally checked out, the same sense of a voyage to somewhere (where did the teacher say it was?) and the same inconsequential chit-chat that precedes a trip. He knew the feeling would not last but decided to enjoy it while it did. The pretty Chinese lass next to him furtively offered him a strangely scented fruit drop in bright wrapping so he swapped it for a chocolate lime and knew the school analogy was spot on.

The final *Lift-Off Safety Training Instructions* (commonly called LOST Instructions) were recited by one of the 7 crew in a stilted fashion as if he was reading a poem in front of the class. Unlike aircraft, though they were less euphemistic, referring openly to disaster potential and expected lifetime (10 minutes on depressurisation at over 20k miles above the Earth). If cast adrift in space, there was no life belt and no whistle to blow (there being no sound waves in space because there are not enough molecules to wave). Even on Earth, there's no known case where the whistle alone has led to a rescue so the manufacturer of emergency aircraft whistles has had an easy ride all these years. Steve realised he was letting his thoughts digress but being all set to go, he was much calmer than he anticipated. He feared that there might be some distress among the paranauts and as chaplain he would be called upon to offer comfort but that proved to be unfounded. In fairness, to Steve, he had gone through the exercise in his mind and worked out what he could say but like those about to have an operation, there is little one can do except emphasis success rates. In this case, there had been no major incidents during the last two manned lift-offs and while an uncomfortable experience, previous paranauts had found it tolerable.

The lift-off itself was indeed stressful but they had all been so heavily briefed it was in some ways an anti-climax. Some thought they had also been mildly drugged.

The pill they'd been given with the obligatory pouch of water 20 minutes before was, they were told, merely a form of aspirin to thin the blood a little, but Steve felt it did not have quite the same bitterness. However, why worry, it seemed to work and the heavy eyes and slight dizziness they were warned about were eminently bearable. After a couple of minutes, there was a half-hearted cheer that went up but it was not as enthusiastic as the success warranted and again Steve thought the *aspirin* must have been some form of sedative. There was a heavy judder as the second stage was released from the craft and then it all went quiet and they realised how deafeningly noisy it had been. As he stared out of the window, he was totally mesmerised by the curve of the Earth and the way it gradually became a full circle. He watched for the best part of an hour as his Earth and all those associated with it glided away into the distance. It was then that he had a really odd and unsettling revelation.

6

Deep Reality Dawns

STEVE LATER EXPLAINED it to his friends in the Mars Bar as suffering some form of relapse during the journey after his initial elation at the successful take-off. He wondered about the drugs he had been given but decided it was much more real and worrying than that and much too real for comfort.

Having peered out of the small port window and witnessed the Earth float away below him, he had begun to contemplate. Now that he was in space, it occurred to him that all of the molecules constituting his body, the atoms constituting the molecules, the protons and electrons constituting the atoms, the quarks and so on down to the infinite smallness of the mass that was essentially him, were no longer part of the Earth but floating away in some double-decker School Bus which purported to be a Spacecraft. He realised that:

He no longer existed on Earth. He had died as far as Earth was concerned because he was no longer physically there.

This might have been a grim thought but it turned out to be most enlightening and comforting when he worked it through. He accepted that he was just as dead on Earth as anybody who had ever lived there. Indeed, for the approximately 150 billion Homosapiens who have lived on the Earth from the start, all except the 8 billion or so now living there were dead according to this definition of being dead, because they were not there anymore. He was just as much *not there* as they were. He might be there in peoples' thoughts, in the electronic impulses in their minds like the memory of a departed friend but that's all. The ministers at funerals referred to the finality of leaving the earth; well, he had left it. If death means not present on Earth, then that was the end of him.

This essential awareness seemed so obvious to him that he wondered why he had not thought of it like that before. While dead to the world, he was still conscious and real, that is to say *alive. I AM,* he thought, *and I know I am because I'm pretty full of adrenaline and chocolate limes at the moment.* "I think therefore I AM," Friedrich Nietzsche had said back in the 19th Century. "I AM who I am," said God to Moses from the burning bush way back 4000 years before that with a warning not to look at the bush for too long. *I AM* it seems is the fundamental tenant of a thinking entity whether it be man or God. So does death simply mean leaving the Earth or is it some state of not being an *I AM.* As he peered out of the porthole towards the diminishing Earth, he continued musing on these things. He was, after all, the chaplain for Mars and would be expected to provide some answers to enquiring scientists there.

Firstly, there are scores of learned books on this topic written by prominent philosophers over the centuries. Some of the authors were atheists, some were agnostics, some were believers and adherents of various religions, including the one in which he believed and of which he was an ordained minister. All that was fine but here in space, for the first time, he was confronted with the real issue in its unadulterated simplicity and clarity, without the swirling mists of beliefs and traditions from ages past that enshroud those on that planet Earth he could still see out there.

Secondly, he knew it was the real him looking out on this Earth. He had been aware from the days of his School physics, that his body was actually a space composed of arrays of minute particles that buzzed around within it. Indeed, the particles within him were spaced in similar proportions to the stars and planets in the Universe. He was a sort of living mini-universe. Yes, that was important; the minute particles of which he was composed were similarly spaced to the matter in the rest of the universe. He was truly a *part of the Universe* which extended from the minutest of a minute to the infinitely large. Stephen Hawking's theory of everything which had sounded so immodest to him when he first encountered it, was partly a realisation that the universe operated uniformly over this vast scale from quarks to stars, that is roughly from 10 to the power of minus 20 metres to 10 to the power of plus 20 metres. We human beings are just a part of this scale somewhere in the middle. (Maybe it extends more than the power of 20 each way but that's as far as we can comprehend so perhaps we are not in the middle). The same rules of physics apply over this enormous scale from the minute to the enormous. It is thus actually the humblest view of us possible; true physics offers a depth of humility unattainable in any other area. The forces, the electronic impulses, the thinking, everything that made up the totality of Steve and even the interactions with thoughts of those who knew and loved him on Earth were all part of this single unified universe. That might have been daunting and totally depressing had it been everything, but it wasn't everything.

Thirdly, Steve knew this was not the whole story. If it was the totality of existence and there was nothing more, then he was a fraud and he should immediately resign his commission as chaplain and go. (In practice though, since he was now en route to Mars there was nowhere to go unless they ejected him into space; perhaps a novel way of being fired.) In his heart, he KNEW that there was more to it than this because it is not possible for a constituent part of something, like him, to assimilate and comprehend the whole. How could one small array of particles like him know that they exist as an entity able to think about everything including the universe of which they were part unless they had a consciousness, that is some embedded personal mini-universe able to think for itself? Clay on a potter's wheel cannot understand the need to form a vessel although it is a constituent part of the whole, because, unlike us, it has no consciousness. Nietzsche was correct, the mere fact that he was capable of thinking meant that he existed. And if he existed and was conscious, then he was more than a group of particles like any other random group of particles because he was a thinking and reasoning entity. So what is the extra thing, this force, this influence, this *information*, this god within the mix of all these things that enables this consciousness? It is not a question of IF it is present because it's demonstrably present, but rather: What FORM does it take and how did it get there? That is the big unknown.

Steve had studied Science before opting for his engineering course at university and knew something about genes and DNA and the embedded knowledge within such systems. Before DNA, there was the more primitive RNA and the belief that way back, life was somehow initiated through molecular interaction involving inorganic matter and ultra-violet rays from the sun. But this has never been achieved in the lab; the Miller-Urey experiment and other attempts are contested and many scientists dispute the possibility. The sheer complexity and the odds of it happening are infinitely small. It's not that it's unlikely to occur (and therefore in theory, quite possible) but rather that it's just not possible at all. The seed of life and consciousness must have been there from the start in some form of abiogenesis. DNA has the seed of life itself embedded in it as *primaeval information*. It was there from the Big Bang and is a *fundamental unknown.*

The very core of life is embedded information and nobody knows how it got there.

Perhaps information science comes closest to bridging the gap between life and no life; maybe thought itself is more real than substance. (We'll come back to this point later.)

Fourthly and finally (as Steve was getting tired of all this thinking), this extra influence must exist *throughout the universe.* If it were confined to the Earth then death, for example, could be defined as not being present on Earth and as we saw earlier, that didn't make any logical sense especially as he was now travelling in space, well away from the Earth and he was definitely not dead because he was thinking. If it permeates the universe then it must exist in some form that allows it to be accessible to human minds otherwise how would Steve be aware of it. Minds communicate with minds and not inanimate things. (We can communicate with another person or even a dog but not a table or arguably a robot.) So the universe has a *mind*, a bank of information which can process thoughts. Whether or not this mind is simply a repository for information like the cloud we all use in our electronic communication or has any intelligence of its own is the big question. It's big because, if this *mind of the universe* has a thinking ability it becomes almost indistinguishable from a god. That's not necessarily the God worshipped by the religions because, however well-meaning, they each clothe their God with attributes that reflect the rites and beliefs of their particular religion. It's rather a universal, omnipresent God with a universal mind that our minds and perhaps others in the universe can tap into.

Meanwhile, as Steve peered out he realised that he could also see the moon or at least some of moon as it was partly hidden by the Earth. He found viewing the Earth and the moon circulating around it one of the most mind-boggling sights he had ever witnessed. He started to wonder drearily about how the moon would wax and wane as viewed from his position on the spacecraft but could not get his mind around it and drifted into a pleasant sleep feeling elated and, well, over the moon that he had gone some way to sorting one or two things out.

7

Problems Ahead

ON THE JOURNEY to Mars, Steve often found his sleep patterns were disturbed and he slumbered in short naps. Early one evening, he was jolted out of such a nap by a general buzz of activity around him rather like waking up on a long aircraft flight and realising dinner was being served. Indeed, exactly like that because the head Flight Steward, one of the scientists whose secondary job it was, came floating along with an iPad collecting meal choices. He accidentally let go for a moment and had some difficulty retrieving the iPad as it drifted away; zero-g was such a pain. In the pre-flight rehearsals, all 40 paranauts had been allocated these secondary activities which they were expected to undertake as their contribution to the day to day work throughout the journey to Mars. Much of this work was basic domestic activity such as cleaning, monitoring the environment, serving food, clearing up afterwards and so on and was not popular. Other jobs involved assisting with scientific analysis, monitoring social communications with Earth and on-board entertainment were less monotonous but they all gave people something to do, a vital part in the quest to alleviate boredom on the long journey and relieve the crew of some tedious duties.

Meals had proved to be an issue since the early days of space flight. Fuel supply for the rocket stages had more or less been perfected, admittedly after countless research projects and years of analysis but fuel for the human travellers was still an ongoing bone of contention. It had caused more international squabbles in recent years than any other aspect of space travel. While the crews on the initial Mars flights had been resigned to sacrificing any thoughts of cordon bleu standards in the interests of the mission, this was not so with the current group that included paranauts and terminauts who were of course paying. In a way, this was to be expected as even on long-haul terrestrial flights the quality of food had a priority beyond its real value and with journeys of several months or so under the most monotonous conditions, it became a key feature of the adventure. Twenty years ago, enterprising companies had developed interesting spacecraft meals which they had made available for sale on the Internet. It had become the fashionable gastronomic experience in cities across the world and Mars had thus seeded an important cuisine development. The chewy bars and compactly-packaged potted food with their various savoury and sweet flavours were popular as they met the modern lifestyle of quick snacks.

Steve had long considered that the main downside of all this was that meals became largely solitary affairs requiring none of the social interaction of previous times; no lively banter about the food itself and life in general and the inadequacies of both. In the early lunar missions, the authorities were inclined to compartmentalise astronauts by confining them to their pods but their attempts were often circumvented. In the ISS, the initial suggestion that the Americans and Russians should have separate quarters was also over-ruled by the astronauts themselves who got along very well and had their meals together on a common table. In the Drove 5 spacecraft though, they seemed to have taken a backward step by serving each person as if they had been on some terrestrial long-haul flight. Perhaps as chaplain, he could raise such an issue on the basis that it impacted on the well-being of the group. Maybe it would not be well received because, as he had noticed in his previous employments, the establishment is naturally suspicious of workplace gatherings. Perhaps it was better to just engineer it himself when the opportunity arose and not ask permission.

On this occasion, after dinner, an announcement was made over the speakers that Captain Peter Reid had an important item of news. There was some discussion about what this news could be and half an hour later he appeared in his official uniform, rather than the casual clothes he normally wore. He spoke from a position near the stairs between the two residential floors in the spacecraft where the maximum number of people could see him and all could at least hear him. Following a few introductory words, he quickly focussed on the news item which he read from a prepared statement:

"Fellow passengers, following the agreement which you all signed, I am obliged under Item 34 to inform you of any incidents or issues as they occur or very soon thereafter so that there is mutual responsibility and trust between all those on the mission. While the launch and subsequent stage releases went well and you will hardly have noticed anything amiss, there was one fault which we will have to address over our journey. I do not wish to alarm you as we have plenty of time, indeed the whole journey, to resolve it."

He paused as if having second thoughts about releasing the information but carried on.

"As you well know, our spacecraft, Drove 5, has three extending legs on which it will land when we get to Mars. It will approach slowly and carefully with the six landing rockets slowing us down over the last few miles and finally 500 metres above the Mars surface the three legs fold out. Unfortunately, one of these legs was damaged during lift-off when the rocket motors below it had a flare back causing it to overheat and twist slightly in its harness. This has not happened before and we are looking at repair options and landing alternatives that will hopefully—"

An audible gasp went around the two decks as they absorbed this unwelcome news. One of them, Erik, a large fair-haired Nordic man in his late 30s said loudly, "Are you telling us there's no way of landing? Like an aeroplane with an undercarriage fault?"

"No, not quite; two legs are fine, it's just one of them and we have the whole journey to figure out how to resolve it."

"But if we land on two legs, the spacecraft will fall over on landing and possibly blow up as it still has some fuel," continued Erik.

"Yes, we must devise a way of maintaining the vertical orientation of the craft but I must now decline further questions as the Earth authorities and the Mars council are working on the issue and are not in a position to give more specific information."

There was general murmuring and Erik, by now clearly very upset, continued, "It seems we were all doomed almost before we left the earth then."

Other paranauts who were presumably also very apprehensive chose to withhold any immediate comment and allow Erik to state and perhaps overstate their feelings.

Captain Reid tried to assure everyone that this was only a blip. Erik who was a mechanical engineer and perhaps appreciated the magnitude of the problem more than most was becoming very distressed and giving voice to his doubts about ever going on the mission. The captain noticed that Steve was seated nearby and asked him to speak with Erik, offering his own office as a location if they wished to go there. This, they did while the captain started circulating among the rest of the paranauts to reassure them.

On entering the captain's office, the only executive office on the Drove, Steve took one of the two chairs adjacent to a large wall screen and invited Eric to sit in the other. He noticed Erik was visibly shaking and after impressing on him that similar things had happened before (had they?) and had been readily resolved, he started to ask about his background and home life and offered him a tea pouch from the captain's supply. After a while, he calmed down enough to explain that as a mechanical engineer, working on aircraft maintenance for many years, he probably understood more than most about landing systems and knew the true dangers of their position.

"That's great," said Steve, "your experience could be useful and I'll mention this to the captain. It's probably in your file but with no expected need it would not have been highlighted."

"I don't think the crew will want advice from us paranauts, after all, we are passengers at the end of the day," observed Erik.

Steve assured him that the crew would become much better acquainted with the passengers on long interplanetary flights of several months than on terrestrial ones and would welcome external inputs. Eventually, Erik made his way back to his seat in the cabin by which time folk seemed to have absorbed the bad news and moved on to mundane issues such as the shower and bathroom booking schedules and the limited time slots of only 15 minutes for their use. Mona, the Chinese lass in the next pod to him did seek his view of the *news* and asked how Erik was now. He assured her all was fine and played down the landing leg difficulties. She ventured that since they were now committed to the journey in any case it was not worth worrying; adding (knowing Steve's Chaplaincy role on the mission) that Far-Eastern religions, as opposed to those in the west, encouraged an acceptance of one's lot without the pressure to constantly change it for the better. Steve was too weary to take up Mona's challenge on that one and suggested it would make a good discussion topic for the future since they were stuck on this ruddy bus for the next four months. Meanwhile, they settled for another chocolate-lime Chinese mint exchange and he settled down for a quiet post-dinner nap.

However, a quiet nap was not to be because The Mars council, in its wisdom, insisted that all the residents on Mars were schooled in the detailed knowledge of previous space programmes. This was implemented by a series of after-dinner lectures and today was the first of these. It started with descriptions of the space missions over the years, the rockets that sent them up, how they came down and what happened on the missions. As if that was not enough it then progressed to the development of the ISS, statistical analysis of the 800 or so folk who had been into space (even back in 2020 it was over 500) and the associated technology and politics. Endless screenings were followed by online *fun quizzes* reminiscent of those that Steve remembered being run in pubs in Scotland. He didn't like them then and he still had no desire to have his rather truncated general knowledge examined in a random fashion; his mind did not work that way. If he needed to swot up the lunar landings of the 1970s for example, he would find the pages on Google and work through them becoming an expert for a day and then more or less obliterating it after the need had drifted away. Random general knowledge, so important in the past was now rendered unnecessary by the Internet. Any rate, that was his excuse for being moderately useless at quizzes.

So, it came to be that, after dinner, Steve was subjected to a lecture by one of the crew speaking via his iPad 22, about the first proper rockets designed by the German genius Baron Wernher von Braun. These were the V-2s that rained on London in the Second World War nearly 100 years ago; essentially the same rockets were used again for more peaceful purposes on his repatriation to America after the war. The space race during the Cold War of the 1950s and 1960s had led to rocketry becoming a key military science and both Russia and America developed the capability of sending rockets into the stratosphere.

As so often with force-fed information, Steve's thoughts, triggered by something he'd heard, went off at a tangent. He reasoned that humans had been leaving the Earth for well over 60 years so perhaps it's not so special after all (except that none of them had been a chaplain). Since the turn of the Millennium, there had been no time when all humans were on Earth, at least one had been out there. It was a sort of replication of a former time some 200 million years ago when a fish, born with strong fins that could be used as flippers, ventured laboriously from the sea onto the dry land. There must have been a first and a second and a tenth and a hundredth doing the same. In thousands of years when folk populate Mars and perhaps other planets, the identities of those pioneers may be lost forever and children at school will be told that curiosity and a sense of adventure led to earth-men in the pre-interplanetary age spreading beyond their local earthly environment. And the children will absorb it into their ROM data centres implanted in their heads like the tags on farm animals and wonder at the primitive simplicity of early times when humans had no such electronic support.

He'd missed some of the presentation and they were now onto the early 60s with animals being sent into space with varying success and then the first human, Yuri Gagarin aboard Vostok 1 in 1961 which placed the Russians ahead. Alan Shepard from NASA performed a manned flight a couple of months later and redressed the difference. From then on, there was divergence in their approaches with Russia tending to explore wider afield and NASA homing in on moon landings with their Apollo programme. This culminated in the first human moon landing by Neil Armstrong, Edwin (Buzz) Aldrin and Michael Collins aboard Apollo 11 in 1969. From any viewpoint, this was a momentous occasion and really brought the feasibility of men going to other planets home to people across the world. The photo of a heavily suited astronaut, actually Neil Armstrong but you cannot see him behind his reflective shield, is one of the most recognisable photos of the early space age.

Steve remembered that his Granddad used to tell him that he worked in a factory in Manchester at the time and they were told several days before that they were allowed to watch the landing on the canteen TV which wrong-footed the union stewards who had not even got around to asking. He wondered if any companies had given time off to watch their own Mars landing or had there now been so many that they were no longer news-worthy even when there was a potential landing difficulty. It's always the way that when something has been done once then those that follow, although the challenge may be just as great, get no special recognition. Does anybody remember who was next to climb Mount Everest after Sir Edmund Hillary and Tenzing Norgay? Indeed within 50 years, thousands had done it and around 200 had lost their lives. He'd drifted again and the lecturer was manfully droning on;.

By 1975, the inefficiency of two leading nations competing independently and the exorbitant costs involved led to an agreement to collaborate resulting in a multi-national manned mission using an Apollo space-craft launched by a Russian Soyuz rocket. The success of this mission led to further collaboration and sharing of data both on voyages and on practical aspects such as the effects of long-duration flights. NASA successfully devel-oped a reusable space shuttle but a disaster at the launch of the Challenger Shuttle at Cape Canaveral in 1986 killed the seven astronauts on board and the American public started to question the viability of the NASA programme which by then did not have the same simple goal of the 1970s, that of putting a man on the moon.

"To be continued," said the lecturer recognising he was losing the attention of his class from the number of iPads turned off. The paranauts chatted for a while with their near neighbours and gradually drifted into a night time silence. Again night had little real meaning when you were not on the earth but the authorities had desig-nated adherence to a diurnal routine largely for manage-ment convenience and partly for the comfort of the trav-ellers who were encountering so much that was new and strange.

Steve lay awake in his pod for some time worrying

about how his allocated flight job, that of dealing with social communications of the paranauts, both between themselves and separately with their family and friends on Earth, would pan out. He resolved to work around all his 40 or so colleagues on board over the next week to check how they were managing. Some were resigned to having only occasional interaction with their folk on Earth for the journey period while others were still trying to have more frequent contact by texting and accepting the frustrating delays.

It had all gone very quiet except for the hum from the various airflow systems and computers and also an occasional knocking sound of which he had recently become aware. There it was again; a sort of metallic cluck as if somebody was tapping on the outside with a small hammer. Nothing to worry about no doubt but what could it be? He decided to mention it to the crew in the morning.

8

Bumps in the Night

IT WAS ABOUT two months into the journey and they were nearly halfway to Mars having travelled over 100 million miles. On occasions, Steve could still see the Earth, now a mere dot in the blackness of space. His early concerns about his fellow travellers suffering isolation sickness owing to the limited communications with Earth had proved largely unfounded and they had settled down to the routine of calls typically once per week and usually by delayed voice. They had accommodated to a style where they said what they wanted to in sizeable bites which were then transmitted to Earth for a reply in half an hour or so. It was almost like making a series of mini-speeches rather than a conversation but that was what the speed of light dictated and they were stuck with it.

Socially, the group within the Drove had evolved into clusters of friends although there were a few loners whom he jollied along on occasions. He had long since come to the conclusion that they would have been loners even on earth. Where he himself was concerned, he found his colleagues slightly cautious and likely to keep themselves in check knowing his role as chaplain as we saw earlier. Their jobs were generally well defined in specific and pertinent areas while his, being in welfare and support, had no clearly defined boundaries. However, he had made a few close friends who seemed to accept him as he was and found he could relax with them. One of these was Ken Markham, from Hampshire in England, who was joining the Mars village as the new principal communications officer with responsibility for the technical aspects of maintaining contact with earth. He had degrees in both mechanical engineering and electronics and like most people on Mars, he also had a secondary or stand-in duty which in his case was monitoring the oxygen levels. He joked that his job was to keep their bodies alive and the chaplain's was to keep their spirits alive. Be that as it may, it was to Ken that he decided to raise his concern about that clonking noise that he sometimes heard in the night.

He broached the matter one evening after a particularly bland dinner or *rations* as they called it. (The paranauts loved to wind up the crew by implying they were in some sort of jail by reference to their *incarceration*, allocation of *rations* and *exercise breaks*.) Steve asked Ken, "Do you find you can sleep right through the night or do you still take those pink sleeping pills?"

Ken admitted, "Yes, I normally do; they said they were pretty mild so we could take them every night for the whole journey."

"I felt they could become addictive and weened myself off them but it does mean I wake easily and hear if anybody makes their way to the loo for example," said Steve, adding as nonchalantly as possible,"I also occasionally hear a distant clonking as if somebody was tapping on the outside of the spacecraft."

"Now I know why you're a chaplain and I'm a technical guy," he laughed, "bumps in the night, approaches from little men out there trying to get in or is it your God with a message."

Ken noticed Steve was just looking at him and not laughing and felt suddenly uncomfortable.

"Oh, sorry, you meant it didn't you? It must be some characteristic of the temperature change due to the radiation on the outer skin. After all, one side can be heated by the sun and quite hot and the other facing outer space is exposed to nearly minus 273 degrees C so there will be many stresses and strains leading to the creaking you heard."

"But that would be random and of different intensity; this is roughly the same type of bang repeated at the same sound level more like a loose exhaust knocking on the bottom of a car."

Ken, remembering the earlier captain's announcement said, "Well, there was that incident with the extending leg at the start of our voyage which they said would be resolved. Have you heard any more about that by the way?"

"I did speak to one of the crew the other day and she said it was practically resolved, then she quickly changed the subject so I didn't like to pursue it," said Steve.

Ken thought for a minute and then suggested, "Maybe I need to listen out for it myself. It is possible that the position of your pod is nearer to the sound than mine and I won't hear it but it's worth a try. I'll make a point of lying awake to see. Let's face it, this bloody journey is becoming unbearably boring so there's nothing lost except the pint of Ale you'll owe me at the Mars Bar when we finally arrive at the village if it's all in your imagination."

"That's a deal," said Steve, "but I understand the rules approved by the Mars council only allow half a pint per person per day."

"Then you won't be drinking that night will you!" said Ken.

Ken's sleeping pod was four removed from Steve's and they agreed to communicate should either hear the knocking. All electronic communication between travellers was recorded *for training purposes* and while neither felt that there was any real need for their investigation to be surreptitious, they both felt it would be better if it was kept between the two of them even if only to avoid the mirth of their colleagues should it be a false alarm. So it was arranged that Steve would unfasten his restraint belt and float back to wake Ken should he hear it. Restraint belts were expected to be clasped during sleeping hours because at zero gravity a person twisting and turning in the night can end up on the floor or the ceiling or simply levitating by the morning. (Apparently, on an earlier trip to Mars one male paranaut had ended up in a female pod owing, he claimed, to levitation which was not believed and led to some levity of a different type among his colleagues.) That night no knocking was heard and in the morning it transpired they had both fallen asleep. The next night too, nothing was heard although Steve claimed he was awake for long periods. Ken did start to wonder if he had fallen for some practical joke or was the subject of some physiological experiment by the chaplain.

It was the third night that catapulted their investigation into the ranks of a full-blown mystery. About three hours after everything had settled down Steve again heard the knocking sound and immediately slipped back and woke up Ken who was grumpy at first but came to once he saw the earnest look on Steve's face . Ken agreed he could just hear some sound but then to their surprise it became a very low whine which continued for 10 seconds or so, stopped for about a minute and then started again.

"That's some sort of drill I tell you," said Ken.

"Maybe one of the crew are working on something tonight; some maintenance item for example," suggested Steve, but then added thinking aloud, "But why do it in the night and why is it preceded by this odd knocking sound; I tell you it's coming from the outside of the Space-craft. It's the same hollow sound with an echo we heard when they tapped on the door of our training spacecraft to tell us the session was finished."

Ken felt sure there was some innocuous explanation and wanted to continue his sleep.

"Let's simply ask the crew in the morning and you could always ask that Chinese girl, what's her name, Mona, across the aisle from you if she heard anything. Meanwhile, I'm going to continue in the land of nod where I'll now probably dream about alien visitors, perhaps they'll even take the chaplain away as a hostage!"

"At least that would be less boring for us all," muttered Steve as he made his way back to his pod.

That evening, after their *rations*, there was yet another educational talk on the history of space development. At least they had now got to the 1990s so there could not be too many left. This time it was by the only UK member of the crew and he felt more at home with the accent. There had apparently been three manned space stations altogether but the last and most impressive was the International Space Station (ISS) which was started in 1998. It provided good experience for astronauts, some remaining there for over a year and was still being used on occasions until 2030 after which it was partly disas-sembled. Countries involved included the USA, Russia, Japan, Canada, several member states of the EU and the UK. On a good night, it could be seen on Earth with the naked eye as it was only 250 miles up and with its solar collectors was larger than a football pitch. Steve well remembered in his teen years following Tim Peake the British astronaut during his time on the ISS when he was communicating with schools directly from space. By then,

NASA's successful space shuttle was no longer flying and the only way of getting there and back was by Russian Soyuz spacecraft which had been around for 40 years. It was again fortunate that the cooling political relationship between Russia and the USA had not extended to space.

It was the first time that many in Britain had taken much notice of space developments since the moon-walks of the early 1970s. In America, most of the population were following NASA, SpaceX, Boeing, Lockheed and others as they launched a constant stream of big rockets to extend the satellite base for the new universal G5 transmission. The subsequent progress of China in becoming a key contender in the space race to Mars had not been foreseen and this had led to more rapid development, something like the race in the 1960s between Russia and the USA to reach the moon. By 2020, over 500 folk had gone into space since Yuri Gagarin including half a dozen very rich tourists. That's not to mention several hundred poor animals ranging from tortoises to monkeys and lots of cats and dogs who did nothing to deserve their fate other than being in the wrong place at the right time.

On the matter of the bumps in the night, Steve discovered after delicately broaching the subject with Mona that she had heard scraping noises in the night but had assumed it was the funny noise Westerners made when asleep. He looked at her and was given an inscrutable grin so he volunteered that he had spoken to others (well, one actually but what's in a number) who had heard it. Realising he was serious, she then admitted that there were occasional very soft noises in the night from the Spacecraft skin but she had assumed it was the cooling and heating they had been told about. She knew it was from the skin because she once went to the toilet (discouraged at night because it woke up others) and it seemed to be equally everywhere within the whole spacecraft, not louder in one place than another. Steve then made light of it by agreeing it may be a temperature effect and, in order to avoid alarming her, deflected the conversation onto something which she had raised before; her fascination with Eastern religions.

Indeed, he discovered that she had interesting views on most things and defended Eastern ways generally, not just the religions, as being intellectually and ethically superior. She even suggested to Steve (was she winding him up?) that the reason why Christians were the only ones who had to be 'born again' was because they were so bad to start with! But then she could see no reason why God, whether Eastern or Western, would purposely make any part of his creation bad in the first place or even endow it with a propensity for badness. She suggested it was just a way for Western religious leaders to keep their followers in check. Steve decided to duck that particular discussion for the moment knowing she could not be bought off with the Biblical argument of original sin. He remembered from his childhood an old Presbyterian preacher in some Scottish kirk thundering from his perch, high up in the woodwork, 'ye are all born in sin and shapen in iniquity'. He knew, as chaplain, he'd one day have to deal with this question of hers in a serious conversation but that would have to wait for the right time – a time when he had an answer, said a little voice in his head. Meanwhile, there was the more immediate and pressing matter of the bumps in the night.

Further discussion with Ken resulted in them deciding to see the captain about the noises as they felt the crew might fob them off with a placatory response. There was a risk in this because it elevated the matter into an issue when maybe it was caused by something very minor.

However, they arranged to meet him a couple of mornings later and found themselves sitting in his wee office, the only one in the Drove, with a properly percolated coffee feeling slightly ill-prepared and apprehensive. (An Italian company had developed, with the help of the Italian Space Agency, a coffee machine for use in Space way back in 2015.) Captain Peter Reid at nearly 50, was older than most of the other crew and had a wide range of experience. He'd been around in the early days of the ISS cutting his teeth on risky docking manoeuvres and had spent long periods managing operational matters relating to the second round of moon trips in the 2020s. His steely dedication to strict quality guidelines and his determined and targeted approach to difficult issues had earned him a formidable reputation for wanting everything spot on.

"How can I help you guys?" he said after a few pleasantries about the mustard and cress and the six mini cos lettuces growing in a tray beside his desk. Steve launched forth with a short account of his concerns about strange sounds in the night and his need to know the reasons so that he could assure others who heard them that there was nothing untoward. The captain listened carefully and made no response but then asked Ken why he had come along too.

Ken was not quite prepared for being singled out but managed to respond,

"The chaplain drew my attention to the distant drilling sounds and I thought I heard them on occasions too. I'm sure it's nothing much but when it's all you hear and it's in the night and you've got plenty of time to think, it takes on a completely unwarranted importance."

Captain Reid leant back in his chair and considered his options. This was the chaplain and a well-qualified mechanical engineer before him, not part of the crew but nevertheless well informed. One of them dealt with the well-being and psychology of the folk on board, the other, judging by his bio, understood well the mechanical aspects of complex systems. Maybe he should risk including them in his confidence circle although this was meant to be the crew alone but a situation like this had not occurred before so the old rules would not necessarily apply. He contemplated this for a couple of minutes then made a decision.

"I'm afraid it's a case of Houston we have a problem although in this case it's Mars being informed not Houston because it concerns our arrival there in a couple of months. Strictly, it is a matter for the crew alone but since both of you could both prove useful I am prepared to include you on condition that, until informed otherwise, you do not discuss the matter with the other paranauts."

Both Steve and Ken nodded their acceptance of this.

"You will remember that we made light of the leg extension damage on the launch, saying we would solve the matter en route. I understand that the absence of any mention since then has led people to assume the damage is not serious and it has been addressed or shown to be no threat to a successful landing. I'm afraid that is not the case and indications are that the whole leg extension mechanism is likely to be non-functional. As far as we can tell, it's a mechanical issue as the sensors on the hydraulic rams convey positive messages and indeed they do actually commence to extend but meet resistance consistent with the leg being buckled by the heat. As you know, we reported a flashback from one of the engines which must have overheated the leg mechanism. I am sorry to have to tell you this."

Ken came in with, "I am sure we would far rather

know and if I can help in any way, being a mechanical engineer please involve me."

"Thank you for that," said the captain, "and Steve may be useful too because, at some point, we will have to inform all the passengers and manage their consequent reaction."

Steve was still trying to unravel his thoughts and asked,

"How are the noises we heard related to the damaged leg?"

"The noises were our space repair drone which can drift about outside the spacecraft with miniature jets, rather than the propellers used on Earth. The drone has a camera and can also perform minor mechanical checks and repairs with its probes. It was developed by a Japanese company for exactly this type of situation. We have been using it to examine and fit small detectors to the outer skin and we do this at night-time because we don't want to draw attention to it at this stage. Seeing a little jet-drone drift past the windows would not inspire confidence once the purpose was revealed."

Ken realised why they had become insistent that the window blinds were drawn at night.

He asked, "At what stage is this investigation?"

"I'm afraid we have concluded after much consultation with the Mars Council, who are effectively our Mission Control from now on as we are so far away from Earth, that we must proceed on the basis that only two of the three legs will operate. This means that on landing, the spacecraft will tip onto its side at best or rollover at worst doing irreparable damage and potentially igniting the remaining fuel in the thruster rockets. Also, the pressurised vehicles for transporting people to the Mars village will then not dock with the craft meaning that each person would have to be suited up individually and transferred. We have seven spacesuits but it would still be a long and precarious procedure as the suits would have to be shuttled back each time. We plan to land in the Mars day when the temperature may be, say, 15 degrees C but, if it extended into the night when the surface temperature drops to minus 100, that would be an added peril. You will now appreciate why we are reluctant to broadcast this more widely until we have a viable solution."

They were silent for a time and Steve remembered Eric's earlier concerns. He asked if one of the crew could make a spacewalk to the damaged leg but he was told that, while it had been relatively common especially on the ISS in the past, the Drove had no facilities for this; a bit like modern cars having no spare tyre thought Steve. Ken asked if the Mars village had sufficient workshop facilities to construct something on which the Drove could land and the captain said that was one area they were investigating but the landing position could not be fixed closer than within a circle about 10 metres diameter so docking onto a structure would be very risky. He looked at his wrist pad and rose to terminate the meeting saying,

"Look, we are not going to solve anything this morning and I need to get on. Please respect the confidentiality for the moment; I will ask you to join us with the crew at the next update on the issue. Steve, I would like you to start thinking about how we release this information and manage the reaction. Ken, I would like you to think about the mechanical aspects of our problem. As you will appreciate they have thought through all the more obvious solutions but a fresh angle would do no harm so you can start right away."

"I can hardly avoid thinking about it," responded Ken,

"considering my own and everybody else's continued existence might depend on it!"

Ken and Steve had made no movement towards the door to leave so the Captain opened it and said, smiling, "Now bugger off and let me continue sending these reports to Earth, not that Earth is much use in this emergency."

Thus dismissed the two made their way back to the cabin but not before they had had a long discussion at the water-cooler.

9

Doomsday Scenario

KEN MARKHAM HAD difficulty sleeping at the best of times and found that he was now waking up every couple of hours through the night. He had managed to find some electronic drawings of the Drove and ascertained that the legs extended far beyond the shell and were essential for landing to avoid the spacecraft toppling. Presumably, three was the minimum number of legs possible and while four might have helped, even then if one had malfunctioned, the spacecraft could have fallen over like a chair with a broken leg. Indeed, four might have led to the craft wobbling precariously once down whereas three would avoid this in the same way that a three-legged stool never wobbles. Ken considered whether the craft could land on some type of platform erected on the ground to replace one leg but with the other two legs extended. This would need the ability to land with high precision while rotating the Craft as it landed and he was not sure that could be done. It was ironic that with all the current sophistication of electronic control systems, in the end, everything boiled down to basic ingenuity and mechanical movement .

Steve, on the other hand, was worried about the Captain's suggestion that he, as the chaplain, should be involved in the release of the serious news that the landing issue was not resolved. He wondered when the

Captain would want the news released, how the paranauts would react, how he could console them if the likelihood of a safe arrival on Mars was low and how would they tell their loved ones on Earth? Maybe others had heard the noises in the night. Explaining that this was a space repair drone attaching itself to the side of the Drove near the damaged leg to take photos while they were asleep might affect the already delicate relationship with the crew members. Getting along with folk is important in any group whether it be in work, in sport or wherever. On the Earth, those that are not happy in one group can move to another but on a spacecraft there is nowhere else to go so they have to stay, potentially leading to serious discontent. One person panicking on receiving the news could upset the psychological dynamics of the whole group. Indeed, he had seen a touch of that earlier with Erik who had since settled down and now even entertained them on occasions with Norwegian songs. As chaplain, they would understandably look to him to manage the welfare aspects of the news. However, his course at New College, Edinburgh and subsequent training was centred on theology and the Presbyterian Christian religion which was poor preparation for being among a group of well-informed young scientists and engineers from all over the world. He would have to rely heavily on his previous experience with disgruntled railway travellers and difficult folk in Dubai in order to scrape through this emergency. He kept pondering how best to deal with it but in the end, events took their own course.

The crew had known for some weeks about the seriousness of the landing problem but they were sworn to secrecy by the Mars Council and Earth Mission Control. The weak link in the information security was, as always in such situations, the avoidance of any hint to their loved ones on Earth. The odd innuendo; 'if we get back okay', 'if you could transfer our savings to another account', 'if anything happens, I love you' could signal a slight concern. The sum total of all this apprehension over a period could seed a suspicion that could lead to anxious questions about the mission from those that knew them best. And it was indeed thus, that one evening a tired crew member hinted to his girlfriend on Earth that there's a mechanical problem needs to be resolved before landing. She is a sharp girl and couples this with the known flame flare which was reported at the launch. Indeed, it could be seen in some of the released pictures. So she twitters her buddies in the Mission Friends Group. This is an informal social group consisting of friends and associates of the crew and paranauts on the spacecraft who keep in touch, although scattered across the world. The tweet only says, 'looks like damage to Drove could cause landing problem,' but it's enough to seed panic within the Friends Group. When accidentally leaked to terrestrial social media it was seized upon with alacrity by the press who were suffering from a quiet news day.

So it was that Ken went rushing across to Steve, or at least as quickly as one can manoeuvre when weightless, with an agitated expression on his face and a news headline on his iPhone:

Drove in Peril as it nears Mars

Steve was surprised that, within a few days of their meeting with the captain, it was so widely known but then, bad news travels faster than good news. He was also disappointed that presumably, somebody must have leaked the information. To be precise, he was in fact only a little disappointed and perhaps just a little relieved as

81

he had not quite worked out how to tell folk about the danger himself and that requirement was now well and truly unnecessary. He quickly perused the article which actually had very little of substance and neither disclosed the reason for the peril nor its potential effect on landing the Craft. Steve decided to see the captain immediately but was met by one of his assistants who seemed to have adopted the task of shielding him. He convinced him of the urgency without disclosing too much and was ushered into the captain's office a few minutes later.

Captain Peter Reid knew about the news release and was exasperated that somebody had leaked it in spite of his request. Like many precise and well-ordered people, he had difficulty managing unexpected events. Steve pointed out that it was probably no one person and certainly not intentional but rather a propagation of seemingly innocuous events that added up to a rumour that became a headline. The captain thought it was important that the whole Spacecraft were informed immediately before they all heard it on-line and that they were given assurance about the on-going work on a resolution. He then, to Steve's surprise, asked him to make the announcement.

Steve immediately suggested it should come from the captain himself but Captain Reid explained that was not the way he wanted it done as it would cause too much concern at this stage. He insisted that Steve as chaplain inform them immediately that there had been an unfortunate news release on earth which exaggerated the problems with the landing gear and that the chaplain would make himself available to assist any of the passengers or crew who were apprehensive, either on their own behalf or because of the effect on their families. The captain did offer Steve one of the crew members, Sid Hawthorn, the person most involved in Drove landing issues, as a 'press officer' to work with him on technical questions. Steve left and found a quiet corner pod (belonging to a friend who was currently helping with the communal laundry facility) and worked out how he would inform his colleagues without signalling a doomsday scenario. After dinner that evening, he proceeded to the position used by the after-dinner lecturers (dubbed speaker's corner by the cynics), picked up the microphone and after attracting their attention gave the following announcement:

Colleagues,

May I please have your attention for a few moments. The Captain has asked me to speak to you about the terrestrial news item doing the rounds this morning in many of the National electronic newspapers. Some of you may already have picked it up. It relates to the accidental flare released by one of the engines on our launch which has left one of the landing legs slightly damaged. The crew, under guidance from Mission Control on Earth and the Mars council here have been trying to repair the faulty leg, mainly at night when other systems are using little power, you may have heard mechanical noises in the distance.

As always, the press has sensationalised it by considering the worst-case scenario and this may lead to folk at home, including your own families and friends, becoming concerned. I would like to assure you solutions that obviate the need for extension of the damaged leg are being explored and there is no need to assume landing will not be as smooth as it has been on the previous occasions. You may remember that previous landings of the droves were uneventful and their crews were much commended.

Finally, I am happy to assist any of you who have

concerns individually or within your families includ-
ing, as chaplain, praying with you for a safe journey
and arrival on Mars. I am happy to take questions but
bear in mind I'm not a technical guy and will, therefore,
deflect any questions on such issues to the crew member
in charge of landing arrangements, Sid Hawthorn.

There was silence for a moment, a lull before the storm, and then the questions started. Most of them had been suffering from acute boredom and while concerned, it at least added a new dimension of interest and excitement. They came thick and fast; why had they not been kept abreast of progress, why had two months gone by before Earthlings were told, why was the design dependent on legs anyway, what happened if it fell over and so on? Why are *you* rather than the Captain telling us they said and also what's this about prayers—even if they worked on Earth they're hardly going to work in space. "We want more information," they said, "so get us some answers and next time, bring the captain with you."

Ken came in and pointed out to them that Steve had done what he could. He then thanked him on their behalf for speaking to them about it and there was a grudging murmur of assent. However, over the next few days, several paranauts sought Steve's advice on dealing with their concerned families and one or two on personal matters which gave Steve the satisfaction of feeling that his role as chaplain was beginning to be accepted. However, this activity did not diminish his own concern about how they were going to find a suitable spot to land this stricken school bus on the rocky Mars terrain.

10

Finding a Parking Space

OVER THE NEXT few days, Ken was included with the crew in the communications between Mission Control on Mars and the UN Mars Committee on Earth. Essentially, the technical difficulties of landing on two legs were still unresolved. The focus of attention was now on devising a mobile platform on the ground which could be manoeuvred by Mission Control during landing to the position where the third leg would have been. Earlier studies of landing on a step had been discounted owing to the imprecise positioning accuracy on the descent. The danger of any mobile platform placed under the leg was the possibility of it not functioning correctly on the day adding further potential for disaster.

One morning, following a restless night worrying about this and the consequence of landing failure, Ken was sitting on his bed letting his mind meander aimlessly for a moment before he got down to the business of the day. It was all a matter of legs he thought. Humanoids developed from walking on four to walking on two and learning how to balance. Man had never had three legs, although three was the most stable minimum number. At this moment, for example, he was sitting on his bed with three points of contact with the ground, two legs on the floor and his bottom on the bed. He had many times been out walking on the Scottish hills and become tired. If there was no suitably positioned flat rock on which to sit he would find a slope and perch on it with his legs pointing down the slope; not the most comfortable position but better than nothing. It needed no platform or seat but he could be stably positioned in this way *anywhere on the slope.* That was the answer! Of course, it could be anywhere on the slope; it was his eureka moment. Land the Drove on a sufficient slope with the legs on the downhill side and the exact position on the slope was immaterial. It relied on being able to turn the drove to that position as it landed and the availability of a suitable hill near the Mars village.

Ken hurried along to see Sid Hawthorn and divulged his thoughts regarding the slope. Initially Sid was somewhat dismissive and said they had looked at the possibility some time ago but rejected it because the control jets were not really suitable for rotational control but only vertical descent. Ken pointed out there was some limited control of rotation by lateral vernier adjustment on each of the jets---it was indeed this that had malfunctioned on take-off and moved a jet a little causing the overheating of the leg mechanism on take-off. Sid agreed on reflection it might just be possible to rotate the Drove sufficiently. Also, there were plenty of hills very close to the Village; it would just be a matter of selecting the right one. Sid saw the captain later that morning who liked what he heard and set the wheels in motion for an in-depth analysis of the idea. Over the next few weeks, it was decided that this was the way to go and the captain made an announcement to the paranauts that he and his team had at last found a resolution. Any credit due to Ken's input at just the right time seemed to have been lost in the noise but Ken himself knew who had nudged the system in the right direction with such a positive result and was happily content in that knowledge.

Meanwhile, Steve had been dealing with the increasing concerns of the paranauts and also one or two of the crew once the real possibility of mission failure began to sink in. The early downplaying of the terrestrial news had somewhat backfired when the true seriousness was manifest and while there was no outright panic, most folk on board were suffering from a general air of foreboding. Partly as a distraction and partly because he was, after all, the chaplain and meant to do such things, he organised a number of short services which he referred to as *gatherings* to avoid the ritualistic overtones that religious services engender. These gatherings were shared social events and folk were simply invited to tune in on their iPads at a given time on the specified evening. He was careful to explain to the multi-national and multi-cultural assemblage on board that these gatherings were to talk about and pray for a safe landing. He had expected half a dozen of the more worried people to tune in but was surprised to have over half of those on board enrolling. In the second gathering, he transferred to an interactive mode so that folk could ask questions electronically and become involved. Since by now, three-quarters of them were on board he asked the captain if he could conduct the next one by word of mouth by assembling everybody on the upper deck and received an affirmative reply. Perhaps it was not so surprising in some ways he thought because in disasters and situations of danger on earth folk would draw together in a local church to share their anxieties whether they were religiously inclined or not. These occasional gatherings became a feature of the remaining two months of the journey.

The sixth gathering on the upper deck was just a

couple of days before they were expecting to arrive on Mars and it became a more intense and deeply probing affair than Steve had expected. No doubt this was partly because it would be the last such gathering before landing and partly because, while the new landing procedure had been widely broadcast, there was still an acute danger. Nearly all those on board were present. Steve conducted the gathering along his own traditional Christian lines with a few minutes of prayer for a safe landing on Mars to *God in all his manifestations* so that the non-Christians were comfortable. He then as on the previous two occasions gave a short 5-minute address on how, as pioneers on a new planet, they had great responsibilities to develop a new kind of society where all could live in harmony. He then played a recording of *Abide with Me* and bid them adieu for the last time before landing.

However, they seemed reluctant to leave and just sat there until a guy named Paul sitting near the front piped up and said, "You prayed for a solution to the landing, which then happened; you prayed for the possibility of implementing it, which then happened, are you sure we're going to get safely to Mars and make it a hat trick?"

He'd said it with a smile and one or two folk laughed awkwardly so Steve guessed he was just probing. He said, "No, you're going to make it happen by *your* prayers, that's the way it works."

"But I'm an atheist and although I prayed, it's only because I'm just as scared as the rest of you. I don't believe all the religious stuff you guys churn out."

All eyes were on Steve to see how he received this challenge.

"If you prayed from your heart out of fear then you are not an atheist. By your silent desire, perhaps not even fashioned into words, you are acknowledging that there is something beyond our physical being that can be reached; something we can tune into? That something has been called God by thinkers for thousands of years. These thinkers may be philosophers, theologians, scientists or anybody in the street but they are all at least agreed on one thing and that's the name, it's God. To some, God may be an omnipotent control centre, to some an omnipresent person attending to their personal needs, to some a cosmic force pervading the universe and to some all three. Very few are truly atheist or even agnostic."

It was all quiet, so he carried on, "If you don't believe me, Google the case of the Chilean Miners Accident of 2010. They, like us, were a diverse bunch of folk trapped in an inaccessible space, in their case some 2500 meters below the surface in a dark cavern with no hope of rescue. They were there for over two months and the whole world was watching their plight. While the technical challenges in the rescue were enormous, the greatest fear was the condition of the miners, not so much their physical hardships but their mental state. Would they go mad in this doomsday situation among the stifling dark passages underground over such a long period and start killing one another? Once communication was established one of the notes of support they received was actually from the astronauts on the ISS. In the end, all 33 miners survived by instituting daily patterns and routines and attendance at daily prayers established by the group.

Private prayers are the very core of the awareness of God. Not public prayers that are of necessity subject to some peer approval but truly private prayers. Religions are merely the gift wrapping; the ornamental box housing a beautiful diamond. Gift wrappings come in a variety of forms and are often gaudy and inappropriate but do not let this detract from the beauty and value of the enclosed gift, the personal prayer diamond inside. Never judge a gift by its wrapping."

Steve suddenly realised he'd slipped into preaching mode as if he was taking a morning service in a Scottish Kirk rather than among his friends and colleagues in a capsule in space. He found himself a trifle embarrassed and closed the gathering, "Please pray for a soft landing of our Drove and in whatever position we find ourselves, literally, may we all be safely escorted to the Mars village reception area. Hopefully, the next gathering will be thanksgiving at the new chaplaincy in the Mars village on Friday."

As he made his way to the water cooler, he met Paul and with a little nudge said, "Trust you'll be at the next gathering, Paul," to which Paul responded, "Only if you keep your sermons short!"

11

Landing Rights

AS THE LANDING day dawned, there was a general air of resignation among the paranauts and indeed the crew. Steve's assurances that all would be well were wearing a little thin but nobody admitted this to their neighbours for fear it might be seen as a sign of weakness or disloyalty. Surprisingly, little had been said about the detailed mechanics of the modified two-leg landing although all by now understood that it was on a sloping hill near the village and a difficult manual manoeuvre was required. In no time, the day was upon them and they all busied themselves getting their own possessions ready and tidying up. Finally, the signal was given that touchdown was in half an hour so they strapped themselves in their seats and chatted nervously about inconsequential things.

Fifteen minutes to touch down, TD minus 15, the first spacecraft manoeuvre thrust was felt and a general air of agitated excitement developed with folk talking to their neighbours in adjacent pods to keep up their spirits. At TD minus 10, with the speed still over 2000 mph, they could feel the deceleration; a distant roar developed and the Drove shook. People were visibly frightened as it entered the thin Mars atmosphere. The outer skin would now be glowing deep red with the heat. Those that could see out of the small windows were awestruck by their first view of the planet with its gently curved horizon above a red ochre foreground. At TD minus 3, there was another frightening lurch followed by a deafening roar as twelve descent thrusters sprung into action. Just before TD itself, there was some rapid twisting movement followed by a crushing noise and then nothing.

There had been so many reorientations and bumps over the previous few minutes that nobody knew what to expect next and they looked at one another apprehensively. After a minute or so of relative quietness, a couple of the crew rushed up from below and announced they were down, which was pretty obvious, but not safe yet as the craft was twisted at an angle with one of the two legs precariously perched on a protruding rock. This was a pretty unstable position and even the crew could not hide their concern. After a fearful half an hour, they were told that a ground buggy from the village was on its way to move some large rocks in position to better stabilise the craft before disembarkation could commence. This would take about a couple of hours but the sand density in the atmosphere was on the high side which restricted visibility. Sand storms are common on Mars and even on good days, the dust could be whipped up into swirling clouds which severely limited the visibility.

While waiting, the crew explained the emergency exit procedure involving three people at a time suiting up and descending into the depressurisation zone at the base of the craft prior to leaving on the Rover transfer vehicle taking them to the reception centre. The spacesuits would be brought back each time on the Rover's return. They were told that they would be leaving their pods in an order that reduced the out-of-balance forces of the precariously stabilised spacecraft but Steve reckoned this was simply an excuse to prevent any misplaced heroics about letting others go first. To help reduce the tension and distract them from their predicament, Ken tried to lighten the mood by chit-chat and banter and he suggested they ate up the best of the remaining food packages. He then spoilt his good intentions by referring to it as the last supper.

In the event, this part of the operation went as well as could be expected given two peripheral difficulties; the height of the exit door was above the transfer vehicle's platform owing to the landing position. This meant assistance was needed in each case (after the first person jumped and damaged her suit). The second was the sand storm that was developing fast. Both of these extended the transfer time and there were fears that the oncoming night would mean it was too cold to continue. The 16 trips over the 500 metres to the village took a total of 6 hours; a brilliant job by the crew and ground staff. On the last trip, Captain Reid shut everything down on a temporary basis so that the ground support staff could return the next day when hopefully the sand storm, which was by them becoming severe, had abated. Much of the freight brought with the passengers was left for later collection when hopefully the craft could more safely be secured in position. As the captain looked back on leaving, he was appalled at the angle of the Drove, leaning like a crippled obelisk against the darkening Mars landscape, and he was extremely grateful that everybody had left in safety.

Steve had left on the penultimate Rover trip and apart from the remaining crew was one of the last to arrive. Once in the reception area, he experienced a strange feeling of utter relief and absolute wonder at the amount of space in the Community Dome. They had been cooped up in a very confined spacecraft and this seemed like heaven on earth, or rather Mars. For four months, they had been able to view the emptiness of the universe and yet they were suffering because they had very little of this vast space in their wee craft. It was the space equivalent of Coleridge's *Old Man of the Sea*, water, water everywhere and not a drop to drink. But now the spaciousness was like a tonic and revived their wonder and excitement at landing on another planet. Once free of their suits, they joined what was effectively a reception party, meeting lots of people and milling about trying to get used to having weight again, albeit only just over a third of that on earth but still causing a heavy almost clumsy feeling after the weightlessness in the Drove so that after a little, the opportunity to sit down was welcome. President Leskovich of the Mars community gave a short address of welcome and referred to their especially good fortune in landing safely following the earlier mishap in the Drove. The new arrivals were then escorted to individual rooms, given a soporific pill of some sort and encouraged to rest. Being thus dosed up, exhausted and absolutely relieved, they all fell into a deep sleep as intended by the authorities for new arrivals on the planet.

The next morning, they ventured out of their rooms bleary-eyed and wondering how they showered, tidied up, got their possessions delivered from the Drove and so on. It was evident from the concerned looks and pre-oc-cupation of the staff that something was amiss. It tran-spired that the sand storm the previous night had been moderately severe and nobody, not even a robotic rover had been sent to the stricken Drove until the morning when visibility was much improved. The rover could not find the Drove's position so mid-morning a manned buggy went to the landing position of the night before.

The Drove was not there, it had gone! On hearing this, panic set in among the staff and managers of the Mars village; this was terrible. Following the euphoria at the successful landing of the crippled craft, it had not been properly tethered by the landing technicians as recommended by Earth Mission Control and in the storm had rocked, become unstable and finally rolled away down the hill coming to rest, after considerable damage to the booster rockets and other external parts, a hundred meters away. Furthermore, it lay with the airlock door firmly buried in the soft sandy Mars regolith so that access was not going to be easily possible. Fortunately, it had not exploded but this was still a disaster. Among the items in the Drove, apart from so-called fresh food supplies, there were the personal effects of the passengers and many other things including replacement technical components and electronic control units which were urgently required for the village.

Steve's general impression of the Mars village to which he was now assigned as chaplain, was on first glance rather foreboding. It was after all the first human community on another planet and was bound to appear horribly grim and utilitarian to new arrivals. They were taken on a tour to familiarise them with their new surroundings and this is what they found:

Essentially there are five large concrete domes connected by tunnels and surrounded by horticultural areas of translucent plastic. Even in the most artificial of environments on Earth, there is always the possibility of a short escape, the momentary nip outside for a breath of fresh air. On Mars, that is not possible although going outside, albeit in a spacesuit, and seeing the wonders of space with the Earth as a steady glowing dot among the twinkling stars (generally planets glow, stars twinkle) might partially compensate.

Four of the domes are for residents and typically about 200 meters in diameter. They encircle a fifth or Community Dome which is somewhat larger at 300 meters in diameter. They are named after cities loosely connected with the research on living in such an environment and in alphabetical order, thus so far; Anchorage, Beijing, Casablanca and Dubai but this is just foreshortened to A, B, C and D. Each resident dome has three connecting tunnels or arcades, one each to the adjacent domes and one to the Community Dome creating three exit points in case of an emergency. The works facilities, fuel stores and back-up air-conditioning systems are some distance away outside the area of the domes but connected by longer tunnels. These domes can each house 30 to 50 people in small private areas called pods which are effectively small bed-sits. All the immediate facilities they need are housed locally in each dome and more are planned as the village grows. With the arrival of Steve and his fellow travellers on Drone 5, the total population was already approaching 170 and growth to several thousand was expected in the next few years.

The Community Dome has three floors with the executive pods and administrative offices on the top floor, laboratories and scientific areas on the middle floor and everything else on the ground floor. The ground floor, where it all happens, consists of further laboratories, housing for the rovers and associated outdoor items and most importantly an open plan area for the community as a whole. This includes a store where Mars money (described later) can be spent, a gym, a health centre, a restaurant, a café and the Mars Bar, which sells small quantities of Mars home-brewed beer (again more later) and very expensive wine imported from Earth in horrible half-litre plastic containers.

Last but not least in Steve's estimation, is the spiritual health centre. This name had been carefully chosen long ago by the Mars Committee of the UN to ensure equality of support for all the religious faiths. In the event, everybody just called it the chaplaincy in spite of the crescent, the squatting Buddha and emblems of other faiths alongside the cross on the wall in the meeting room. Leading off from this room is Steve's pod and a small private study with its spare bed for emergency use which came in very useful later. The chaplaincy meeting room is a cosy retreat from the big community area outside and has become widely used for all sorts of purposes. It can accommodate a score of folks at a push and is used as a lecture theatre and for gatherings of all types in addition to a chapel for services of all faiths.

Steve gradually settled down over the next few months to his role in this strange environment and, although it was all so alien, it began to feel more homely once some semblance of a routine was established; human beings are essentially creatures of habit. It was at this point that Jo Thanawala entered the scene as we saw earlier, having been referred to him with suspected acute homesickness called Celestial Depression or CD by the authorities.

12

Banter in the Mars Bar

DR JO THANAWALA made a renewed effort over
the weeks following her meeting with Steve to take more
interest in her work in the biochemistry lab, however
boring, and to arrive on time in the mornings. She found
herself wondering in a curious way about the tall Scottish guy with a dark beard who had ended up in such an
odd role on Mars. She resolved to follow up the acquaintance and a couple of weeks later she casually appeared
one afternoon at Steve's office in the community centre
and reminded him that he had agreed to tell her how he
landed as chaplain on Mars. She had meant rather than
as a Parish Minister in some leafy village in Scotland but
he mistook her meaning and spent the next half hour
describing exactly how he had landed in Drove 5 on Mars.
As it happened though, she was also interested in hearing
his account of this because she had only heard disjointed
versions from others so her original enquiry was put on
hold for a future occasion.

Although it had only been a few months ago, the
landing of Drove 5 had become folk law among the Mars
community and indeed on terrestrial news too, in spite
of the authorities both on Mars and the control centre
on Earth suppressing part of it (from corporate embarrassment it was said by some). She listened intently as
Steve recounted the details of the landing and subsequent

toppling of the craft and how they had to excavate the regolith to access the door. He explained that they eventually righted the spacecraft and found the damage was reparable but it initiated a blame game about who was responsible for a spacecraft once docked on Mars. The resulting animosity between Captain Reid and President Leskovich of the Mars Community became the subject of much speculation by the news channels across the world and it developed into a media soap opera. Being key personnel in the Mars venture and both having a meticulous approach to compliance with the rules led to constant disagreements when the rule book was inadequate for the task in hand. People assumed it would all die down after they had managed to dig a passageway to the Drove door and gain access. However, the news channels were not going to give up on a good storyline and even after the two protagonists had found a workable way of getting along, they continued to exaggerate every mild difference for the fun of it. Jo and Steve continued to chat for a time until Steve excused himself, explaining that he had arranged to meet John Abraham her line manager at 6 pm in the Mars Bar. She was disappointed not to be invited too but realised that it might have been more than purely social and wandered off saying in passing that she had things to do.

When he got there, John had not arrived so he settled into a corner seat with a regulation half-pint of beer. As noted earlier, this restriction was not due to the lack of ingredients on Mars, for the small micro-brewery was operating well, but rather the increasingly puritanical stance taken by some members of the Council on this and many other issues. He was just beginning to space out when big John joined him with a cheery suggestion that his Scottish friend had already tanked up. John was born in England but his family had moved to Canada where he had spent most of his younger life. As a PhD student at Imperial College, London, he renewed his association with England and although subsequently working for NASA for many years, he often reminded folk that he was an Englishman. As a section head on Mars, he had to deal among other things with conventional people-management issues and John had occasionally turned to Steve for off-the-record advice. Steve had explained that he was no better equipped to advise on people issues than anybody else but John had argued that, as a chaplain having some training in church management, not the easiest bodies to manage, he was an excellent sounding board. From their conversations, Steve also suspected that John was something of a deep thinker although he had never probed the matter.

After some man-chat about world football and the pre-eminence of Rangers following their slump on the world scene many years before, they degenerated into moaning about the miserly beer allowance. To add insult to injury, when there was no barman it was dispensed directly into their plastic mugs from a steely robotic device known unofficially by Mars folk as Greta, owing to it being so unlike any Bavarian barmaid they'd ever seen. The conversation then drifted on to their work and people issues.

"I see you off-loaded your bright young assistant to me as soon as she upset your staff attendance tick list," said Steve with a smirk.

"Yes, she is brilliant at her job but seems to suffer more than most from terrestrial nostalgia. Indeed, she had real trouble on the journey over here."

"Didn't we all?" asked Steve.

"It is the little things of life that we had got used

to and hardly noticed but are now no longer there that constantly remind us we are in a type of post-Earth experience—on which point," exclaimed Steve, "have I lost it or is that a fly on my glass!"

"It's sure a fly all right, Steve, but that doesn't mean you haven't lost it," chided John.

"I heard the other day that somebody had seen one."

"But that's terrible. All this effort to avoid seeding Mars with earth's microbes and the precautions we have taken as paranauts and yet it's failed. Is not everything meant to be biologically screened—surely flies would be noticed?"

"Apparently not," said John, "The eggs are less than 1mm across. Do you know the female housefly only copulates once in her life (let's hope she enjoys it) and secretes the semen for subsequent egg fertilisation? She can lay hundreds of eggs every few days over her lifetime so that's why they're everywhere on Earth—there're bound to get transported with something sent here now that a lot of ordinary stuff needed by humans is arriving."

Steve was hardly listening as he was thrashing around trying to swot the fly with a plastic menu, but John admonished him.

"Just let it be, it's a small reminder of home and you need to preserve these links with life down there, even the flies." John continued, "Talking about flies, I was once in a pub with an Englishman, a Welshman and a Scotsman."

Steve gave an exaggerated sigh and muttered something about here we go.

"Three flies flew in the window, one landing on each of their three pints. The Englishman got a teaspoon, delicately eased it out and continued to drink. The Welshman waited for it to get to the centre and then, in a show of wild determination, flicked it out using his thumb and forefinger with such force it was impaled on the window pane. Your countryman, the Scotsman, he just waited until the fly's attempts to swim subsided and it lay immobile on the surface. He then squeezed it out over the pint, wiped the residue off on his kilt and drained his pint."

"OK, OK" said Steve, "actually, we call it fly fishing." He then added, "And did *you* hear about the two Scotsmen, two Welshmen, two Irishmen and two Englishmen who got stranded on a desert island. After three months the Scotsmen had made a whisky still and were selling it to the others; the Welshmen had started a choir, the Irishmen were still fighting on the beach but the Englishmen still hadn't spoken to each other as they'd not been introduced."

John realised he was not going to win this line of banter and after a pause returned the conversation to flies.

"Isn't it amazing that fly's' eggs can survive the journey here."

"It's no more amazing than me surviving it," said Steve. John looked at him oddly.

"We've all survived that, what makes it so special for you?"

Steve put down his beer.

"Well, physically, it was not too bad, a bit cramped with 47 of us in a space not much larger than a double-decker bus. You eventually get used to all the minor frustrations, the hanging on to everything to stop it floating away, drinking through funny straws, pissing into plastic bags, constantly having to catch your screwdriver every time you do a repair job and so on. No, it was seeing the earth getting smaller and smaller until after 3 months you only saw it occasionally and only then as a wee dot in the sky. That dot was my total existence, my total life and now it is nothing."

John responded thoughtfully, "Most of us spent so much time sorting out the petty annoyances of every-day living on the Drove spacecraft that we had little time for philosophical thoughts like that. But I suppose that's part of your job and you have got to deal with it and to have answers. I really don't envy your role as chaplain but drink up and I'll get you another one before you become melancholy."

"I thought we were only allowed one half-pint per day. That's the rule, isn't it? And I of all people must be seen to observe these ruddy rules," he grinned.

"The rules are made by folk on the wee dot you mentioned just now so I should not fret about it. I'll tell you what; I'll order two for myself from that damn machine that thinks it's a barmaid and then you can offer to drink one of them to avoid me sinking into the wanton sin of disobedience to our masters---that's what you folk are meant to do isn't it?"

John had to over-ride the voice-over warning on the beer dispensing machine in order to extract two more beers, one of which he placed in front of his friend. Steve said nothing for some time but after a while, he made an admission that he had told nobody else.

"Since you ask," he said, "I had no trouble with lift-off but about an hour afterwards I found I was totally emotionally drained feeling horribly alone and somehow disconnected. Basically, I suppose I was shit scared—excuse the non-liturgical language."

John was used to jollying his oddly pious friend along with rib-digging insults and targeted jokes but sensed this was not the right response at the moment. He was just wondering how to handle it when he was saved by

Mary who joined them with no sense of interruption and asked why they were looking like two jerks planning a bank raid. John glanced at Steve with a 'maybe we'll continue some other time' look and they gave Mary, a lively, personable American girl in her late 20s working on organic chains or some such boring subject, their full attention.

Later, Steve pondered on the psychological effects of going to Mars. John was right of course. As chaplain, he not only had to deal with his own emotions on leaving the Earth but he had to give assistance to others suffering from extreme disconnectedness on departing from the planet on which they were born, possibly forever. In his profession, he had to attend the dying and, as postulated earlier, if that was equivalent to leaving the Earth, then going to Mars was akin to dying.

13

Who's in Charge?

JO WAS STILL bored but she had the feeling that this period was the calm before a storm. She had been there before as a schoolchild but that seemed to be another world, as indeed it was. The school was in India but the schooling was Tibetan owing to her being the child of a liaison between a lapsed Tibetan monk and a local Indian girl both from Dharamshala. This was highly unusual and led to Josephine growing up in a cultural environment very different from her compatriots. Her mother had become inspired by the history of the Tibetan folk of Dharamshala and their desperate flight across the Himalayas a century before to escape the oppression of the Chinese. The Buddhist community in the Pradesh area employed some locals and she became an office assistant when the first computers were being introduced. She worked closely with a young Buddhist monk who discovered he was skilled at using the new electronic systems but the two of them found they had other interests and he was tempted away from his vows of celibacy as a practising member of the local temple. The two eloped to a remote village in the mountains to escape their disapproving families and communities. Josephine was born a year later and the family returned to Dharamshala after a time to find that the communities were less opposed to them than they had thought. Her father's brilliant computer skills were of use to the Buddhist community and he was employed as an external consultant to them. While he could never return to the inner sanctum of the Temple, he was well respected throughout the region as is the Buddhist way and they all doted on little Jo as she became known. She attended the best School in the area where she excelled , particularly in mathematics, but after a time, she became bored with all the study, feeling like now, that it was a quiet lull before life really got going. This it did and she went on to university, the Indian State Space Programme and finally, to Mars.

Now, here she was, late afternoon, becoming bored again, so she decided on a whim that a diversion was needed and made her way to the chaplaincy on the weak excuse of informing Steve about some news from her friend in New York. She had picked her time fortuitously because, as she arrived, Steve said, "This is about the time of day I sometimes go along to the Mars Bar for a beer. It's just opening and you're welcome to come along, they serve coffee and tea too."

She tried not to appear too keen, "Yes, maybe, thanks. I've got to check out something in the lab, but that's not for an hour."

Once they were settled in with a beer for him and a coffee for her, she said, "Your account the other day of the landing was particularly interesting because my friend who lives in New York told me that all the news programmes clearly blamed the captain for being responsible for ensuring the safety of the Drove including when docked on land, be it Earth or Mars. Yet, it would seem that the Mars council had assumed they had authority over the craft once on Mars because the technicians responsible for securing it are employed by them."

"Yes, I agree. I think it's similar to Port Authority

responsibilities for securing sea vessels when docked in harbour, not that I know much about maritime law," ventured Steve.

"Or even Mars law," said Jo, smiling.

"Maybe not, but as it happens, I did, as part of my preparation for coming here, read up about the constitutional basis of the Mars authority and the council. I know folk find the council's puritanical rules a little irksome but it resulted from concerns about the management and social structure of the Mars village when first established some five years ago. Every society needs governance and rules in order to exist in harmony and Mars is no exception just because it is a long way away."

"Yes, but why do we have more socially intrusive and limiting rules than those on Earth?" asked Jo.

Steve settled back in his chair.

"Well, if you've got the time, it's like this. There was much concern in the early days of Mars exploration that the main issues would be the ability of people to get on with one another in the limited social environment for the first few years. Living together with a handful of others for a year on the International Space Station or an isolated research base in the Antarctic was one thing, surviving on Mars with the strong possibility of never going back to Earth was another. This was mainly because living under conditions when your stay is deemed an experiment involving reporting to a controlling body is very different to emigration when you are committed to living far away with only the odd holiday back home. The first pioneers of five years ago had bravely agreed to consider Mars as their home but the social infrastructure was hardly established and it was all totally daunting. As we know, there were fatalities in the early 2030s caused by technical failures but in two unfortunate cases by mental breakdown and collapse."

"And even those that returned have not been quite the same as they were," injected Jo.

"That's true, so they had to revisit the core features of social interaction and the academic sociologists had a field day. Take the two key events of everybody's life which define the fixed points of its existence and which cannot be avoided; birth and death. On Mars, there are no midwives, baby clinics or medical facilities to facilitate the birth of a child. The attitudes on Earth since the late 2020s have become very intolerant of unplanned (and in some countries, unapproved) births following the sophistication of modern non-contraception aids and the grudging acceptance even among Catholic nations of early-stage abortion. On Mars, this had led, as on the ISS and on remote earth stations, to an acceptance of a period of celibacy while on a mission because the consequence of liaisons could create social instabilities. Some cynics had called the ISS a space monastery. (Somewhat inaccurately because, of the 120 astronauts to go there up to its demise in the mid-20s, nearly half were women. It could equally have been called a space nunnery!). Even to this day, there has been no claim of a conception in space but then perhaps that was not something you'd broadcast too widely. No births were expected on Mars and this gradually became, *no births are allowed on Mars*, because, as rules are developed rule makers always want to turn anything out of the ordinary into a restriction. Currently, should there be any of those electronic check-ups that reveal a pregnancy, the Mars instruction is that *abortion must be undertaken*, ostensibly because of the lack of childbirth facilities. So it remains that there will be no births on Mars.

"Before the acceptance of terminauts, deaths on Mars were expected to be few and far between. The demographic age spread had been narrow, largely 25 to 40, and in any case, the health of candidates was assessed at the selection stage and those suffering from any ailment were rejected. However, that does not prevent the possibility of death from one of the four anticipated causes of life termination on Mars, these being accidents, disease, undetected health issues and ageing. To date, there have been fatalities due to accidents but not the next two, although one person on the first group was found to have a weak heart. Ageing, on the other hand, has become predominant now that the doors have been opened to allow terminauts to come for the express purpose of dying here. They are generally self-funding and pay several million dollars which help to make the missions viable. As you know, some of them are ailing and soon expect to see their days out but others seem to improve because the conditions on Mars suit them and then forget what they came out to do. My job description includes conducting their funeral services and I've spent much time swotting up the ceremonial procedures of various religions in readiness for such an occurrence.

"Then there's the grim matter of the disposal of the body after death. The Mars council had many discussions with a wide range of religious and secular bodies among the nations on earth regarding this sensitive issue. The general consensus was that the body should be ejected into space if death occurred on a spacecraft unless the remaining time to the destination was less than two days. When on Mars, the burial should be in a regolith concrete sarcophagus which is the only allowable way of preventing the spread of Earth contaminants apart from cremation which requires fuel and oxygen. The bodies could be lodged in Mausoleums as time progressed (named *Marso-leums* on Mars to differentiate them from earthly ones). It might be thought that this was a trivial and boring aspect of Mars colonisation."

"It might indeed," said Jo.

"Oh, I'm sorry, I'm getting onto my hobby horse. All ministers, vicars, priests and so on have a certain morbid preoccupation with death. It is after all the grand finale, the curtain drop on their duties. Mind you, lawyers do quite well out of it too."

Steve paused as Jo looked as if she wanted to ask something relevant to the topic, but she said, "You got yourself a beer but only offered me a tea or coffee earlier."

"Oh, sorry again, but Indian girls tend not to drink alcohol and, er…"

"Indian girls, did you say—and how do you know that? There's only one way you can redeem yourself!"

"OK, What can I get you?" he said.

"They do a miniature bottle of house red wine; that would be great, thanks."

He winced inwardly, it was very expensive and while getting it, he realised she had obviously been to the bar before although he had not noticed her there. On his return, she said, "Pity you can't have another beer. The Mars council's restrictions on this and other things, for example, casual one to one attachments, unless author-ised and registered by them as an approved *couple-bond*, are totally unnecessary in my view. They seem to enjoy making annoying and petty rules for no reason and they are often honoured in the breach as there's no effective way of enforcing them. There was, of course, an infringe-ment recently if you believe the rumours that go around."

"Are, you mean the moonlight flit, yes I heard about

that but was spared the details—-probably because I'm the chaplain. What actually happened?" he enquired.

Jo drew closer as there were others around and conspiratorially elaborated.

"Well, a male engineer and a female computer operator (names withheld) considerably exceeded their alcohol limits in spite of the regulations and in the interests of science, according to them, donned spacesuits and went outside for a moonlight walk. During this walk, they discovered that their suits could be combined to form one unit by cross zipping and sealing them, engineers being good at this sort of thing, and they attempted a moonlight hug. Unfortunately, the suits got seriously entangled and they had to be rescued by the Village Emergency Team (VET). In the subsequent investigation carried out by the council, the two accepted that the experiment had failed because Mars has no moonlight any rate because as we know the two moons, Phobos and Deimos, that circulate Mars are both very small and look like stars from the surface. Hugging, as we know from our infamous Rule 98, amendment 3, is not allowed in the village among non-couple-bonded adults and even then, not in public. At the hastily convened Mars minor court, they argued that, being technically outside the village, they were not subject to the rule of the village and not bound by its jurisdiction. They thus escaped any official reprimand but the rule has since been extended to include the environs of the village. They were, however, obliged to make a sizeable donation to the VET equipment fund."

"Very amusing," said Steve, who realised he was enjoying his chat with this Indian woman who seemed genuinely interested in his views although he wondered if he had talked too much and been too full of himself. He had noticed from her bio following their last encounter that she had been selected by the Indian Space Agency in New Delhi to study long term psychological effects of Mars habitation. That sounded interesting and not a hundred miles away from his *raison d'être* for being on the Programme. But had she not just mentioned she had been in New York---that was a long way from New Delhi. Maybe he should find out more about her.

He said, "I would like to hear the reaction on Earth to the Mars development up until you came here if you can spare the time one day."

"Sure," she responded positively, "but not until you have told me more about what you expect to achieve as a chaplain on Mars."

"OK, what about Thursday evening in the Mars Bar restaurant?"

She consulted her work schedule.

"Yes, that looks possible, say 6:30–ish."

"That's a date then."

"A date?" she said with a teasing look.

"I mean as a fixture in time," he replied quickly, "You know the strict engagement rules laid down by the authorities here about any *tête-à-tête* meetings; not that I necessarily agree with their petty ways. It's almost like brave new world in some ways and really silly when it's just two professional people talking about their work and—"

"Bye, chaplain," she interrupted as she left wearing the hint of a smirk.

14

Chatting in Space-Time

STEVE SAT THERE for some time wondering about the Mars community and what effect the abundance of rules and regulations would have on the people. He came to the conclusion that their remoteness required stricter than normal regulations to reinforce the foundations of their social order and their everyday existence. Life in the remote Scottish islands was similarly strictly regulated and remained so for hundreds of years until broken down in modern times by improved communication with the outside world and hence removal of the remoteness. A further difficulty is that communication between Mars and Earth is fraught with a fundamental problem which Steve had to get straight in his mind.

The Earth Communications System (ECS) was established right at the start of the village development and since then had been highly developed using the latest technology. Interplanetary communication is encumbered with the difficulty its speed is limited to the speed of light. That's the highest speed any electronic wave can be propagated and a fundamental tenet of our universe. For non-scientists, there's always a subconscious question formed when some scientist states something like this, after all, he's only human and may have it wrong. The question is *who says so?* The answer is that all the scientists of recent times. The speed itself, of about 186,000 miles per second, was recognised (in metric units) as this in 1983 and it was universally agreed by a committee of international scientists. Cynics might point out that a little over 100 years ago they said the atom could not be split. The scientists then correctly respond to this by pointing out that that's different because the atom was not fundamentally the smallest division. Thus:

The speed of light is a fundamental characteristic of the Universe. As such it can never be exceeded.

However, any such statement is often seen as arrogant by those not schooled in the concepts of science. What right have scientists to pontificate on these things and come up with such a restriction? This is particularly so with many of the religious folk whom Steve used to meet, whether Christian, Muslim or any mono-theist creed because they would argue that God is omnipotent and can do anything including altering the speed of light if He so wishes. Such an argument though is ingenuous and inadvertently disrespectful to God himself. That is because fundamental characteristics are by definition fundamental, that is they indisputably exist and are fixed by the nature of the universe itself. For example, the sum of 1 plus 2 is indisputably 3. To say that an all-powerful God can make it equal to 4 reduces God to some trickster and is disrespectful. The same could be said of the circumference of a circle being 3.14 times its diameter, the sum of the squares of adjacent sides of right-angled triangle being the square of the hypotenuse or, as here, the speed of light being the value it is. It is perfectly rational to say God made the universe and it is also perfectly rational to say He did not. Whatever the truth, both statements could form the basis of a reasonable argument. What is not meaningful is to say that God is irrational and he made an irrational universe. That would be saying God

116

can alter facts such as 1 plus 2 equals 3; the ratio of the circumference of a circle to the diameter or the speed of light. (Steve knew this point was uncomfortable for some of his theological colleagues because it seemingly limited the extent and range of miracles. That's partly true but it does not preclude *extremely unlikely and almost impossible events happening at exactly the right time, o*ne for later.)

Moving on, this limitation on the speed of light (and all waves in space) has practical implications for Mars. Being an average of 140 million miles away (it was at its nearest in 2003 at 34 million), a simple division shows that on average, it takes 750 seconds or about 12.5 minutes for electronic waves to get to or from Mars. That means if you're on Mars and you're rolling pastry for an apple pie and you ring your mum about the required oven time, the message takes 12.5 minutes to get to her, say 5 minutes for her to reply and 12.5 minutes for her answer to come back; half an hour in total. The conclusion must be that it's difficult to rely on Earth for any practical short term help (and you should download a cookbook before you go).

This explains why *communication* is a further reason why the government of Mars must be local and self-sufficient. No doubt the authorities on Earth will be less than happy about this as indeed were the government departments in London with the gradual independence of their British Colonies a hundred years ago. Put another way, the half-hour communication lag not only means it is difficult to have a normal conversation or online conference but more importantly, it means that any timely response to an unexpected event on Mars cannot be made from the Earth. Thus, for logistic and safety reasons, control on Mars has to be self-contained.

Furthermore, the advancing development of social

media using visual techniques in the early years of the century and holography from the early 2030s, will not work between Earth and Mars. True, if Steve were in Australia say, he could have a hologram conversation with his mother in England but this could not be done if he were on Mars. The reason being that electronic transfer from Australia to England, a distance of about 5000 miles, takes 0.1 seconds whereas it takes about 12 minutes or so to Mars. It is true that Tim Peake, the British astronaut spoke to classes of school children in St Albans in 2016 from the International Space Station in outer space. It was possible because Tim Peake was only about 250 miles above Earth and thus a fraction of a second away. So, with Steve being on Mars, the only way for visual and audio communication with his mother is for him to make a presentation which could then be transferred and watched by his mum 12 minutes or so later and for her to then do the same in response. This leads to rather stilted communication and not conversation as we know it. Information transfer is therefore limited in a very practical way by the speed of light.

It follows that all those space fiction books and the Star Wars series in which there was conversation with folk on Earth (*beam me up Scotty*) are therefore misrepresenting the communication possibilities because it is just not possible to talk in the normal sense of the word. (Not that it matters too much because it's fiction and it would be a pity to spoil a good storyline.) Furthermore, it's impossible, not because we haven't got the technology yet but, harking back to the earlier point, because it would contravene a fundamental characteristic of the universe.

Finally, but importantly, this delayed information transfer is interconnected with the conclusion drawn earlier (Chapter 6) that there is more to the universe than meets the eye for several reasons. If, for example, Captain Reid were to report to the Earth authorities that owing to leakages, they were running seriously low on oxygen reserves in one of the domes and to seek their advice, he would not get an answer for half an hour or so. This may be too late so spacetime concepts can have very real effects on people. Secondly, there's the problem of relative time. When Captain Reid's message leaves Mars but has not yet reached Earth, say after 5 minutes (as measured on Mars), where is the information and in what form? Is it in electrons or quarks or something somewhere in space on its way to Earth and everywhere else for that matter? Could it go astray and get lost forever? Is space full of such messages? And, since there's no real difference between a message and a thought, is space full of thoughts? On Earth, one can avoid all these conundrums, even if you're a chaplain or priest because they don't impinge on everyday life but out here on Mars or for that matter anywhere else in the universe they have to be thought through and addressed. Steve realised he would have to do some deep thinking and praying in order to answer these key questions to the satisfaction of the good scientific folk on Mars.

15

The Chaplain's Assistant

MEANWHILE, THE DINNER with Jo on Thursday in the Mars Bar Restaurant started off well but had a rather unexpected ending. She, at last, managed to extract from Steve his life story and what led to him becoming a chaplain on Mars. She listened intently and while he was happy to divulge the facts, including his time with Margo and her son Bobby, she occasionally questioned the reasons for various actions and decisions. She wanted to know if he had run away from life by becoming a Scottish Church minister and he found himself explaining that his Christian upbringing, followed by his commitment and belief that Christ embodied the God in whom he believed, meant it was a natural progression for him. Then she suggested his acceptance of the job on Mars was him running away again, this time from being a normal church minister as he would have to abide by restrictive beliefs and he again explained that it was his mission, although with slightly less conviction this time. As it progressed, Steve was beginning to find the conversation too personal and probing. While he was essentially extrovert by nature and very much a people person, like so many such, he kept his inner reasons and thoughts to himself and Jo, however charming, was chipping away at his resistance. She even asked more about Bobby back in North Berwick and he realised to his horror that he had not contacted him for a couple of months in spite of his promises long ago. He would have to correct that.

In order to deflect attention away from *his* life he, perhaps rather too obviously, steered the conversation to her background and her reasons for joining the Mars team.

"Ah, now I've started to prick your bubble so you're going to prick mine," she joked.

Following a starter of spiced leek and potato soup, they were awaiting the main course to be served. Soup was popular on Mars because it made the limited supply of fresh vegetables grown in the Mars mineral-rich regolith go a long way. Soup in one form or another is present in most cultures, is easily digested and easy to serve once made. Leeks and potatoes grew well as did root crops whereas brassicas were more difficult. They had both ordered the curry, *special of the day* advertised in several languages above the bar, although the same special always seemed to be there. Also, the price of about twenty marks was low compared to the phenomenal amounts charged for anything with the most minor ingredient from Earth.

(It should be explained that marks form the base currency of the Mars banking system which is very simple and very boring but nevertheless occupied thousands of hours of international negotiations by the financial folk who found it exciting. Essentially, there is one bank, the Mars Monetary Bank, acronym MMB (commonly termed the Mickey Mouse Bank by the cynics). It issues and accepts monetary units of Marks, a compromise after the Chinese argued for Myuans and the Americans for Mollars and a bonus for the Germans who were not even at the meetings. Since all exchanges are electronic anyway and largely undertaken by swipe wrist-watches, the name of the unit is immaterial except for indicating prices on

Mars and in particular on the chalkboard in the Mars Bar—yes chalk, some things are embedded in ancient protocol).

The main course duly arrived and Jo suggested that they concentrate for a little on the steaming curry. Afterwards, she recounted her background in the Buddhist community in the Pradesh area of India, her subsequent progress to university and her selection for the Mars Programme. He was fascinated by her path through life, so different from his, and her Buddhist slant on moving to another planet.

"Tell me one thing though," said Steve, "did you have to leave your own close family and perhaps a close friend to come to Mars?"

She looked at him inquisitively.

"I have no family dependent on me and no partner if that's what you mean. My mother and father have accepted that I'm odd and eventually gave up expecting me to settle down in India. After all, I left to study in New York and then I left the Earth which confirms to them that I'm way out in every sense. My parents, uncles, aunts, cousins and ex-boyfriends have all accepted this and I definitely have no children, it's not the sort of thing you'd forget! But why do you ask?"

Steve wasn't sure why he'd asked, it seemed to come from nowhere so he made up a cock and bull story about needing to be aware of whether Mars people had dependants as part of his chaplaincy pastoral duties.

They were debating whether to have coffee when they noticed President Leskovich in the restaurant. He seemed to be looking for someone and when he saw Steve, he came over to him. Steve thought he wanted to ask about somebody else he was trying to locate until he said,

"We've been calling you on your pager. I'm afraid we have a real emergency and need your input."

Steve started to get up.

"Yes, sir, of course, I can come now, I've nearly finished any rate."

"Sorry to spoil your dinner with—"

The president had met her but was lost for her name.

"With Dr Jo Thanawala who is assisting me in the chaplaincy," added Steve feeling the *tête-à-tête* dinner needed some explanation in the rather puritanical atmosphere which, as we have seen, had developed in the community.

"Pleased to hear it, I know you're over-loaded like all of us but perhaps you could come to my office—and you too, Jo, if you're assisting the chaplain," said the president as he turned to go.

As they both abandoned their table and followed the president back to his office, Jo whispered mischievously to Steve, "So I'm your new assistant am I?"

"Yes, so it seems. Sorry about that."

"It's OK. I was going to offer some help as it happens so it must have been meant to be," she added.

16

Camp Fever Fatality

IN THE PRESIDENT'S office, they were joined by two safety staff members. One was Angela Berko, now the Safety Officer for off-site operations who came from South Africa and had previously been in the Biology Section. The other was the Chief Safety Officer, Ken Markham, with whom Steve had teamed up over the drove landing crisis a few months before. The president hurriedly outlined the issue. A scientist named Fred Albright who had come out to Mars three years before in an early drove had gone absent without leave late the previous day, donned a spacesuit, left the village and walked off across the Martian sand. This had happened before with others for short periods but they had always come back after the sheer craziness of it had sunk in and the bleak ochre rocks stretching to the horizon had become intimidating. It had become known as letting off steam (with unintended accuracy as the confines of their spacesuits became increasingly humid and uncomfortable). It generally received a cursory reprimand from the president followed by in-depth psychological questioning of the offender and this usually deterred further offences.

On this occasion, they were expecting something similar and had merely waited for Fred's return. When, after several hours, this did not happen and his oxygen supply would have become perilously low, they sent a couple of VETs to find him. These were staff on call that evening from the Volunteer Emergency Team which was established to give rapid assistance in the event of any difficulty. One was a burly guy named Ben Forbes, the other, a young and super fit black American girl named Sophie Brown. They were instructed urgently to don their spacesuits, search for him and bring him back. An hour later, they were dealing with one fatality and one injured person in the emergency bay (an area of the community Dome designated for this use when needed). A doctor was attending to the injured party and the president then requested Steve to come and administer the last rites to the person who had died.

Steve later pieced together what had happened. The volunteers, Sophie and Ben, knew from the automatic location system roughly where Fred was so they took a rover which was already charged up for emergence use and followed his trail to a small valley about a mile away from the village called Boulder Pit on account of its rock-strewn terrain. When they got there, they could not see him and spent over half an hour meandering about searching for him with increasing concern about his draining oxygen level. They were checking in with base when seemingly from nowhere a rock the size of a cricket ball struck Ben forcibly enough to damage his helmet. It was immediately followed by another and they ran as best they could in their spacesuits for cover behind a nearby rock protrusion. Peering around, they had their first glimpse of him as he appeared threateningly from behind a massive rocky mound holding yet another boulder ready to launch towards them. Fred had obviously gone berserk. In a hurried exchange between them through their intercoms, Sophie and Ben agreed they would have to confront him and if necessary return him to base by force.

That was easier said than done because he could not be contacted through the intercom as he was either ignoring them or had disabled it. Ben bravely approached him in the recognised surrender position with hands above his head but received a rein of smaller rocks for his trouble. One of these ripped his suit arm covering as they were not designed with physical protection in mind. Sophie, thinking quickly, had managed to move off to the side unseen and so he continued to keep his arms aloft giving her time to creep around behind Fred. After about 20 seconds or so, Fred became suspicious and looked around to see Sophie who had skirted between the large rocks protrusions and boulders and was now within about three metres of Fred. He would be unlikely to know who it was because of the Sun's reflection in Sophie's visor; whether or not he did we shall never know because he viciously attacked Sophie who had to use her kickboxing skills, at least as best she could with a suit impeding her. In the resulting affray, Fred fell heavily against a large boulder smashing his helmet and gashing the side of his suit.

By now, Ben had arrived and the two of them managed to overpower Fred who was staggering around but still able to land the odd blow on them. To ensure he was sufficiently restrained, they pushed him to the ground and crouched on him while turning his helmet to face upwards towards them so that by shielding the light they could see his face. To their horror, they saw that his eyes were dilated, his skin was dark red and he was mouthing something at them in a demented way. They decided to get him back to base as soon as possible but Ben was having his own problems as, in seeking to restrain Fred, he had cricked his neck and also partially dislodged a breathing tube within the suit. They managed to drag Fred onto the Rover where he totally collapsed and offered no visible signs of life. Ben was weakening and having breathing difficulties but Sophie managed to get him on the rover after a struggle and drove back to base with both of them on board as fast as the rover would go while calling ahead for assistance. The remaining members of village rescue team had been alerted and were anxiously waiting beyond the airlock in the Village. Ben was still conscious and they quickly removed his helmet and administered enhanced oxygen from the inhalation equipment while still in his suit to save time. Fred appeared lifeless and his eyes were rolling in an uncontrolled way so they stripped off the upper part of his suit and gave him CPR treatment while feeding him enhanced oxygen as best they could.

When Steve and Jo arrived, a doctor was attending to Ben whose space suit was now being removed although Ben was responding and even helping them—a real relief for all concerned as lack of oxygen can only be tolerated for a very short period. It took some time to extract Fred from his damaged suit and Jill, a part-time nurse, was applying defibrillator shocks in the hope that some sign of life would be restored. It was soon clear that this was not going to be successful. Other folk around were clearly shocked and while offering assistance really did not know what to do. Steve quickly assessed the grim situation and suggested that, owing to the sad death of Fred and the required medical treatment for Ben, those around could meanwhile assemble in the community area where he would join them shortly. All except the doctor and nurse, the president, Steve and Jo, reluctantly drifted off looking pale and upset.

Fortunately, Ben was recovering well from his few

minutes of reduced air supply following the damage to his suit. He had become very faint and, should the flow of air and therefore oxygen been cut off entirely, he could have suffered brain damage within 5 minutes so there was always a risk when accidents occurred on walkabouts. His neck was painful but nothing life-threatening and he was severely distressed about Fred and concerned that they had been too rough with him. It later transpired from post-mortem analysis that Fred had had a hypoxia fit out there in boulder pit owing to the prolonged period with a low oxygen level, long before being restrained by them.

The president drew Steve aside and confided that he had a concern and that Fred's unfortunate demise had brought it to ahead. He had noticed that several folk who had been on the first and second groups and had thus been there longer than the others were becoming restless and developing some strange character traits. While poor Fred's actions today were extreme, the president felt that serious forms of CD were gradually becoming more prevalent and he was worried that there may be uncharted long term psychological effects of being on Mars, perhaps caused by the radiation levels or similar. He asked Steve to do some discrete research and make some suggestions to address the matter as he was becoming worried that it might spread through the village following the death of Fred. The president then had a quick word with Ben who was beginning to look himself again and also thanked Sophie Brown for her cool-headed action in safely bringing back Ken and doing all she could for Fred under such difficult circumstances. Steve went off to the chaplaincy to quietly absorb all that had happened and start thinking about the things to be done, condolences to Fred's family, informing the news media and the arrangements for committal and interment although it was as yet early days.

He was also left wondering how on earth he was going to deal with the president's concern about widespread CD and any other form of interplanetary camp fever.

This was actually the second death on Mars because some three years before, just a few months after Drove 3 had landed, one of the three older travellers who had funded the trip out of her own resources had died. She had cancer and had paid several million dollars for a one-way final trip to Mars. Acceptance of such passengers had been much discussed in the early stages of Mars development but sheer commercial considerations had won the day and about a dozen *terminauts* were now on Mars. In the subsequent three years, there had only been this one death and it became evident that being on Mars seemed to extend life expectancy but nobody knew why. As there was no chaplain at that time, the funeral and cremation of this first terminaut was conducted by the President Leskovich himself who followed the procedure used for death at sea. The woman involved had no living relatives on earth and while sad in its way it had consequently caused no great distress among the fairly small population then on Mars. As it happened, the terminauts, while accepting they had gone to Mars to die, were finding the swan song exhilarating and some had indeed forgotten why they went there. They objected to the term terminauts and requested a change of category to senior astronauts but the Mars management had already reserved that title for themselves.

Fred's death was of course entirely different. Although there were by now over 160 people on Mars and Fred was known to most of them and pretty well-liked, he was seen on occasions as a little morbid. Steve though, felt the funeral would be a reminder to all of them that they were living on another planet under precarious conditions.

The manner of his demise would ring a chord with many because they were all to some degree aware of being on a psychological knife edge with one side hankering after the green green grass of home and the other side stoically performing their duty to the community on this remote and lonely planet. A poor night's sleep and a wee mental lapse the next day or a tiny change in the chemical balance within the brain and any of them could be Fred storming out of the village across the Martian landscape in some stupefied trance. The same was, of course, true on Earth but there the daily routine, the proximity of family and friends either geographically or by social media (less feasible on Mars owing to the long delays) and the calming effect of mutual interests in their work and leisure kept most folk reasonably sane. The pressure was on Steve too because the President seemed to assume his role as chaplain placed him on the spot as the person to avert the danger of rampant camp fever and steer those who showed signs of distress back to an acceptable level of a rational and happy existence.

17

Consequences on Earth

ON TOP OF this, there was trouble brewing with the Earth. Relationships had been declining for some time over a host of petty issues and misunderstandings and now a fatality, under what they considered avoidable conditions, would not help. Camp fever on Mars would undoubtedly have its effect, not only on those on Mars but by reflection those on Earth. Most of the residents of the village had kith and kin on Earth who were following the progress of their remote relatives with interest and were sometimes frustrated at what they saw as the obfuscation of the authorities.

In Steve's case though, his mum and dad were well abreast of the news on their son's activities. He had indeed effectively become one of the key players in a media soap opera which, while not programmed at regular times, was frequently shown on TV so that he became a well-known character on the world stage. This was inevitable because, from the day a few years before when man first walked on another planet and became an interplanetary species, the public had been enthralled with it all. The experiences of the first few adventurers and the construction of the first domes had been pawed over relentlessly and their families subjected to interview after interview providing ever more detail on their background, their feelings about them going and their expectations for the future. It was frustrating for the media folk being unable to interview the main characters remotely on Mars and however much one explained that the messages could not go faster than the speed of light making normal conversation impossible, they tended to think this was some temporary limitation rather than the consequence of a fundamental feature of the universe. When indisputable facts clash with the ill-informed popular opinion, it is, unfortunately, the latter which presides in the short term. The media had to make do with prepared statements from the Mars inhabitants which they found acutely inhibiting.

Fortunately, by the time Steve went to Mars, the media had reigned back a little but his parents were still newsworthy personalities and felt mildly under siege whenever they went out and about. The questions developed into a monotonous stream; had their son always been interested in space, how often did he report home, was he tired of Mars food, did he have a girlfriend there, and now, how was he going to conduct Fred Albright's funeral. His ex-wife, Margo and son, Bobby, were also subjected to attention but less so than it could have been as Steve was seldom in touch with them.

Steve's parents were involved with local folk in their English village and his dad would sometimes tell Steve the current views of the locals. This provided a plentiful source of stories to raise as light relief for his friends in the Mars Bar in the evenings. So much so indeed that his mum and dad became celebrities by association which was really great for Steve as it made him feel less remote from it all. Indeed, he made a mental note to chat with his friends about their families as a way of engendering a more homely atmosphere for them on this barren planet. For example, his father's account of a visit from the Pastor of the nonconformist Baptist chapel along the road from where he lived, once he discovered the Church of Scotland's Man on Mars was his son, particularly intrigued them. The Pastor was strongly evangelical and felt it was his duty to emphasise the abominable sin of his son going to Mars. God so loved the world and that is where we should be, he insisted. It was, he said, like Jonah running away from Nineveh and that Steve should have stayed and prophesied to the unconverted on Earth. However much his father argued, he was no match for the arrogant assertions of this Pastor with the staring eyes of those with a mission from God. His father reckoned it was a reciprocal case of the father's sins being visited upon the children!

The Church of Scotland for its part argued that the reason for Steve being on Mars was the spread of the Gospel to what they considered their most distant parish. As he was technically a practising minister within their employment, albeit on extended leave, they felt responsible for him as he was their *protégé*. He was still attached to the Edinburgh presbytery of the church and on occasions, reported to them. However, the general media were so informative on Mars matters there was seldom anything in the reports they did not know by the time of the Presbytery meetings. They were also delighted that their famous minister had conducted himself so admirably and by association, it brought much approbation upon the Church of Scotland. It had also indirectly seeded much debate and some changes of approach among the friends of the church. (The term member with its club association had been gradually phased out after many years.) Space exploration had largely driven out the concept of a God *in our own image* and of God and Jesus residing *above in the ether*, even for the most diehard traditionalist. Pragmatic liberalisation on this and other features had removed the requirement of belief on things that were clearly not possible and adherence to 4th Century Creeds and 17th Century Articles was not expected. As a result of this and other changes, the church, as a society of *Church Friends*, had gradually regained plausibility among thousands of folk who wanted to believe without the barriers imposed by ancient tradition. It was an irony that in the 2030s the very science which the church had so damned over the ages should, as an unintended consequence become its saving grace.

Steve's request to them for advice on the forthcoming funeral of Fred Albright left the Church of Scotland Committee on Church Procedures somewhat nonplussed. There were clearly stated orders of service and guidance on bereavement on their web pages for both Christian and non-Christian funerals and surely it was just a matter of the chaplain doing more or less the same on Mars but avoiding references to anything too... er... earthly. However, as always, the devil does not reside in the full glare of religious work but in intricacies and procedures and especially in the corners of obscure committees. Here, among the petty incompatibilities and minor peccadilloes, the devil could sow the seeds of rampant adversity. It could cause otherwise good honest folk to hate one another with an intensity that only the strongly religious can muster. Steve wisely chose to avoid the over-prescriptive practices which emanate from such committees at all costs and this was best done by simply not forming such committees so that He had nowhere to hide on Mars. Hopefully, this particular devil would then be confined to Earth and not contaminate this wonderful planet in the heavens above.

18

Fred's Obsession

STEVE WAS SOMEWHAT drained following Fred's death and dealing with the consequent emotional lows among many of the Mars population. One evening, he made his way the short distance from the chaplaincy to the Mars Bar with the idea of draining a glass of ale to go with his drained emotions. However, John was there studying his iPad with such intense interest that he did not notice Steve for a few moments. Steve was about to accuse him of playing electronic war games when John looked up and beckoned him over in some excitement to look at a Web page. It was a well-known Mars Web Site although primarily aimed at bringing readers on Earth up to date with Mars events. The main headline was about a new rocket development; strange, he thought, how *new* creeps in everywhere, a development could hardly be old. Every baby born on Earth is said to be a new baby, indeed, he had never heard of somebody having an old one. If ever one is born on Mars it will presumably also be a new baby; not that one ever could, there being no facilities and such strict rules on termination of pregnancy as we saw earlier. That, however, was not what John was excited about. Underneath the headline articles were subsidiary news items about this and that including one which proclaimed:

Fred Albright had visited Boulder Pit twice before his fatal rampage.

Steve put down his beer and read the article at once:

Some mystery has surfaced regarding the recent death of Fred Albright after his solo breakaway from the village to the Boulder Pit area and subsequent death under strange circumstances. Analysis of his recent movements as part of the ongoing investigation reveals that he had been to the region twice before. The first time was with the group of geologists studying the unusual rock strata exposed by the cliffs in the region. The second time was, it appeared, a few days before the final, fateful time and it had not been properly recorded in the log. It was indeed a solo visit and while lone trips outside the Village are not banned they are not common and are usually for a specific well-defined purpose such as retrieval of something left outside. On this occasion, Fred had returned after two hours during which he had used a rover for transport each way and spent about one hour at the site.

Following this revelation, his movements prior to his final visit have been re-examined and it was found that all the safety checks and procedures required for a safe exit from the Dome had been meticulously undertaken. Given that Fred had become overwrought and finally berserk, it must have been occasioned by something that occurred afterwards while at the site. On his final visit it appears that he meticulously followed all safety checks so his state of mind must have been fine at that stage. This throws into doubt the supposition that his death was the result of an extreme case of Celestial Depression.

Steve read the article again and could not hide his annoyance. This had been leaked to the news and the President would rightly be furious. Presumably, the earlier forays had been in secret but known to the person who leaked the news. This put a new perspective on the whole incident. What had Fred seen or what momentous event had occurred out there or perhaps in his mind that had brought on the collapse of his reason to the extent of putting himself and others in danger? Maybe they would never know but they should at least try to find out.

Steve had been so absorbed that he failed to notice that Ken and Ben had seated themselves at a nearby table so he beckoned them across to join John and himself. Jo came in a few minutes later with Angela, the Safety Officer who had been present at the meeting with the President following Fred's disappearance. He noticed that Jo had struck up a most unexpected friendship with this South African girl with Dutch routes and a broad accent. Steve raised the matter of the article he had just read but they all said they knew about it and he felt slightly miffed that he had somehow been missed off the circulation loop. He also wondered who had leaked it to the media. After a minute though, he put that thought aside and asked the group, "What do you actually think happened out there?"

"Maybe nothing," said Angela.

"Maybe he just had to get away from these bloody great domes we are stuck in for the next year or two," ventured Ben, who had now fully recovered from his ordeal rescuing Fred but was still rather grumpy.

Jo said, "OK, but why visit the same desolate spot which is nearly a mile away? It must have been something there and, given his low state, it could have been something pretty minor but sufficient to tip him over the edge. It appears he had been there before with others."

"That's right," said Steve, "should we not be asking those with him on that first visit whether there was anything they noticed in his actions or response while he was there? Also, we should be questioning those who knew him best."

Angela suggested, "That's one for you, Steve, as it's really up to you to explore every avenue so that we know why he had this attack, if only so that we recognise the signs in others or even ourselves."

"Hang on, I'm a chaplain, not a head shrink."

Ken quickly interjected, "What's the difference?" to the amusement of all and the conversation quickly degenerated into basic banter as so often happened in the Mars Bar after a stressful day. Jo put in a word for Steve.

"Actually, it's a good job somebody is looking after your mental and spiritual state or you'd all be out there wandering about like aimless zombies."

"Sure," said Ken who'd heard how the president had appointed her as chaplain's assistant by default, "in which case, you would have to don your spacesuit and come and find us while your new boss prays for us in the chaplaincy."

Searching for a way to deflect the conversation, Steve said, "OK, I'll have a word with those closest to him to see if there are any clues as to why he went back to this spot twice and also his state of health and mind at the time. Meanwhile, have all of you folk eaten because I'm famished?"

They agreed with this sentiment and asked for the menu. Jo who was observing a dry week for Vesak, Buddha's birthday, nevertheless obtained her allowance of Mars ale but generously poured it out for the others. Steve complained that the Menu was rather old so the stoic Danish guy, who was acting barman cum waiter for the night, gave him a newer one which was not really what he meant. John asked if the *special* was changed every Earth year or every Mars year (nearly twice as long) and earned himself a withering stare from the waiter. Nevertheless, the shortcomings of the dinner did not detract from the lively conversation and it was agreed that they should all meet up each week to relieve the monotony of life on Mars.

The next morning, Steve asked Laurie if she would pop by and see him. Laurie was a biologist working on plant diseases who was reported to be a close friend of Fred and had been with him on their first visit to Boulder Pit. Steve had met her before (there were very few folk whom he hadn't by now) but had never really had a sustained conversation with her. She guessed why Steve wanted to chat with her on this occasion and immediately outlined what she knew about Fred. He was a first-class graduate from Caltech who had achieved his PhD at UCLA and became a principal geologist at the National Science Centre before being invited onto the Mars programme. She knew Fred was an only child but he had never discussed his home life nor any girlfriends or anything like that. He was rather intense and introspective having a fascination with the primaeval formation of the planets and how we came to be on one of them; it was indeed this that directed his interest towards the Mars programme and after a time a job on Mars. She had once joked about previous life on Mars in some former geological era and remembered that he had become quite serious and explained there could never be life elsewhere than on Earth because it was statistically impossible. Their conversations always seem to drift into one horror scenario or another which would befall us and as a result, she found him rather depressive. Occasionally, he would lighten up but even then he exhibited a sort of black humour which she found uncomfortable. Although she was one of those who knew him best as she happened to be in the adjacent pod when they come over to Mars, she explained that this was only the case because virtually nobody else knew him at all. He was very much a loner and seemed to be forever reading books on his iPad.

On their geological trip to Boulder Pit, Laurie said he kept wandering off purportedly to check the contours of the strata which had been found there although he kept examining odd boulders rather than the rocks which they were meant to be studying. He said these boulders were from extremely old rocks formed in the very early days of Mars over 4 billion years ago but still appeared to be time-zoned and possibly sedimentary in nature. Several times, he split boulders into two with his chisel to examine the rock formation inside. He seemed fascinated by the black and dark brown streaks which were embedded in the granular rock.

Laurie explained that she, as a biologist, was included in the party of four involved in the first trip because they were wanting to check if there were any biological spores or germs from the village that had spread to a point a mile away. For this purpose, she collected samples of soil from the valley to take back to the lab. She also included some samples taken from a depth of half a metre down under the regolith for comparison and she was currently working on this in the lab.

"Did you notice anything which would have any bearing on his unfortunate death a few weeks later?" asked Steve.

After some time thinking she said, "Of all the folk I've met here on Mars, he was the guy I would consider most likely to have a breakdown. He was friendly but had an odd wide-eyed look on occasions, and—"

142

Steve could not help noticing how pretty she was and looked at her quizzically but she read his thought, "No, it was nothing like that, that at least would have been more normal, it was a sort of fearful look. You know he had some theory he would go on about that mankind was unique, a once-off aberration of evolution and that we must eventually degenerate into animals and become extinct as a species. The only thing that keeps us human he would say is the belief we are something special, one of a kind in the universe. Psychologically, if that is removed, we go insane because there's nothing else."

Steve said, "Tell me, was he a confirmed atheist then?"

"I've no idea," she said, "I had not thought of it in that light, but I can see as a chaplain that could be your take on it. Did you not know him at all then?"

"Not really," responded Steve, "I wish I'd known him better, although it may not have made any difference and as you say he did keep himself to himself. On the trip, did he show any oddities apart from his intrigue with these ancient loose rocks lying around?"

Laurie answered, "Not really but there was the hammer and chisel which he forgot when we left the Boulder Pit area. On the way back, on the rover, we offered to go back and get them but he made some play of feeling unwell and muttered he could collect them on a future occasion. That was a little odder than it sounds because as you know tools have great value here as they all have to come from Earth, hence using up the drove weight allowance and therefore have an enhanced worth. He would have had to borrow tools from others for his day-to-day geological lab work. I now realise he was probably engineering a reason to return to the area."

"That's very useful, thank you," said Steve wanting to draw the meeting to a close.

143

"For your interest, I got a report on him from Earth yesterday and as you say, he was the only child of a single mother who died two years ago so has no family. He was a most brilliant student specialising in the pre-Cambrian era, right at the dawn of evolution and the seeding of life on Earth. He appeared to have made no close friends, being completely dedicated to his study. He shared a flat with somebody who said he was always civil but seemed to spend all his time on the screen except for occasional forages for food and never even opened the window blinds in his room—the archetypical loner."

As Angela left, she commented, "I like your set up here, what do you actually do though?"

Steve said, "Come along to our coffee gathering next Friday and you'll find out. Meanwhile, have a good Mars day."

Steve reported these findings and other things he had discovered about Fred from various discussions to the Mars council. The council decided that they should send a task force out to Boulder Pit and investigate what went so wrong that it led to a brilliant Geologist, albeit an odd and disturbed character, going berserk and attacking his rescuers. They also decided in the circumstances that the internment and memorial service for him should be held over to a date several weeks ahead. Since he had no family connections, this presented no issue except that some of the news media began to assume that foul play must have been involved and a post-mortem was needed. In order to divert this assumption, the Mars council hinted that the funeral procedures on Mars needed to be finalised. This was at least partly true as their chaplain was still busy endeavouring to extract advice from the Church of Scotland on procedures for funeral committals conducted on other planets.

19

Turning over a New Leaf

FOLLOWING THE LEAK to the news media about Fred and the circumstances leading up to his demise, the president called an ad hoc meeting of the Mars council. It was decided that a group of four should visit the Boulder Pit area to search for anything that would throw light on the incident. The two original VET volunteers, Sophie and Ben were selected together with Angela who dealt with the safety aspects of Off-site operations and Dr Wayne Hill. Wayne was an oil and gas geologist in a former life but had been enlisted onto the Mars programme to work on the extraction and processing of constituents to produce rocket fuel from the indigenous rocks. These rocks had the necessary elements of carbon, hydrogen and oxygen in abundance but devising ways of synthesising them into suitable fuel was proving very difficult. The president had a feeling that his general knowledge of sedimentary rock structures beyond this fuel project might be useful.

They met up in the chaplaincy, it being a conveniently private meeting room, and did not seem to mind Steve being around although he had volunteered to leave. He made himself useful by supplying coffee and biscuits and thereby picked up the vibes of what they were planning. The consensus of opinion was that Fred got excited about something out there in Boulder Pit valley, stayed much longer than he should have done and started running low on oxygen. They were hoping to find the exact position of the attack by Fred on his colleagues and to examine the area to try and throw some light on the incident. This involved a comparison of his Mars-Nav movements recorded on the village tracking system with the disturbance of the sandy regolith. Unless a dust storm had occurred his tracks should still be visible.

The next day, the four of them donned their spacesuits, loaded their equipment onto the largest rover, a laborious process needing each item to be taken through the airlock and carefully packed, and then set off towards Boulder Pit. It took about half an hour while the rover was steered around the many rock protrusions and large boulders, some bigger than a motor car until Sophie recognised the area of the altercation with Fred and explained to the other two exactly what happened and the precise sequence of events. Ben managed to find the spot where he had stood and thought he even found the rock thrown at him although he could not be sure as he was protecting himself as best he could. For a moment or two, they all just stood and considered the absurdity of an attack by a deranged human being upon other human beings in a grim and barren environment on a remote planet. Then Wayne broke the spell and explained that the valley had probably been gouged out by ice flow several billion years ago exposing some of the oldest sedimentary rocks as boulders on the surface. These rocks were extremely dense and hard and similar to old red sandstone from the Pre-Cambrian age on Earth.

Sophie's thoughts had drifted back to the attack itself and the position of Fred as he emerged from behind the massive protruding rock with the flat top to the left of them.

"You know it's almost as if he was protecting or hiding something as if in his disturbed state he didn't want us going there," Ben added.

"Yes, you could be right. Perhaps we should all explore the region from here to the left first and then widen out afterwards."

Wayne was already making his way to the left and the others followed not knowing quite what they were looking for but not wanting to become separated from the others. The primaeval instinct to avoid being isolated at all costs in this remote region meant they would stay close whatever happened. The whole land felt dark and eerie, rather like the foreground in mountain landscapes by 18th-century Scottish painters except there was no hint of greenery underfoot, just sandy regolith. They had only just started to explore behind the massive rock from which Fred had emerged when Wayne drew aside to look at an upturned boulder on the ground about half a metre across which had been split in two along a strata plane like a piece of slate exposing stained dark brown and charcoal black areas. They gathered around and were all staring at it when Angela exclaimed, "My God, there's his chisel, just tucked under the edge; he must have been working here—in fact, he must have split the boulder in half to see what was inside."

Sure enough, a couple of meters away lay the top half of the boulder. She was about to retrieve the knife when Ben said, "No, wait, we must record everything as we see it like an archaeological dig."

They were really too intrigued to be diverted but Ben insisted he at least took some photos first, which he did. As they peered at the broken surface, Wayne, who had brought a magnifying glass with him was studying the charcoal deposits. The others could see nothing much except a blackened surface but Wayne with his experienced eye was examining the stained parts of the surface. After some minutes, he slowly stood up and made a pronouncement:

"Friends, I think Fred made a highly significant discovery. The black streak through this boulder and presumably others around is largely carbon and within it are what I believe is evidence of some primitive plant life although the patterns seem to be in the form of a strange lattice growth. If this proves to be correct, it is the most important discovery on Mars to date. We know already that these rocks predate the earliest Carboniferous periods on Earth and this implies that there was molecular carbon, oxygen and hydrogen interaction, possibly indicating primitive molecular life formation, on Mars long before it occurred on earth."

"Wow, that's quite a discovery," exclaimed Sophie as they all gathered around to inspect the growth taking turns to borrow Wayne's magnifying glass. It was, in fact, a leaf-style impression with four sides, each one concave and unlike anything they had seen before. It was only a few millimetres across but there were the remnants of others around it, some of which were larger.

"OK," said Ben, "that's not totally surprising in view of all the hype about possible early life on Mars over the years, so why did Fred flip when he made this discovery?"

Angela, although present in her operational role, was a cell biologist and had done her PhD on emergent life forms based, like ours, on carbon/oxygen/hydrogen combinations but evolving differently to those on earth. (She had originally assumed this was the main reason for her selection and was disappointed that it had become her secondary role). She now sensed she might have some inkling why Fred in his perilous state was tipped over the edge by this discovery. She said,

"It was probably not the nature of the fossil plant life itself but the fact that it had developed so much earlier than we thought along the evolutionary route. The consequent implication of this for all living matter including the human race is enormous and the sudden realisation by Fred could have seriously affected him. He may have made the discovery of the century."

Their conversation had been somewhat stilted because it was only possible through the little microphones and speakers embedded in their helmets owing to the absence of sound travel on Mars. Realising this conversation could become rather involved and not being quite sure what Angela was getting at, Ben advised, "It might be better if we considered all this in the comfort of the Dome so let's go straight back and meet around the table in the Chaplaincy Centre."

Wayne agreed and added, "Meanwhile, I'd like to arrange to get the two halves of this Boulder into the lab in the Village. They are too heavy for us to do it today but if two people could come back tomorrow and collect it using the rover with the pick-up arm, that would be great."

Ben took a large number of photographs and they returned to the Village, divested themselves of their spacesuits, completed the required safety reports on their trip and made their way to the Chaplaincy Centre.

As they arrived, Steve was in a deep *tête-à-tête* discussion with the beautiful Jo and Ben was not slow to rib his friend a little;

"Hope we are not disturbing anything, we can always come back after an hour or two if we're not wanted."

He thought he saw a touch of embarrassment on

Steve's face so he quickly went on, "We have made some important progress into the possible underlying reason for Fred's actions and wondered if we could discuss things here. You and Jo too are welcome to stay if you wish."

Jo immediately nodded that she would like to stay.

"Of course," said Steve, clearing off the table and inviting them to sit around it, "but first, I must arrange for the tea capsules to be heated and dig out some more biscuits."

He had noticed that they seemed a little on edge and he knew sweet biscuits were always a calming influence whether fed to a two-year-old having a tantrum or an over-wrought executive.

Wayne took it upon himself to describe their trip to the site of Fred's incident and to describe the discovery of what he considered to be a mini coal-like seam in a boulder. Within the seam there appeared to be lots of rhombic stem or fern shapes but with curved sides typically two to three millimetres across. If indeed it is shown to be fossils of primitive plant life in these very old rocks, it would be the first incontrovertible evidence of some sort of previous life on Mars. He described their feeling that this was not that unexpected and had been postulated for over 20 years so could not really account for Fred's reaction but Angela persisted in thinking otherwise. Steve thanked Wayne for the update and then asked Angela what she thought could be so mind-bogglingly important (literally in Fred's case, unfortunately) about finding strange fossil fern-like impressions on Mars. As it happened, she had been thinking about this while riding back to the village and gave this explanation:

"People have been talking and writing about life elsewhere for hundreds of years. It has led to a whole branch of science fiction leading to best-selling books and films and we have come to assume that extra-terrestrial life

(ETL) will be found in due course. However, Fred, as a prominent geologist, had been arguing that the likelihood of evolution somewhere else yielding similar beings to ourselves is infinitely small and should be discounted. Finding a well-developed leaf of some strange plant would constitute the first real evidence of ETL and meant that he would be credited with finding one of the greatest discoveries ever made. He had the power to manage the release of this tremendous discovery and wanted to keep it secret while he pondered what to do about it. But power corrupts even the most studious and academic of human beings and the excitement at his good fortune simply sent him over the top. When he thought that others may find it before he could announce his very own discovery, he attempted, in his befuddled low-oxygen state, to defend his position with an uncharacteristic resort to force. Remember when Archimedes discovered, while in his bath, the way to check if the King's gold was being substituted for lesser metal, he ran naked through the streets in excitement. It seems great discoveries can expose the less seemly side of those responsible."

20

Jo's Revelation

THEY WERE SILENT for a moment following Angela's prognosis and Steve asked if anybody had any other views on why Fred was so distraught following his discovery. Jo was sitting just beyond the group around the table and they had forgotten she was there. She piped up from the background and asked if she could venture a different interpretation. They looked mildly surprised but she went on to explain by way of introduction that she was brought up in the Indian border state of Himalaya Pradesh under the influence of Tibetan Buddhists and that consequently, she saw things somewhat differently to the West. Sure she had studied astrophysics like others and this led eventually to her place on the Mars team but she had always retained a fascination with the philosophers of the East and their emphasis on emotional knowledge and the spiritual aspects of life. The West had homed in upon physical aspects, the elements of carbon, oxygen and hydrogen and their interaction in a primaeval sludge to produce the origin of life. But maybe the East was nearer the truth all the time, maybe it's the embedded information that's the key, not the atoms. It could be this incipient information or spirit permeating all space that is responsible for life or indeed is the very horme of life itself.

"And does this have any direct bearing on Fred and his

actions?" asked Angela, who felt that they were in danger of drifting into the realms of the ethereal and away from finding a reason for Fred's mental state.

Jo responded, "I am not sure but I believe it may well. However, I'm happy to leave it until another time as I expect you're busy—"

"Yes, we are," interrupted Steve, "and I guess we should report on our findings to the council early tomorrow morning but I'm intrigued to find out what Jo has on her mind and happy to hear her out even if it's rather late."

The others nodded their assent and they made room for her to move in around the table. Jo leaned forward, swept her long black hair to the side and in her clear Indian-English quietly enunciated why Fred's discovery of life similar to that on Earth but in times past on another planet had such a monumental impact on him.

"Quite simply, the realisation that this find upended the accepted balance of religion, philosophy and science was too much for him; it was his flash of understanding on the Damascus road." She paused as if about to give a well-rehearsed lecture and went on, "Our solar system was formed some 6 billion years ago and the planets cooled into the spherical forms that we now see about 4.5 billion years ago. On Earth, by 4 billion years ago, cell life was developing in the Carbon, Oxygen and Hydrogen mix but it was not until 2 billion years ago in the Carboniferous age that plant life evolved. That period from the nano-cell to recognisable plants was the result of evolution progressing through millions of Y junctions, any wrong turn of which would have made the outcome of life as we know it impossible.

"Some (let's call them Group A) say that it was natural selection alone, all the other paths being less successful and dying out. That's a neat answer and therefore popular because folk like clear simple solutions.

"Some (Group B) say there must have been something influencing the evolutionary path towards life as an outcome, some incipient knowledge within the universe that imparted prior information for RNA and DNA. That is to say, the universe has or even is, a *Mind*. (The spiritually inclined may think of it in terms God, Allah, Karma, etc. The computer scientist may think of it in terms of information theory and the psychologist as thought itself but let's stick with 'Mind' as a catch-all term for this.)

"Now, logic dictates that positions A and B are not mutually viable, that is to say, it can't be a bit of each. If you're in group A then you believe it's natural selection alone and the slightest hint that B is possible means, it's not *alone* so you would enter group B. If you're in group B then you can't be a little bit in group A because that is reserved for those that believe in natural selection alone (Those in group B can, of course, accept natural selection; they just do not think it's natural selection alone)."

Jo paused a minute but then continued, "OK, I'm getting tied up here with the logic, but don't forget, Fred had a great analytical mind and would instantly have realised all this. Let me put it another way: Once the plant stage of evolution had been reached, it was not so surprising that it developed into fish and animals and eventually to intelligent beings like us. That is not to say it was inevitable, but it was much more likely to occur than the first stage of going from inorganic, inanimate material to complex plant structures. That's the really incredibly amazing part of evolution, the very first part.

"Now, suppose Group A is true and it's due to natural selection alone. How does Fred's discovery of the oddly-shaped leaf affect this group? On Mars, the cooling from its formation about 4.5 billion years ago was more rapid as Mars was smaller and conditions were amenable to such evolution much earlier, maybe as much as a billion years earlier. Again, for life to progress from an inorganic mush to the plant stage on Mars, it requires development through myriads of Y junctions and the odds of it happening by natural selection alone are again billions to one as they are on Earth. Now, without going into the statistics too far, the chance of such life developing in two places Earth and Mars (or for that matter anywhere) is obviously many times less than that in one of the places alone and is billions of billions to one. It is often argued that there are possibly billions of other planets so this reduces the odds. However, the chance, even bearing this in mind, that similar life would develop *independently* on two *adjacent* planets (Earth and Mars) within the universe again increases the odds and this time to billions of billions of billions; that is to say, it's just not going to happen. So natural selection alone cannot account for independent development of similar life *on two adjacent planets.* So Fred's discovery is the end of the road for Group A— essentially they're fired! All that supposition over the ages that nature alone has the answer is reduced to nothing."

She paused but they seemed enthralled so she carried on, "Sorry to labour this point but Fred would have instantly appreciated all this as he was after all obsessed with his work on the origins of life. He would have known that his discovery of similar plant life on Mars would have been the death knell for his firmly held view and life's work that natural selection alone accounted for everything. The only alternative was B which left room for some other influence within the universe, some other factor beyond matter and energy alone. That for Fred was a mind-shattering realisation. He tried to hide the evidence, perhaps until he felt he could get his head around it and manage it. But the stupendous effect it would have on his view of the world was too much for him, it blinded him because his world, indeed his universe had fallen apart. It was indeed his Damascus moment and unfortunately, unlike Saint Paul who was blinded by a stupendous realisation over 2000 years ago, he was encased in a spacesuit. Poor Fred had seen the way things are but alone and remote from the Mars village, remote from Earth and remote from friends who could have helped him like they did St Paul. Fred's find was his nemesis because it has also sealed for him a place in the progress of mankind. His discovery is the first real evidence of extra-terrestrial life. It was fatal for him in one sense but has yielded him a form of immortality."

Jo felt it was time to summarise.

"In a nutshell, if with the odds of life evolving by natural selection at all are minuscule, then the odds of similar life at any time evolving independently on an adjacent planet are infinitesimally small. Such a situation could only be the result of information transfer across space and this requires space to have or be a *mind*. Stephen Hawkins' quest to develop a theory of everything led to one of the greatest works of science ever produced. However, it does not signify the grand finale because his everything is not everything, it does not include the *mind* of the universe which somehow permeates all space. Maybe our own little minds can interact with this *mind*, or maybe we are part of it and it's the sum total of all of us, we just don't know, but what we can say is, it definitely exists."

Jo stared at a point in the centre of the table and seemed overcome by what she had discovered. They waited but she said no more and they all just sat for several minutes. Eventually, Steve broke the spell with an impromptu vote of thanks.

"Thank you, Jo, that's going to take a bit of time to absorb. I've got Fred's funeral to conduct in a few days and I'll keep all that in mind. As a chaplain, what you say is of course music to my ears, particularly as I'm currently reading up about astro-information theory and panspermia; it all seems to fit together. Your familiarity with Eastern culture and its greater weight on mind and thought yields insights which are strange to Western ears. We'll all have to meet again and talk further about this sometime."

Rising, he added, "Meanwhile, we have been asked to report the facts as we see them to the council tomorrow morning at their weekly meeting, after which I imagine the discovery will be broadcast widely in terrestrial media by late afternoon and we'll see what that brings forth."

As they dispersed, he noticed that Ben and Angela were in deep conversation about some aspects of Jo's rendering of the situation.

21

Fossils and Guinness

STEVE WAS BEGINNING to feel comfortable in his rather odd position as the Church of Scotland's Man on Mars. OK, it was not exactly a typical Scottish parish and the issues he had encountered were unlikely to figure in the books of advice to parish ministers but he was becoming generally accepted as a chaplain in the Mars community. The president and council members were friendly and supportive of his work and even those members who had been most doubtful about the need for a chaplain grudgingly accepted there might be merit in somebody taking care of what they dismissively referred to as welfare issues. He was delighted to be asked by the council to be present when they considered the release of the news about the fossil leaf. He lay awake that night thinking about the implications of the discovery on different societies on Earth.

He reckoned that, at one level, the scientific community would be overawed at the knowledge and start numerous research programmes at Universities on the nature of the early life on Mars. At a deeper level though, most of the mathematicians, astrophysicists and particle physicists who were all wedded to a quantum particle view of the Universe would be totally nonplussed at this disturbance to their equilibrium. Maybe the *mind* is also energy packages in space but that would need a lot of working out. Similarly, the religious community (at least the established theist religions) would, on the one hand, be delighted by the realisation that God's care extends to life elsewhere in the universe. On the other hand, their religious structures, the rites and rituals practised with such dedication over the centuries, would be fatally disrupted. The politicians might welcome the drawing together of minds from different cultures and views in a unified wonderment of life elsewhere. It sometimes happens in international sports events that create a certain togetherness for a period. On the other hand, the *raison d'être* of politicians lies in the differences between groups of people and anything which diminished this could be detrimental to their profession.

In fact, he reckoned that generally, the *on the other hand* folk would be less than happy and being cautious and averse to change, would offer resistance to acceptance of the news. While they could not label it fake news because the evidence was irrefutable, they would discredit it in many subtle ways so that it became a taboo to mention it. The church successfully used this approach for several hundred years after it was incontrovertibly shown that the world was a sphere; surely that could not happen again in this enlightened age. But Steve was getting tired and not thinking too clearly. He gradually drifted off into a somewhat restless sleep in an uncomfortable position in his chair from which he awoke in the middle of the night and clambered into bed to get proper rest.

Consequently, the next morning, sitting with the others around the table in the Mars Council Chamber, he was not at his best. Ben took the lead in reporting all that had occurred on their visit to Boulder Pit, their discovery of the split boulder, the strange leaf fossil and their meeting afterwards. The president immediately requested that the specimen be retrieved and brought back to them at the council if possible, later that day and two council members went off to arrange the transport. He then asked them to continue and Ben outlined the discussion they had had but did not mention Jo's rendering of the wider implications of the find on the current thinking of life in the universe. Steve guessed Ben and Angela had agreed to this as they were uneasy about Jo's view. Steve though felt it should be reported to the council and added,

"The view was also expressed at our meeting last evening that the discovery of previous life on Mars beyond the evolutionary incubation stage and indeed to the early plant stage showed that there must be other factors guiding it's development in the universe way beyond natural selection alone."

"How do you make that out?" interrupted one of the council members.

Steve replied, "Because the statistical likelihood of life developing from inanimate molecules in the first place has been shown to be one in billions and the likelihood of it happening again on an adjacent planet and in a similar way, judging by the leaf pattern, is virtually impossible."

"And your conclusion?" said the president, who had understood Steve's point.

"I don't know for sure" answered Steve, "but one possibility is that the development of life is steered by some force or knowledge or mind in the universe that has hitherto not been determined but is nevertheless present."

"Do, you mean a God? said the president,"And, of course, you might be biased in that direction being the chaplain."

The others were agog at the President's directness although he did have a reputation for getting to the kernel of the matter.

Steve said cautiously, "Yes but I'd rather call it a mind for this purpose, an omnipresent mind within the universe that our wee minds can tune into. The word God has preconceived meanings soaked in rituals and tradition among the religions of the world; I actually mean something more than that, much more than that."

"Oh," broke in the president, "that's getting too philosophical for this time in the morning; let's get this fossil here and have a look at it and work out what we are going to say in the press statement to the media. I want you all back here as soon as this boulder arrives at the village and meanwhile, no mention of this to others until after the news statement."

They all dispersed to attend to their daily business but Steve found he was too excited and keyed up to concentrate. This was rather unfortunate for the person at his next appointment who, like others, had been diagnosed with CD because she received a slightly less sympathetic reception than would have normally have been the case. Steve did see her the next day and was able to redeem himself by explaining first hand his involvement with the new discovery which was on his mind.

The split boulder was duly transported albeit with some difficulty to the council chamber by early evening and the same group reconvened. The two halves of the boulder split almost horizontally along the strata line, were laid out on the ground for them to see under a light which shone at an angle onto the surfaces. A casual glance showed nothing unusual and was disappointing in view of the excitement it had caused. That's when Wayne, who as a geologist had been allowed a little time before the gathering to examine the find more closely, came forward and spent the next half hour waxing eloquent on small indentations and shapes he had observed. Most

162

of the surface was sandy brown and granular but heavily compacted. There were also small areas with a dull black flaky streak through them and one place where this was about a centimetre wide. This, he explained, was carboniferous and essentially a mini-layer of compacted coal but from a much earlier geological period than our carboniferous period.

Close examination of this mini-seam revealed several areas of leaf-like shapes, each one overlapping the others and about four millimetres across. Sure enough, the shapes were almost square but with the sides being slightly concave rather like a sheet stretched out at the four corners. Veins could just be detected in the best specimens and they looked decidedly unfamiliar and oddly weird; nobody could remember seeing four-sided leaves before although Steve made a mental note to do a Google search. One of the biologists was sure there was no such leaf in terrestrial nature and ventured that slightly different evolutionary paths could have yielded these different shapes. Three, five and subsequent numbers of apexes and sides of leaves were common and a few flowers and grasses had four leaves but not leaves with four sides. Four is not the most common number in nature and of course, a four-petaled clover is a fortuitous find in folklore. Wayne drew everybody's attention back to what he saw as the key issue. This was evidence right before their eyes, of life on Mars in an era long ago and not only primaeval cells but life developed to the plant stage and, he ventured, to what looked like land plants rather than sea plants. This constituted a momentous discovery which he felt should be publicised as soon as possible.

The president who had been in the background as they all peered at the two slabs then sought their attention and gave a little speech in which he thanked them all for their parts in finding this evidence and expressed his sorrow at the demise of Fred in the process. He then added that the council would have to consider how and in what way this news was released. He said he would need to speak with his Earth colleagues about this and he asked the group to keep it to themselves until then. Steve felt very uncomfortable about this as he recalled his fears of the night and wondered if the council had already alerted Earth to some potentially exciting news and been asked or even told to hold for the moment. This assumption was further supported when the president added that Fred's funeral should be postponed until the way forward was clear. Steve was about to raise his concern but the president left and returned to his office. The others hung around inspecting the boulder surfaces and one or two took photographs on their iPads which surprisingly nobody had forbidden but Steve, feeling a little frustrated and tired after his lack of sleep, left and returned to his comfortable room in the chaplaincy.

While this room was pretty basic, essentially a bed, table, chair, en-suite toilet and shower at the back of the Chaplaincy Centre meeting room, it had become his home, his place of retreat when he needed to ponder. There was also the small study which doubled up as a consultation room when necessary and also led off from the Chaplaincy central meeting area. He knew the Chaplaincy had done rather better than other services in space allocation. As he passed through the centre en route to his room, he was surprised to see Jo sitting at the meeting table. A tinge of guilt passed over him; he had recounted her revelation on the philosophical importance of the find to the council but had not given her the full credit for it. He started somewhat clumsily to explain how he got carried away when she cut him off.

"That's no matter; I just wondered if you would like to chat about the day's events."

"Yes, sure," said Steve, realising he had got off lightly.

"Over dinner," she added.

Ah, he thought, *not quite so lightly then.*

They decided to go to the restaurant area in the Mars Bar for a bite rather than in the Bar itself. The establishment of this restaurant was a new development initiated by the Mars council to address complaints by the villagers about the standard in the Bar. In addition, Patrick, an Irish mechanical engineer had volunteered to take over the running of the Mars Bar and restaurant and had drawn up a rota of people willing to act as chef for a night, thus providing a constantly varying menu. Patrick, or Pat, as he had become known to his friends, also initiated the production of a new drink on Mars and this became very popular with the villagers.

Pat had approached the president sometime before about serving home-brewed Guinness in the Mars Bar. This would effectively transform it into an Irish Pub. The president, to give him his due, was not opposed to this idea but was concerned about the impression it would create with the Earth committees. Over the course of the next few weeks, he seeded the thought with Earth that every respectable place on their planet had an Irish Bar and Mars should have one too. Furthermore, it would attract more terminauts on which the economics of the colony partially depended. Earth eventually gave way on condition that the opening hours were restricted to certain times. Having overcome that hurdle, the president was now intrigued to see how on earth Pat was actually going to brew Guinness on Mars!

Pat had all that worked out though. He had been emailing the Guinness headquarters in Dublin for some time and found they were enthusiastic about their brew becoming the first interplanetary stout in the world. The limited supplies of barley grown within the Mars ecosystem (about which more later) were sufficient and with some slight adaptions, the Mars Guinness could be A1 quality or even A1 star (The Mars Bar was after all a long way from the Guinness quality inspectors). He was also keen to offer some Irish specialities including a stew which would be unique to Mars. To cut a long and successful story short, he eventually introduced these items to the Mars Bar so that villagers could enjoy a Guinness and an Irish stew. Apparently, Guinness was good for you, even if the stew was less so, and although it was provided in plastic bottles which were then poured into plastic mugs (Guinness not the stew), it was well-received on Mars. He made a great issue of knifing off the froth on each mug and letting it settle for 5 minutes as they used to do in Dublin bars before the European Union got involved. This also ensured that customers were thoroughly thirsty in anticipation by the time they got their hands on their drinks. So the Mars Bar became an Irish Pub in all but name and Steve argued that, as part of his professional need to mix with the villagers, he should frequent the Mars Bar.

On this occasion, in the Mars Bar restaurant, Steve and Jo dined on this very stew followed by locally regolith-seeded strawberries. He described the Inns he had visited in Ireland in the past and the ins and outs of new developments on Mars, not least Fred's great discovery. They swapped tales about their very different backgrounds and Steve told her more about his parents, his college friends and Bobby. They had a second Guinness each, which was not allowed under the strict Mars guidelines, but Pat had engineered a relaxation of the rules for Guinness alone as (once again) it was good for you. By the end of the evening, Steve could not help noticing how much he was enjoying being with her but knew he must not give voice to such feelings which were frowned on by the Mars establishment and him being a chaplain too. So he contented himself by giving her a peck on the cheek as they left which she pretended to hardly notice and Pat who was washing up at the bar also pretended not to notice.

22

News Briefings

STEVE'S SUSPICION REGARDING the prior
briefing of Earth was corroborated when he searched
the United Nations web site and noticed that an ad hoc
meeting of the Mars Committee of the UN had been
called for two days' time. This Committee was formed in
the early days of Mars human exploration and included
a handful of countries involved at that time including
the USA, Russia, China, India, the European Union and
Japan. Once exploration got underway, other countries
did not want to be left out and the membership had risen
to 24 by the mid-2030s. This made it somewhat cumbersome and difficult to make decisions quickly so the Mars
council based on Mars itself started making unilateral
decisions on minor but urgent matters. The UN Committee tolerated this for pragmatic reasons although it was
never actually written into the constitution. So when the
council drafted the news briefing about the discovery of
previous life on Mars, duly sent it to the UN Committee for comment and received no response, not even an
acknowledgement, it assumed the Committee had considered the wording of the communication a minor matter.
It was, therefore, finalised by the Mars council members
and released to the electronic news media the next day. By
precisely 12 noon, it was winging its way to all the news
stations on Earth at the speed of light.

The news briefing as the name implied was short and to the point. The hand of the president could be seen throughout the two short paragraphs from the council and particularly in his reference to research by scientists on Mars. He had been arguing for increased funds for research staff and equipment and this gave him a golden opportunity to press the case. The briefing, read as follows:

Following the death of Fred Albright, on operational duties in the Boulder Pit region about a mile from Mars village (as broadcast previously), a fossil he found has now been examined by the scientists on Mars. The fossil within a boulder of very old Precambrian rock includes several clear specimens of plant leaves with a four-sided concave rhombic shape hitherto unrecorded on Earth. Mars scientists are continuing to examine and analyse these fossils.

The Mars council consider this to be the first direct evidence of life on another planet. The biological similarity to life on Earth, although evolving independently of Earth is particularly significant and Mars scientists will examine the possible reasons for this keeping an open mind to all possibilities on how this life form was seeded. These will include inter alia, biological cross-fertilisation between the planets, panspermia and the presence of previously undetected influences on the development of life within the universe.

On Earth, one hour earlier that very morning, the UN Committee had agreed that they, the UN Committee itself, must take charge of this research and release of the news around the world rather than the Mars council situated on Mars. This was due to its potential destabilising influence on politics and world markets. An urgent message was sent to the Mars council at 11:45 am instructing them to hold the release. However, the speed of light limitation when communicating with Mars meant that their instruction did not arrive on Mars until 12:05 pm Earth time, as unfortunately for them Mars was nearly at its furthest distance from the Earth that month. This was 5 minutes too late to stop the news release although technically sent in time from Earth's perspective. So it was, that by mid-afternoon that memorable day, the whole World knew about Fred's fossil. The Mars Committee of the UN was furious, particularly as it made them look ineffective. The UN Secretary himself, being no scientist and not understanding the inherent delays caused by the speed of light was highly critical of the Mars scientists for countermanding their instruction. The representatives of the nearly 200 countries, being largely career diplomats, were queueing up to make speeches supporting the Secretary. Several countries pledged their support for a new UN-sponsored research programme aimed at increasing the speed of communication using so-called wormholes in space which delighted several universities who were desperately short of research funds.

There has to be a culprit for every unfortunate event and this role was adequately fulfilled by President Leskovich. He was after all the key representative on Mars, he could not defend himself face to face on Earth owing to the communication problems and he was Russian (although this was often forgotten owing to his excellent command of English). The UN was miffed that, yet again, the Mars council had acted unilaterally and decided they had to show who was boss. After a short ad hoc meeting, they agreed that the president had exceeded his authority and that his tenure in the post should be terminated with

171

immediate effect (In the event it could not be immediate because it took a total return trip time of over half an hour for the message to get to him and his acknowledgement to get back owing once again to those damn physicists and their speed of light). This took some of the heat out of their ire but proved difficult to implement because if you get the sack on Mars there is nowhere for you to go unless they send a special drove spacecraft from Earth to collect you. They endeavoured to find an immediate replacement for the president but the available recruitment market, being only those currently on Mars, was limited. Furthermore, the president was respected and popular within the Village even if he was a stickler for the correctness and somewhat puritanical in his ways. Consequently, nobody applied for the post and it lay empty until Earth reluctantly agreed that he should be offered the post of *acting president* until a replacement was found. The ex-president himself was somewhat reluctant to accept the new post and had to be financially persuaded and so it was that he ended up as Acting President doing the same job as before but on a higher salary.

On Earth, the big news release about the fossil leaf initially had a rather muted response. After all, they had been talking about life beyond the Earth for a hundred years and it was by now half expected. Indeed, it was rather an anti-climax that, when finally discovered, it was merely some unusual foliage. News can be like that; there is an eerie silence as the facts about, for example, some disaster sink in and then as the full enormity becomes evident and the fatalities mount up, the media machine picks up and the headlines buzz. In this case, it was fortunately not a disaster of any form, except for Fred, and folk could go about their business in the normal way and accept that there was now proof of life elsewhere. Steve felt the full realisation that life on Earth *was not unique* would gradually sink in over a longer period resulting in a paradigm shift in philosophy, religion and all manner of blue skies thinking. This would lead, in due course, to implications and unintended consequences for most branches of human endeavour.

When it was realised that the UN had tried to suppress the truth about the discovery leaking out, there was much bad press in countries all over the world. It came at a time when the UN's credibility had hit an all-time low and simply added fuel to the increasing dismissive view of such authorities. It was part of the popular belief that most establishment institutions and indeed the government itself was potentially corrupt and essentially self-seeking. This spilt over into universities and research institutions who were no longer viewed as the unbiased arbiters of scientific knowledge. There was a growing drift away from acceptance of the views of the *expert* to the extent that the man in the street always felt there was an ulterior motive to views expressed by professionals and their associated authorities. This embedded cynicism had taken root twenty years earlier with recognition of the power of fake news for propaganda purposes and while most people were by now savvy to the unreliability of headlines, they had assumed that the UN at least was above all this. Now it was evident that, like others, they were managing the news rather than openly releasing it.

Where Mars was concerned, some leading politicians of minor nations started challenging the international agreements of 50 years before that Mars like the Antarctic was an internationally neutral zone. Some viewed the USA, Russia, China, India, Japan and others as effectively hijacking the new Planet with them being left on the side lines. They argued that the colonisation of America had led to numerous wars over the next few hundred years and it might, therefore, be better to apportion Mars in the early stages to all the countries of Earth, not a special few. Some even started to argue among themselves as to whether this should be pro-rata based on territory or demography. The UN decided that they needed to take a practical step to recoup some authority both on Earth and also with the Mars villagers themselves who had become somewhat disaffected.

Consequently, the UN foreshortened the planned Mars visit schedule and funded the early launch of Drove 6 from Cape Kennedy to a date in six months' time. This Drove would include several internationally renowned geophysicists to assess the new discovery of fossil vegetation on Mars. One difficulty was that the five domes of the village were practically full and the arrival of a further 50 or so people would create logistic difficulties. In the event, this was reduced to 35 people which had the advantage that more freight could be included. Some of this *freight* was extra core ingredients for food to appease the Mars council who had pointed out that while the UN was preoccupied with their own political standing the food situation on Mars had seriously deteriorated. One or two of the more disaffected villagers had hinted they might work to rule by withholding scientific information if conditions did not improve.

23

Food for Thought

THE INTERNATIONAL POLITICS unfolding on Earth with respect to the Mars Colony were in every sense remote to those on Mars. The Earth was more or less at its furthest distance from Mars in the cycling of the two planets and this was reflected in the attitude of the villagers. Indeed, they were generally more preoccupied with their immediate surroundings in the domes, their day to day work, good housekeeping and, not least, their food than the small globe they sometimes saw in the sky. Unlike our good-living Texan member of the flat earth society, they did not deny the reality surrounding them but they preferred to leave the deeper thinking to others. After all, as Plato had observed long ago, you don't want too many thinkers in the market place. In fact, it's fair to say that in the overall scheme of things, food for the humans on Mars is equally as important as fuel for the rockets; poor food leads to poor functioning and ultimately to poor thinking. You do need—food for thought.

Steve recognised this and took it upon himself as part of his duties to be a champion of better food on Mars. On his earthly pilgrimage (as he loved to call his time before Mars, with a nod to John Bunyan), he had several theories why his beloved Church of Scotland and for that matter, some other establishment-based religions were losing their flocks. Apart from the deeper matters of belief discussed earlier, there was their poor standard of food and drink. The way to the heart is through the stomach and if God resides in the heart then food has a religious significance. The Jews, the Muslims, the Hindus, in fact, many of the really old religions realised this long ago but it obviously takes thousands of years to appreciate this as some haven't got there yet; food and drink is just not their cup of tea (so to speak). Whatever your tastes, a *kosher falafel*, an Arabic lamb stew or a Hindu *vindaloo* are all catalysts to conviviality. Methodist, Baptists and Presbyterians have no dishes which are a patch on this and indeed patronise other cultures and religions whenever they go out for a decent meal. Presbyterians are by far the worst, favouring well-fingered biscuits and instant coffee to wash away their services. (A Presbyterian bun sounds more promising but turns out to be a rather severe hairstyle favoured by its stricter members in times past).

So, back on Mars, Steve found there was limited cuisine because there was no incentive to use core ingredients and no scope for ingenuity. Some Italian company had cornered the market in interplanetary packaged food and boasted over 157 varieties wrapped in plastic and brought to soggy life by adding water which is, in any case, is in short supply on Mars. They can be prepared in 5 minutes but that's no advantage because the Mars folk have hours of leisure time and nothing to do and nowhere to go. His campaign to get more core food ingredients from Earth was having some effect but only by assertive action and the threat of strikes. Many of the villagers were in their thirties and were inspired in their youth by The Martian film (from the book by Andy Weir) where a stranded Earthling manages to survive by growing vegetables.

Indeed, Steve was still lobbying the council only this

morning at their weekly executive meeting (which he was now invited to attend).

"Before we go," said the acting president, now widely abbreviated to AP by the Villagers, "are there any other items which cannot be left until next week?"

"Yes," piped up Steve, ignoring the AP's *I-want-to-finish* look.

"In view of the increasing problem with boredom and lethargy, requiring pep drugs which are now running low on Mars until Drove 6 arrives, I suggest we apportion the growing zone beside Dome B to those who wish to have garden allotments so that they can grow their own food and sell it if desired."

Steve usually tested out his ideas on his colleagues first, but not this one as he had only just thought of it.

The president, now getting to know Steve well, guessed as much.

"And what is your considered policy on prevention of contamination between domes, your selection procedure for applicants for these allotments and the pricing of the produce?" he asked.

"All in a report which I'll submit in due course."

Well, it was not quite a lie because he didn't say he'd finalised or even started the report yet.

"In that case, we'll look forward to receiving it before our meeting next week so that we can consider it in depth at the Meeting," said the VP as he got up to go.

Steve dealt with the usual chaplaincy matters over the next few days; advising folk on family issues back on Earth, consoling those who missed family events at home or lost a parent while they were away, arranging weekly Christian and Islamic services as best he could. He was not seen around in the evenings, declined a dinner with Jo and was noticeably absent from the Mars Bar. The reason was that the report on his allotments' idea which he thought was probably a non-starter and thus not worthy of much time, had become not only feasible but very attractive. It was finished two days before the next meeting which gave council members time to study it and him time to have an evening off. Accordingly, he wandered into the Mars Bar to enjoy a well-earned reward and had just ordered when he was surprised to see the AP sitting in the corner by himself. Steve thought he must have rewarded himself too but his reward must have been for something very special as he hardly ever went there.

Although the AP was known for his somewhat correct and prudish ways, Steve risked a jokingly familiar greeting.

"What brings you here to this den of iniquity so early in the evening?"

"It's hardly that. The surroundings are grim and I've decided to get rid of Greta and have a full-time rota manning this place although those Earthlings will probably try to prevent it. In answer to your question, it's their petty bickering at every committee meeting that has driven me to seek refuge here. I've spent all day trying to convince their Conveyancing Department to send more core food ingredients. The deadline for finalising consignments is a month before taking off date, why I don't know, and they are still arguing about it. They did agree to send more barley grains among the other things though."

"And why barley in particular?" asked Steve.

The AP did not answer but raised his glass of dark stout. Steve realised that Guinness ingredients must be getting low.

"Patrick is always pestering me to place it on higher priority but I have to be careful." He then added, "We also thought we would try some fruit in the greenhouse. The yield per square metre has to be high to make the case but we are going to experiment with intensive strawberries in layered trays, pineapples and also raspberries as the canes can straddle around other items in unused spaces. Potato plants on which tomatoes can be grown as well as they are essentially the same plant have come into their own and we have been asked to test them."

Steve asked, "All this along with the existing strains of root vegetables will need a lot of care and attention. Do we have the facilities and spare labour to support this? From my perspective of keeping people happy I believe it is very important because food is a crucial feature of life on Mars."

"I can see you think that," said the AP, viewing the large pasta which Steve had ordered.

"Yes, well I hope you included ample stocks of Penne pasta in the order or I'll be no use to you."

"On that point, tomorrow, I might support the proposal in your report with two modifications. Firstly, you must explain what an allotment is because people from some countries will not appreciate that it is land divided up into small plots and allocated to those, often with no garden, who wish to cultivate them for flowers and vegetables. Secondly, to be efficient with the limited cultivation land available here there must be some degree of collaborative cultivation. In other words, some can specialise in fruit, some on root vegetables, some on rice, some on green plants and maybe even some on… pasta plants.'

Steve smiled and responded, "Some of these intensely focussed astro-scientists here would probably believe your last example! But I see what you mean; maybe they could be specialist in one crop but still have a small area of their allotment for anything they liked.'

The AP agreed that could work and then, although Steve offered to get him another Guinness (knowing full well that was beyond regulation levels), and said he never normally had more than one and left. Steve did wonder about his use of the word *normally*.

Steve sat a little longer contemplating how his life on Mars was becoming reasonably comfortable although he still missed much on Earth. Bobby had emailed him to say he was moving up to the next year at school and had been appointed a space monitor reporting to the class on space developments and especially on Mars. He had helped Bobby by sending him some pictures and explained to him how much he would love to have been there with him chatting about it. Not being able to chat to folk on Earth owing to the speed of light thing was a real disadvantage. Sometimes, he longed to pick up the visiphone to his mum and dad and see them at least electronically face to face but that was not possible and only emails with photo attachments were feasible, like Earth communication over thirty years ago. He would have loved to go for a walk in the cool, fresh evening air of his native Scotland. Maybe he should not stay too long but then he had an uncomfortable premonition that some event would ensure that any return in the reasonable future was out of the question.

24

Mars Flu

MOST OF THE disaster scenarios that could occur in the small remote Mars community had been analysed to the point of death, literally. These included those occasioned by external causes such as extreme sand storms, asteroids, volcanoes and earthquakes although none of the latter two had been recorded to date. These were seen as *acts of God* and were designated as such in the small print of the contracts signed by all the villagers prior to embarkation. They also analysed those occasioned by accidents and, as on Earth, these were not seen as acts of God but caused by humans and thus avoidable. They included operational failures of air conditioning (including on Mars oxygen and nitrogen proportions as well as temperature and humidity), structural collapse of a dome, explosions due to leaking gas and so on. Widespread disease leading to a Mars pandemic was not analysed in spite of the Coronavirus catastrophe in the early 20's and yet it was this that struck such a blow to the emergent community. It was assumed that diseases would not be transported to Mars from Earth owing to the extraordinary measures taken to prevent it but this did not allow for home-grown viruses caused by the particular conditions on Mars. It really should have been foreseen because there was a precedent for emergent colonies suffering from unencountered diseases in a 'New World' from long before.

Just over one hundred folk came to Jamestown, Virginia in 1607 to found one of the first colonies in America. They were from different backgrounds and social classes and were skilled in different areas. However, most of these people died from various diseases. Jamestown was located near a swamp, which made the threat of disease even greater owing to the unsanitary drinking water. The colonists were forced to use infested water for cooking, washing, and drinking purposes and as a result, they developed various strains of typhoid and dysentery. To a lesser extent, this was the case with many of the early colonies on the American continent and deaths from illness far exceeded those from starvation or other causes.

In the Mars village, it started with one of the terminauts, Shane, suffering from what the two resident doctors thought was just a bad cold. Shane, an Australian who had made his millions in sheep farming at the turn of the millennium had already had serious prostate cancer and thought he would like to leave the earth in style. In spite of pleading from his remaining family to stay with them, if not in spirit at least in the body (correct way round), he nevertheless pursued his wish to die on Mars. Once there, he started to enjoy his grumpy old man status and decided to delay the reason for going there as long as possible. He was not best pleased when some deadly disease similar to Covid-19 took hold of him just when he was beginning to settle down.

Within a few days, six other villagers had contracted the so=called Mars flu and the alarm was raised on Earth at a special meeting of the Mars Committee. The terrestrial health advisors insisted on complete segregation as soon as possible but this was not easily achievable on Mars owing to the proximity of the domes to each other.

Once the number of cases had reached a dozen, the acting president overrode the various committees who were dragging their heels in the hope of evading the need to declare a state of emergency. He declared Dome D an emergency infection unit and instructed all the unaffected residents to move to the other domes or the Central Community Dome. Dome D was selected because 8 residents there already had the disease but this meant the remaining 35 folk needed to relocate. The council set to, arranging temporary accommodation, commissioning the use of anything that could class as bedding and arranging toiletry and other facilities as best they could. Fortunately, each dome had its own kitchen facilities so segregation was feasible from the catering perspective. Many of these 35 residents were employed on computer-based activities and had to abandon their work stations leading to delays of the scientific research programme.

The chaplaincy's contribution to finding space for evacuees from Dome D was for Jo to move into the little study/consultancy room just off the chaplaincy. It was large enough for a bed and minor furniture. The toilet and shower facility used also by Steve just off the chaplaincy centre area had to double up for combined use. It did mean he could not leave personal paraphernalia lying around to the same extent and had to tidy up on occasions but this was a small price to pay compared to the cramped conditions some of the others had to endure. Jo was easy going and he enjoyed her company, although her strange Indian scents tended to infiltrate beyond her room. Having the odd image of a swatting Buddhist here and there took some getting used to in spite of the chaplaincy being a home for all faiths. At least there were no African tribal religions to date and the humanists, of whom there were quite a few on Mars, seemed tolerant of the religious icons. There were practical advantages too as Steve and Jo had fallen into the habit of planning their chaplaincy visits and other business on three mornings each week, these being the three days that Jo was formally released from what she called her proper job as one of the biology team.

Meanwhile, Shane had become very ill and had serious respiratory issues. He was put on a monitor and four nights later showed a serious decline. Being 85 years old and already weak before his trip to Mars (some said he should have been refused in spite of the 28 million dollars he paid to come), it was feared he was dying and Steve went to see him and administer what comfort he could. Steve, like others caring for the infected patients had to don a white Hazmat suit which made him look particularly foreboding. Shane was not religious and assumed Steve was seeing him as a caring visitor as he was after all the chaplain. However, on his second visit within 24 hours, Shane perceived that Steve must be performing an expected or required duty or even administering the last rites. This made him even less happy.

"Might have guessed that some Pommy bastard in a white suit would turn up when I'm really down to earn himself a kudos point," he growled.

Steve stared at the gaunt man lying there with a mix of sympathy and annoyance.

"I'm Scottish so not strictly Pommy and I'm not a bastard, I'm the chaplain," said Steve, stiffly.

"You're probably both, retorted the frail voice."

"And what are you then?"

"I was the biggest sheep farmer in Western Australia."

"Well, you're not the biggest sheep farmer now," said Steve as he looked down on the emaciated frame in the bed. Shane opened his eyes—they had been almost closed and peered at Steve for a moment with interest.

"Thought you guys were meant to be all sweetness and light."

"We are, but not to crusty old sheep farmers even if they did own half of Australia."

"So what happens to me now? I've cashed in my fortune for the last trip to Mars (which really upset a few hangers-on who were waiting to get their hands on it) only to die of common flu in this God-forsaken planet."

"Well, it's not God-forsaken because God loves Mars too—" but Shane cut him off.

"No, I don't want all that religious stuff, I want to know what happens to ME. They can't bury me owing to contamination and they can't eject me into space as it's too expensive, so what happens to me, this me here?"

Steve paused for a moment before admitting.

"I really don't know for sure."

"Well, that's a first, a chaplain who doesn't know what happens to you. At least I suppose that's honest."

"I'll speak to the council and let you know their latest position. The last I heard was that they were going to build concrete Mausoleums," said Steve feeling somewhat inadequate. He stared at the floor thinking but was summarily dismissed,

"Well, get the hell out of here and find out then or I'll be gone without knowing," complained Shane.

Steve visited one or two others in the infected Dome D on the way out but kept thinking about Shane's worrying question. Once he had removed his protective clothing and had a shower, he decided to see a member of the council who might inform him of their current position.

It was two days later that Steve tracked down the member responsible among other things for the disposal of waste. This was a major part of the Facilities Operational Section and included all rubbish and recycling aspects of the Mars village. Consequently, the remit extended to human waste including whole body disposal when required. The procedure, apparently agreed several years ago, was to place the deceased in a plastic body bag which would be placed in a large concrete sarcophagus. These, in turn, would be placed in a specially constructed bunker or mausoleum. Owing to the absence of bacteria and the low level of oxygen in the atmosphere, the bodies would hardly decay for at least 100 years by which time it was felt some more permanent solution would be found. Other options considered had been ejection to space whenever the next spacecraft left but this was rejected by NASA because it constituted further littering of space. Cremation was impossible on Mars having virtually no oxygen in the atmosphere unless use was made of the valuable stored oxygen. One option still under consideration was to place the body outside the spacecraft in the bag so that it froze, vibrate it over a long period until it was dust and then release the dust it into space (thus complying with the dust to dust elements of several religions). The mausoleum won out in the end and became the preferred method owing to its ease of implementation. As we saw earlier, the Mars folk immediately transposed it to Marsoleum (after all, what's in a letter change?). Steve had not been included in these discussions and had to go along with it, but felt a little miffed that, as chaplain, he had neither been consulted nor informed.

The next day when he revisited Shane, he duly informed him.

"You mean to say I'll have my own temple on Mars?" he whispered, having now become very weak.

"Not quite," said Steve, "because it will have to be

shared with Fred who's already been cold stored for a couple of months and any others that come along but you'll be in the Marsoleum for over 100 years and will have your name inscribed on the front, or the side, with an appropriate inscription of up to 20 letters—for any passers-by to read!"

He was not quite sure why he added this; sometimes things just come out in spite of yourself; even to dying man. To Steve's consternation, Shane started to shake a little and it took him a moment to realise that actually, he was laughing.

"How about... *I'm on the other side.* Is that less than 20 letters?"

He then added, "You realise I'll have left the Earth without dying. I'll be like Elisha, he left the Earth without dying didn't he?"

"You're right," said Steve, somewhat taken aback, "but how do you know about that?"

"Us farmers in the outback all went to Sunday school; we know a thing or two about these things; it's not just you chaplain types with all your learning. I want to die out here in space because I'll be halfway there."

"Yes, I know, I understand and you're right, it's all a journey and Earth's just a stop en route and no you haven't lost your way, your right on target."

"Thank you, Chaplain, much appreciated. Now bugger off as I've become tired and want to sleep with my thoughts."

"And what's the inscription to be."

Steve lent over and just heard him whisper, "*Forgotten, but not gone.*"

Over the next few weeks, a further six folk died, four terminauts, one crew member and one scientist. Twenty were ill and in a distressed state as they knew how serious the Mars flu strain had become. Dome D (some now said D for disaster) became a fully segregated section with access only sanctioned to those really needing to enter. Steve was very busy and had to increasingly rely on Jo to undertake much of the general caring work while he concentrated on the most serious cases. The strain of flu had still not been isolated by the laboratory technicians who were working in conjunction with those on Earth and unfortunately, even if it were, the chances of a suitable antidote being available on Mars was slight. The possibility of a lockdown as practiced on Earth was not possible because recourse to the natural environment on Mars would be fatal. Steve, Jo and the nurses and doctors all had to wear masks which somewhat dehumanised them. Those who had so far evaded the virus were understandably becoming anxious and needed reassurance. There was really nobody able and prepared to give this comfort except Steve and Jo so they were consequently very busy and becoming weary under the emotional strain of attending to the ill and dying. He had become quite close to Jo, partly because they had to work closely together and partly because she was so ruddy attractive but he went into denial with his feelings knowing the strict rules in the village and him being the chaplain and all that. Beyond Dome D, life continued as normally as possible with people going about their day-to-day business as if all was well.

25

Wayne's Revelation

THIS DAY TO day business for the majority of the villagers was scientific analysis, engineering calculations and assessment, operational activities and communication with Earth. Additionally, people were expected to multi-task between functions and as we know, Jo, a biologist, had ended up in the part-time role of assistant chaplain. Even the Mars council members, although managers of sections, were expected to help in other areas. For example, Dr Wayne Hill, although he was primarily involved with rocket fuel production, his knowledge of Mars rocks was key to the investigation of previous life on Mars. He had often assisted with fieldwork beyond the village owing to his knowledge of the terrain and, as we saw earlier, he was one of the team of four who travelled out to Boulder Pit after Fred's unfortunate breakdown. He was sometimes away from the village base for many hours on these field studies and he, therefore, had the opportunity to experience the beauty and wonder of being on another planet more than most. It was on one such trip that he had a flash of insight that provided a further step in understanding the existence of consciousness in the universe. Like most days though, it had started with the mundane things of everyday life, even on Mars.

The Mars flu was still prevalent and Wayne's Section was down three staff so they were overloaded. On the day in question, he awoke early with the sun shining through the portholes high up in his dome. (It should be explained that the Mars day, taken as the sidereal day, is 40 minutes longer than that on Earth but the Mars year is about twice as long. As the seasons are not particularly evident in the barren landscape, this does not really matter but it does have the effect that it is light in the early morning for a terrestrial year then dark until later in the morning for the next terrestrial year). By 7 am, he had risen, attended to toiletry items and tidied his small bed-sit pod. The pod was not dissimilar to the student room he had occupied at university some 20 years before. It had the regulation bed, chair, computer base, sink, fridge, shower unit and a cupboard for everything from computing screens to clothing and dried food. The ceiling had a warm *daylight* fluorescent surface specially developed for the Mars habitat. All this was packed in a stipulated volume of about 10 square metres although he actually had a little more owing to the curvature of the dome.

Today, he dressed in his yellow Gortex Gilet and dark green trousers. He normally dressed in a pale blue Gilet and navy trousers as his core role was a scientist for whom this was the regulation dress of all whether men, women or unallocated. The engineers, including techni- cal and operational staff, wore green and the service and administrative staff yellow, hence his yellow over green this morning. The Mars council had devised this system some years ago in spite of constant objections by the villagers. He realised that on Earth, the lads would have given him a hard time, probably calling him the sunflower kid or worse, but not on Mars where, in any case, there were no sunflowers. It appears that fashion and proto-col are so deeply embedded in the human psyche that it persists even onto another planet.

The day's mission was to make an exploratory visit to an area hitherto unexamined to the South of the Mars village and bring back loose rocks for analysis. Wayne was joined by two scientists, Yousef from Mumbai University, an expert on mineral formation in the early solar system and Mary, the young American professor from MIT working on self-replicating organic chains, the same Mary who had interrupted Ken and Steve in the bar one evening. By eight o'clock, they had assembled near the exit of the central dome where most off-site preparation was undertaken and were checking their individual rovers that were to transport them over the rough terrain. Their clothing colours from now on were immaterial because all the external spacesuits were the same silver-grey so fashion had its limits. Half-an-hour later, this international threesome were in the air pocket and waiting for the outer doors to open.

Wayne had done this many times before and found the routine unchallenging. As he crept along on his rover, he had time to view the bleak surroundings, the yellow-tinged regolith and the open dark blue skies above this remote planet. There was a surreal beauty to the surroundings and he pondered the thought that here was he, a human being, a representative assembly of molecules from Earth but with the kernel of life within them, now traversing another planet. He paused and let the other two go ahead while he just sat soaking in the ethereal majesty of it all and explored a few thoughts. While human beings are complex bodies composed of particles buzzing around in space, not unlike every other body, their one difference is that they have consciousness and are aware of their state. I think therefore I am. Such awareness cannot be concocted by the particles in our bodies without information. This information can only be in the arrangement of the particles, the DNA and RNA. The difference is attributable to the information rather than the particles themselves hence it must come from *outside the particle domain.* Most scientists are very reluctant to accept that there may be influences within space that they have not discerned or cannot explain with the current view of reality in the universe. This is odd because scientists are meant to be open to all theories until they are proved incorrect. History shows (as we saw earlier) that science does not have a good record in assessing off the wall ideas. The respectable theory that accounts for all, we are told, is evolution by natural selection. The evidence that it works is indeed irrefutable, species most certainly evolve as time progresses. But it does not account for the presence of information and how that started nor does it offer an explanation of how the information is transmitted such that consciousness is possible. Maybe it is *information* that was there at the start and the Big Bang is firstly an information explosion and then only secondly a matter-energy explosion.

Wayne continued pondering and then reluctantly forced himself from his musings and started to drive his rover on towards the others who were a fair way ahead. Then, out of the dark blue sky, a realisation came to him like a thunderbolt. He stopped for a moment, letting the other two progress even further ahead before pulling himself together. He contained his excitement until he could talk to them face to face. That was over two hours later after they had collected several rock specimens and returned to base. As they were sitting in the entrance and debriefing by recording their visit on their iPads, he could contain himself no more and he excitedly explained to a bemused Yousef and Mary the significance of his discovery.

"Hey, Folks, while we were out there something

occurred to me that could have deep significance following Fred's discovery of early life on Mars."

Yousef interrupted, "You mean you could have lost your marbles like poor Fred and started lobbing stones at us?"

"No, not quite, although it does involve Fred. You remember that Fred's leaf showed for the first time that similar life had developed independently on two planets. Well, the rock that contains that fossil leaf is very, very old, nearly 4 billion years indeed and radio dating in our Mars lab has now confirmed this. Evolutionary biologists tell us it takes about half a billion years to evolve from core cells with DNA to a structure as complex as a leaf which means life was seeded nearly 4.5 billion years ago. Well, as you know this was not long after our solar system was formed. So, it's likely that life was seeded then, at that time. That means from the very beginning, the information code was there and it is not a by-product of chemical reactions between the elements subsequent to the Big Bang. That is to say:

The seed of life, the kernel of consciousness, the very horme of human existence was there when the universe began.

Mary, who had spent many years of research on this exact issue, had been listening intently to all this with increasing fascination and interrupted with a thought of her own.

"That would explain the failure over the years to simulate the creation of DNA or the more primitive RNA from core elements. Over a hundred years ago, experiments by Oparin in Russia and Haldane in the UK showed that organic chemicals could be formed from inorganic gases. However, the evolution from these organic compounds to living cells encompassing protein, DNA information and the ability to replicate has not been demonstrated with any certainty and indeed the complexity involved is enormous. Proponents of this process take recourse in the likelihood of various constituents in the primaeval soup of mud and clay acting as catalysts but this is still simply conjectured. On the other hand, if some elementary form of life cell or information carrier was initially present in this soup then the evolutionary development to our present state, while still outstanding is at least feasible."

She paused, a little embarrassed that she had taken over the conversation but they were listening intently so she carried on.

"There is a possibility that it could have been seeded very early on by asteroids from outside the solar system transporting living microbes. The likelihood of this accounting for life on two adjacent plants is low but even if this were the case, it still leaves open the problem of how life started elsewhere in the universe, in other words, how did the microbes obtain the necessary information? Furthermore, the conditions just a few millions of years after the Big Bang were not conducive to the survival of complex molecules, let alone microbes. So the key question remains; how did this *information* get there?"

She then added a thought stemming from her childhood years attending a little Southern Baptist Church in Alabama.

"Yes, in the beginning was the information— you know if Steve was here, he would explain that St John had pointed this out 2000 years ago. His Gospel starts: *In the beginning was the word...* but Christian folk simplify it by saying the Word, the Logos, is Jesus, whereas it's much more encompassing than that. It's the very life within the universe. To Christians, Jesus embodies the full extent of this which is neat and simple but to the millions of others far removed in religion, culture, geography or time, it's the Word, the God, the information, the kernel of life. And it's everywhere, on Earth, on Mars and throughout the universe."

Yousef, who was studiously analytical and not inclined to excitement of any kind then came in with a concern following Mary's last observation which showed that he was not only on board with the concept but was thinking well ahead about its implications.

"OK, but thereby lies a practical problem. Suppose you are right and the life-generating molecular information was there on day one, then it means that there was a consciousness or a mind there from day one too. If that were true, I'm afraid it would be a non-starter with people because both the scientific community and the religious community let alone all the others would find it unacceptable."

"I'm not quite sure what you mean," said Wayne, "surely, it's clear enough."

Yousef explained, "Yes, clear enough to us out here by ourselves on another planet with nobody else around except a few other folks in the village but you have to recognise that it will require a paradigm change for many scientists schooled in the evolutionary development of consciousness. Furthermore, every evangelist preacher from the most fanatical creationist in America to the most ardent advocate of reincarnation in India is going to misinterpret the idea and claim that it corroborates their particular brand of religious theory about God and creation. The true significance will just become submerged in a plethora of inaccurate media reporting and fake news. I'm not religious but if I were, I would find it frustrating that any deep understanding becomes trivialised by claims that it substantiates this or that faith or this or that denominational creed and hence all the associated rites and practices. If it's shown to be true that life is an integral part of the universe from the beginning, that's an astounding discovery of Wayne's and we will have to reset our thinking and accept there is more to the universe than we thought. If that's religion, then I can grant it that credence. If that's a manifestation of God, then I believe in God but It does not follow that all the paraphernalia associated with established religions is also true."

There was a long pause in the conversation. They realised that something significant had been revealed as it can on occasions when folk with no agenda delve into mysteries of life. Wayne, Mary and Yousef continued to mull over this spontaneous discourse for many days following the trip. It had significant implications for science, philosophy and religion because *who we are and how we got here* was important for each of them. Wayne, who had after all started the conversation, rounded it off with a suggestion that perhaps in view of its significance he should report their ideas to Steve as he was the resident chaplain no less and obtain his views on the matter. Unfortunately, though, Steve was about to blot his copybook and it was some time before he could give such weighty thoughts his full attention again.

26

Steve Yields to Temptation

AFTER A FEW weeks, the flu epidemic had begun to subside although there were still several very ill folk in Dome D. The evacuees were asked to remain in their temporary quarters for a further month as a precaution. Attention was being paid to the problem of burial now that it was agreed that no less than three Marsoleums should be built. The construction people were already starting to produce the necessary regolith bricks similar to those used earlier in the construction of the domes and several designs were being evaluated. In the end, a classical gothic shape was selected not unlike those in some British country gardens, largely because they were the only ones the British designer had ever seen before and nobody else had any better ideas. The Muslim folk later objected and some small minarets were added which were hardly compatible with the Greek columns.

These Marsoleums were assembled in a few weeks using the Mars Lego method devised some years ago and based on a popular child's construction toy of the time. Bricks on Mars were standardised from the beginning and this ensured rapid erection as stocks of bricks were usually on hand but restricted designs to those shapes that could be achieved using them. The Marsoleums were built some 100 metres from the village in a dip behind a hill in what was meant to provide a serene setting but the Mars folk with their ever-present sense of mortality, termed it Death Valley and unfortunately, this name stuck.

Increasingly, over the flu crisis and also on other matters pertaining to social life on Mars, Steve had become the spokesperson for Mars to those on Earth owing partly to his natural ability at coming up with the right words and partly because the others, being mainly scientific and technical people, were only too happy for him to do it having no interest in this role. Consequently, he became quite a celebrity on the terrestrial news media. Steve was beginning to enjoy the attention and began to consider that he had too modest a view of his place in the management and social structure. Somebody had to maintain the ethical standards on Mars and he, the chaplain, had been chosen to be the guardian of these standards. Once or twice, he had cautiously reprimanded Mars council members for their overly tolerant attitude to moral deviations by the villagers, after all, it was important that the rules were obeyed to the letter. He had even begun to draft a written code of conduct for Mars to which all new arrivals should sign up and this he felt would ensure good standards were established and maintained. Deviations would have to be punished appropriately and guidelines on these punishments should also be drafted. He was developing a sense of pride in his achievements which were, of course, all aimed at improving the moral standards of his colleagues and he was pleased that in his monthly report to the Church of Scotland he could report that their Man on Mars was doing God's work effectively. The Mars council were not enamoured by the concept of a Code of Conduct for Mars but he was sure he could wear them down to accepting it given time.

It was one evening a couple of weeks later that Steve,

feeling tired and slightly below his best, sat with Jo at the large centre table in the chaplaincy. They were in the process of sorting out the programme for the seven scheduled burials of the poor folk of various religions and none, who had died of the flu. After an hour and a half of concentrated effort, they had more or less finished the plan and decided on procedures for the *burial* services. Steve suggested they had earned themselves a treat and produced two of the plastic bottles of Patrick's Guinness that he had stashed away for a stressful day. These, they drank and a further two were consumed as they relaxed and swapped stories about their past lives on Earth. Jo decided to have an early night and on impulse, Steve gave her a kiss on the cheek as she went to her temporary room off in the chaplaincy. He wondered why he had done this but rationalised it as a wee *thank you* for the extra work on the burials.

He took the burial plans off to his own room in the chaplaincy to go over them once more and lay on his bed for a short rest but fell asleep before perusing them. He woke up an hour later, made his way to the shower room, opened the door and was inside before he realised to his horror that Jo was standing there, sopping wet and as naked as the day she was born. He had never seen a naked Indian girl before and was mesmerised by her dark skin and goddess-like looks. He manfully tried to mutter apologies but the words just wouldn't come out and she, for her part, just stood there and smiled and made no attempt to preserve her modesty. He was just about to retreat (at least that's what he told himself afterwards) when she came over to him and gave him a cuddle, a proper cuddle which he had not had for a very long time. Then he responded with a proper cuddle and then… a less proper cuddle. After that, it was all a blur but he remembered that they somehow ended up in his bed with the Marsoleum plans scattered all over the place before he succumbed to the occasion and later fell into a deep sleep.

It must have been about six o'clock that he awoke into the real world or rather, Mars with a momentary shock at seeing beautiful Jo lying beside him and the bedding and the plans all scattered about. And then, the worry set in. This sort of thing was not allowed under the strict social code on Mars unless they were registered as a *couple* and he was the chaplain to boot. In all consciousness, he would have to resign and that would be a disaster, not only for him but for the many folk who had come to view him as setting the standard and latterly writing those codes. And what would they do with him; if he was defrocked for seducing his assistant he couldn't just leave Mars and...

Jo had woken up and was smiling at him in a slightly concerned fashion.

"Good morning," he said, adding, "I can't pretend I'm really sorry, but that was really not my plan. Now I'm in real trouble."

"Yes, I thought you were looking worried."

She sympathetically moved in towards him.

"Tell you what, you have an English expression, something about one might as well be hung for a sheep as for a lamb, so why don't we cuddle up again?"

He laughed but then realised, she meant it.

Later, after tidying up they discovered, as is the way, that they were starving and proceeded cautiously to the Mars Bar where, being nobody else about at this post-breakfast hour, they had an earnest discussion about what to do. Steve admitted that, while he felt completely deflated with his pride and self-respect in tatters, he also felt completely human. No longer could he occupy the high ground as chaplain over what the church patronisingly termed his flock when he himself had so gratuitously yielded to temptation. How could he have been so arrogant and assume that his position would protect him from such temptation? She, on the other hand, was becoming irritated that her love which she had hidden for so long and surely his too would, in the light of day be downgraded by some stuffed shirts on a committee to a *temptation*, a deviation from some moral path laid down by a bunch of Mars councillors and their controllers on Earth. Who were these moral arbiters anyway and what rights did they have?

"If we love one another, we will just have to ask the AP to register us as a couple," she said, "It's a major step for us but no big deal for him; he's conjoined several people over the last few months I believe."

"Yes, maybe, but it will be frowned on by the Mars council who have, at my suggestion, formed a Moral Committee that scrutinises all such proposals. Also, my home church committee will wax righteous and—"

"What do you mean *maybe*? That's hardly the outburst of romantic enthusiasm I was looking for. Last night, you said—"

"OK, OK, sorry about that. I'm just taking time to adjust to all this and work out the implications."

They were interrupted by the arrival of Captain Reid for his morning coffee, a fortuitous intervention for Steve, and the topic of discussion was quickly changed to the current state of the flu virus and its effect on day to day operation on Mars. Not quite quickly enough perhaps because the captain did not seem overly sincere when he asked them whether he was interrupting anything.

27

Grave Problems

CAPTAIN REID HAD repeatedly asked folk to just call him Peter but the title had stuck although they did amend it to Captain Peter. This was probably due to genuine respect after landing the damaged Drove 5 so successfully and because he was a member of the Mars council. Indeed, he had become the AP's right-hand person on operational matters. Steve had had conversations with him before and probed a little on how the council perceived the way forward on Mars now that the possibility of living there had been demonstrated. There had been recent discussions on this but Steve was only invited to attend the council on occasions when his input was needed and had not been included when the sensitive issue of the future was discussed. The captain was reluctant to release this information but in view of the recent deaths, Steve was particularly keen to know whether the council's plans had changed as a result of the epidemic. He decided to have another try at probing Captain Peter for the council's view.

"As you noticed," said Steve, "Jo and I were in deep discussion. That's because we have to finalise the arrangements for the six recent flu victims and of course not forgetting poor Fred who's still in the deep freeze mortuary."

Captain Peter said, "Yes, that's right. What's happening about the disposal of the dead and how are you managing to placate their families on Earth?"

Steve looked him in the eye.

"I'm afraid that's confidential to the chaplain; on the other hand, I would not mind getting a view from a friend. Similarly, I need to know the council's plans for the future although they are kept under wraps because they could affect the committal arrangements at the funerals."

Captain Peter smiled to himself.

"I do believe our chaplain is offering to trade information."

Steve said nothing. After a moment though, he conceded: -

"You could say that would be exchanging grave secrets for live ones but if it helps the greater cause—"

Jo made a polite excuse at this point and left giving Steve a long look which he was not quite sure how to interpret.

Steve continued, "Where possible, the relatives on Earth have now been contacted and have accepted the proposal to build Marsoleums which is just as well as their construction is well underway. One British family wanted cremation and return of the ashes. Rather than give an outright *no*, we agreed on a temporary internment in a Marsoleum pending possible cremation at a later date. Another wanted their loved one launched into space but they were dissuaded by the cost of one million dollars plus VAT. (Don't ask, the authorities just add it for good measure where Mars is concerned)

"But what about the ceremonies, there's quite a buzz in the Village about that. I mean they are different races and cultures and it's a sensitive time and folk get quite precious about such things," said the captain.

Steve responded, "Well, if you really want to know the detail, it's a total minefield of different practices. After much deliberation involving all the people involved, I suggested it should be like a death at sea where the chaplain or captain of the vessel performs a simple international service using prescribed words. The old Anglican version though would have to be changed. The original is here on my iPad."

He read it out,

"Unto Almighty God, we commend the soul of our brother departed, and we commit his body to the deep; in sure and certain hope of the resurrection unto eternal life, through our Lord Jesus Christ; at whose coming in glorious majesty to judge the world, the sea shall give up her dead; and the corruptible bodies of those who sleep in him shall be changed, and made like unto his glorious body.'

"We've been working on this in the context of Mars or for that matter in any modern perspective. Working from the end back, even many evangelical Christians would baulk at the sea giving up its dead so that would have to go and then the second coming is always contentious and of course, the Muslims deem Christ a Prophet but not the Lord. Many religions don't really do resurrection and then there's brother although presumably sister is deemed acceptable too and finally there's Almighty God which atheists and humanists deny (while in many cases, worshipping Mother Earth). Jo and I worked out a different form of words as a compromise but like all *multi-faith and none at all* compromises it came out very wishy-washy and practically meaningless. So, we finally took the bull by the horns and drafted the following."

Steve hunted through his electronic files and handed his iPad to the captain. It read:

We are today gathered to commit the bodies of (names) to burial here on Mars, a distant planet from the Earth on which they were born. They come from different cultures and different religions each with their own rites and practices which normally would be conducted in the homely presence of their families and friends on Earth but here in this distant place, they are together as fellow travellers.

I, as your chaplain, have been authorised to conduct this committal and can only do so in the way I have been ordained by my home Christian Church while fully accepting that other faiths have different beliefs and would do things equally sincerely with other words. In this, I seek your accedence.

As Christians, we commit the body to death but the soul to everlasting life through Jesus Christ who showed through His teachings the Way to God, the mind of the universe. This regolith, that we now scatter on the remains of the departed, signals the end of the body and the release of the soul which exists forever.

The captain said, "I can't imagine anybody will object to that. It's pretty honest and straightforward and, don't take this wrongly, nobody will know what's going on and what to do in any case. No doubt, some liturgical committee will dissect it at some future date and argue about the *mind of the universe* for example but for now, it's fine. I would advise you to go with it and if they criticise, say you sought the advice of a council member—which you have of course!" he added,

"Thanks for that. Now it's your turn; so what are

the Mars plans for the future?" said Steve, in keen anticipation.

"I have to go soon as I'm on a field trip outside today so I'll give you a brief summary of the current thinking; I would prefer you to keep it strictly confidential for now though."

This, Steve agreed to do and the captain continued,

"The International Mars Committee, that's the UN one, met last week as it happens. The main topic was terraforming Mars so that within a time period of about 85 years its atmosphere and conditions become more friendly. As you know, the idea is effectively a controlled global warming of Mars to make it more habitable because by then, the Earth population would be about 11 billion and the Earth will be ravaged by violent climate changes. However, after many presentations by experts and much deliberation, it was decided by a sizeable major-ity to abandon terraforming largely owing to the sand-storms and resulting dust levels on Mars. They decided to concentrate on enormous man-made Bio-Domes rather like ours but several times larger. These would be partly underground and partly above for two reasons. Firstly, it overcomes the dust issue as residents remain inside for most of the time. This is now already the case in many Middle Eastern cities owing to the rising global tempera-tures and is therefore established technology. Secondly, it allows the possibility of an incremental development, that is to say, adding domes as needed rather than commit-ment to a grand scheme that might not be successful.'

"Sounds like more of the same then," said Steve.

"Yes, that's the gist of it but remember, there's a host of technical and social issues to be addressed. How big can the domes be? Will they withstand large meteorites? What are the long term effects of non-exposure to the sun on humans etc? And on the social side, how will the village or perhaps by then, small towns formed of many interlinked domes provide acceptable living environments? Should children be allowed rather than mandatory abortion as at present and will future Martian children be schooled on Mars or transported back to Earth? As time moves on, will these native Martians become different to us Earthlings with their own distinctive Martian identity? You can see how it becomes other-worldly quite early on in the development; the sociologists, philosophers and not least religious folk like yourself will have a field day!"

After a short pause, Steve observed, "Yes, it's complicated from a terrestrial perspective if you're trying to fit everything on Mars into earthly thinking but actually, on Mars, it could be quite straightforward. When the first colonies developed, their social structures on the East Coast of America, I don't think they worried too much about their home nations, they just lived as a community, dealt with deaths and births as they came along and carried on. History has shown that humans are very adaptable and very good at survival under new conditions."

"You have to go, I know, but you said I should keep this to myself and I'm wondering why; much of this is already well appreciated by folk here."

Captain Peter was rising to leave.

"Yes, the continued development of further and larger domes over the next 20 years is expected to be confirmed shortly. It's the birth and death issues that are sensitive. Once you remove the current abortion restriction, for example, you have to return babies to Earth and that is problematic and expensive. And once you restrict the current euthanasia rights of rich earthlings and advertise *Mars to stay* missions as advocated long ago by astronaut

Buzz Aldrin, then you're in difficult territory. The Mars council is concerned about all this as it will be upon us pretty soon and they want to be one step ahead. It's one for you as first chaplain here on Mars to consider too."

"Thanks," said Steve, "now enjoy your field trip and don't get lost out there."

As he left, Captain Peter made a mental note to ask the Council to consider including Steve in their discussions. Steve, however, had aspects of his own future on his mind before he could concentrate on the future of Mars.

28

A Day Out

FOLLOWING HIS DISCUSSION with Steve, Captain Peter Reid arrived slightly late at the exit door of the Central Dome. One of his current responsibilities as a senior engineer was overseeing the structural integrity of the domes. They were made of interlinking bricks of cement made from the Mars regolith and while the rock dust which covered so much of Mars was ideal for cement, the bricks had to be made with the minimum amount water to conserve stocks and this could leave them less consolidated than necessary. The compressive stress on the bricks was high and widespread crumbling due to say long term solar exposure could be catastrophic. Today, the captain, with another engineer, was due to examine the outside of the domes by climbing the aluminium and wire steps up to the top of each dome. Small transducers were to be fitted at selected points so that any surface movement, possibly caused by this deterioration, could be monitored. This was laborious rather than dangerous and when on top there was the reward of glorious views over the rocky Mars landscape.

He and his assistant for the day, Chen, a young Chinese project engineer, donned their spacesuits and left the safety of the Dome to commenced their climb. They were each tied by safety line to the steps and they could communicate as needed by radio linkage. The lack of much atmosphere and hence, no sound transfer meant they climbed in eery silence. Halfway up they drilled a small hole for the first radio transmitting transducer and rested for a moment. While the lower gravity meant the climbing was theoretically easier than on Earth, the spacesuits, although more flexible than earlier ones, were still somewhat cumbersome and confining. After 20 minutes, they moved on to the top where no less than six instruments were to be fitted. This, they did efficiently, then peered at each other through their heavy plastic visors and clasped hands as it was a job well done. They sat down right on the top in the glorious sunshine observing the view over the rocky terrain stretching into the distance, feeling on top of the world, or at least Mars.

After a few minutes' silence, the Captain, whose mind was still preoccupied with aspects of his earlier conversation with Steve, said to Chen, "You know, it's possible that with the increasing number of terminauts coming out to Mars, we will be looking out over a graveyard of earthlings in years to come. I heard that one American space company is thinking in terms of thousands coming out, each paying over two million dollars per head to spend their last days here and be buried in the regolith. It will become a final pilgrimage to the promised land, the trail of Pandava, an interplanetary Hajj for those who can afford it. And it could really take off, particularly if the religions of the Book, the Christians, Muslims and Jews each trawl through the Bible, the Koran or the Tanakh for texts that allude to heavens beyond the Earth. It will be a catastrophe for colonisation of Mars though because it will be largely peopled by old folk. It won't so much be a matter life on Mars but rather death on Mars."

Chen made no immediate response but just sat there. Maybe he would have commented given time, but at that moment there was a Mars-shattering vibration from somewhere down there below them in the Dome. Not that they heard much in their ears through the atmosphere as you cannot hear in the open on Mars, but they felt the shock wave in the vibration of the Dome itself and looked at one another in disbelief. They immediately started scrambling down the ladder as fast as the spacesuits would allow not knowing what to expect. They hurried to the air-lock door to swing it open but found it firmly closed. They peered through the round observation window in the door but the inside seemed to be uncannily dark. Then they really started to worry. Obviously, something serious had happened and they only had one and a half hours before their spacesuit packs would start to deliver reduced levels of oxygen. Theorising about the promised land was one thing, arriving early was another.

They were a little out of breath and sat down on a ledge around the base of the Dome to assimilate their predicament. Fortunately, their own microphones were working and they could communicate with each other but could not raise a response from anybody in the Dome. After a while, Chen ventured a possible explanation.

"The vibration felt like one I experienced when working on a power substation some time ago; like a fuse blowing in a fuse box but more substantial. That would account for the darkness in there and the lack of communication."

The captain responded, "But surely there's a back-up at least for the electronic side and the shock was much too much to be a circuit breaker?"

"Well, I'm not fully aware of all the systems as I'm the new boy among the project engineers but I understand that while there are lots of small circuit breakers, there is one over-riding all the others which cuts everything off in event of a heavy voltage surge. This is to protect all the delicate systems in the village against a large solar flare which can be a real danger because virtually all the energy comes from solar generators. On earth, the atmosphere protects against this but on Mars, with its much-reduced atmosphere, there is no such buffer."

The captain interrupted, "While we were sitting on the Dome, it was pleasantly warm, in fact, as warm as I've known it, but there was no obvious sun surge."

"That may be so, however, you would not notice a few percent increase and that is all it would take to cause a cut-out. It's just like your 240-volt supply in your home on Earth; just a 10% increase or 24 volts, may bust your TV and computer unless they are voltage protected. Having said that, I understand the main breaker has only blown once, that was soon after its installation and it took hours to get it all going again."

The captain exclaimed, "That's terrible because we can only last another hour or so, we must find a way in. I can't believe the door locks from the inside and can only be opened when power is available. They must have made a fail-safe system with this in mind."

He got up and went over to the door to examine it more closely. Chen, however, sat thinking for a few minutes before he joined the captain who was by now rattling and pulling the handle and looking around for any hidden catches or bolts that could be operated in such an emergency. Chen had had a horrible thought. He remembered there was a fail-safe device for manual operation in the event of a power collapse but it was on the inside on the assumption that in the event of a fire, it would allow folk to escape. Needing to get in was an emergency that may not have been considered. Or, worse still, it may have been thought of and even built into the design so that the village could be closed to intruders. Humans had a psychological need to close the drawbridge at night which persisted through the ages and, it seemed, even to another planet where there were no others. They were therefore totally at the mercy of those inside and would have to hope somebody remembered them and realised they could not get in unaided. He explained to the captain that they would have to wait patiently until somebody opened the door from the inside and that they would use less oxygen by sitting down quietly.

The captain accepted this point and began to view Chen, who had seemed so inexperienced, with more interest. They sat down on the edge of a deep gulley near the base of the Dome to await developments but not without some apprehension. To create some temporary diversion, he continued his earlier conversation and outlined how the commercial viability of the Mars colony would in the future depend on both the migration of terminauts from Earth and exporting the rare heavy elements on Mars back to Earth. Chen picked up on the thought of swathes of old folk dying on Mars and gave less than a serious description of the domes being surrounded by graves like some weathered stone church in a graveyard. They even discussed in passing whether one reason why folk years ago deserted churches and mosques in the countryside was the need to wend their way through stone reminders of former members. He could not imagine a successful company on Earth that buried all their dead directors around the factory ever being successful. He had a nightmare vision of old folk coming out in their droves, literally, until there were Marsoleums as far as the eye could see.

He was just beginning to feel uncomfortable about

discussing dead folk around the Dome while his oxygen level was draining away when he noticed a small movement of the regolith in the bottom of the gulley. For a moment, he thought he must be seeing things owing to the depleting oxygen but then it moved again so he drew it to Chen's attention. They walked down into the gulley which had probably been formed during the construction of the Dome and poked around at the base. The regolith was damp and as they scooped out a hole with their gloved hands, some water formed in the bottom like wet sand near the sea. They looked at one another in surprise and chatted about it excitedly through their spacesuit intercoms. It was, of course, to be expected, after all, the midday temperature was about 20 degrees and it was bound to melt the residual water for a period on occasions. They knew about the water streaks that had been spotted elsewhere on Mars but they had never actually seen water, or more accurately brine on the surface. For a moment, it made the surroundings seem less cold and foreboding.

As time wore on, though, the sun dropped below the horizon and they began to get cold. While the temperature can be pleasant for a period, it soon plummets to negative values. While their spacesuits offered some protection, they would not protect them through the night time temperature of below -100 degrees even if the oxygen held out. They also began to feel lonely and deserted as they sat looking out on the bleak environment of this gradually darkening planet. Chen had not spoken for a quarter of an hour and the captain wondered if he was okay; was his oxygen leaking a little or was he becoming depressed? He remembered Fred and how he had become demented relatively quickly only a few months before. The captain decided to stretch his legs and move around even if it used more oxygen. He also needed a pee but had so far resisted using the spacesuit diaper which was decidedly uncomfortable after use. He went across to Chen and in an attempt to lighten the mood suggested they should knock on the door. He then did exactly that, tapping on the metal with a piece of rock which was lying nearby. Being on the outside with no air, they, of course, heard no sound but on the inside, the sound would carry because there was an atmosphere, at least there was if the far door of the airlock was open. There was, however, no response which meant there was nobody near the door to hear them; hardly surprising because it was unlikely that anybody would be in the air trap.

Seeing the captain tap on the door triggered a thought with Chen who was attempting to put himself into a vegetative state by dozing off to conserve his limited oxygen. The cracking sound of the main circuit breaker would have been loud but not at an ear-splitting level and yet he had felt it through his body while perched on the Dome. He remembered the noises that Steve and Ken had noticed in the spacecraft on the way over. That was due to a tapping on the outside of the craft. He put all this together and mulled over it for a minute and came to a decision. He explained to the captain that they had to attract the attention of somebody inside or it would be too late. It could be done visually but there were only a few windows (Glass portholes had to be brought from Earth so they were very expensive). Furthermore, they were placed high up in each dome and the chance of reaching them and attracting attention was low. The only other way was by sound, they had to make a noise that would be heard inside. This could be done by climbing the steps again and hammering the outside of the Dome with the rocks that lay around. Captain Peter reckoned the climb would use too much energy and they should just try the lower levels.

It was thus, after about 90 minutes in the harsh environment with the temperature dropping and dusk falling that two intrepid humans from Earth were to be seen hurling sizeable rocks onto a concrete dome. It was a desperate attempt born out of sheer frustration at being left outside and seemingly forgotten owing to the preoccupation of their colleagues with their own problems inside. Furthermore, they were beginning to suffer from breathing difficulties and took it in turns to lob the rocks as best they could and as high up the Dome as possible. After about 5 minutes, a flickering light appeared at the small window in the door and they moved towards it eagerly. It took another minute for the airlock to be depressurised and the door to be opened manually but that did not matter as they were over-joyed with relief. They edged in as the door could only be held ajar manually and were met by two operatives with LED torches who helped them through the airlock and eventually out of their spacesuits. Very few lights were working and they were helped through to beds in the medical area nearby where they were given oxygen masks and some injections. There seemed to be chaos everywhere but they were both becoming drowsy and soon lost interest as the injections kicked in.

It was two weeks later that Chen and the captain were attending the first of several investigations on the great voltage surge as it was called. Things were more or less back to normal except that the whole community had become more cautious and there was an air of foreboding about the future that had not been evident before. Yes, it was caused by a minor solar flare as Chen had suggested but the safety systems were all having to be reassessed.

The whole village had been brought to a halt and hundreds of software and hardware issues were having to be addressed involving about half the workforce. Nobody had admitted that the safety of the two people stuck outside had simply fallen between gaps in the responsibility remits of the staff. The captain and Chen felt a trifle forlorn that their ordeal was hardly recognised. Fortunately, there were no fatalities directly attributable to the voltage surge although one of the patients who was still weak following the flu epidemic had died during the chaos as medical staff adjusted dialysis and other machines following the switch to temporary generators.

The incident did, however, lead to a rethink about interlocks and the logic of some safety procedures. The safe operation on Earth of transport and other systems has developed over hundreds of years but on Mars it was new. Even on Earth, flaws can occur owing to some unforeseen event. A classic case was back in 2015 when a mentally unstable pilot of a German-operated airbus aircraft locked himself in the cockpit while the first pilot left to go to the toilet. The door could not be opened from the cabin side because the perceived threat was from terrorists on the outside. Frantic efforts to get into the cockpit were to no avail and the plane was steered into the Alps killing all on board. Back in the village, the external doors were quickly modified and if one day some passing alien decided to break into the village, then so be it.

29

Steve's Revelation

BOTH STEVE AND Jo had discussed their newfound attachment several times over the last few weeks. Neither had been able to give the day to day matters their full attention owing to an undercurrent of pre-occupation with the unfolding of events between them. Steve finally decided to take the bull by the horns in the traditional way and to propose that they form a conjoined *couple* as defined by the council. It, therefore, came to be that one evening, back in the Chaplaincy Centre after a meal at the Mars Bar restaurant, that Steve said, "Jo, I do have something to ask you having now thought things through. As you know I do love you and in fact, I would like to ask you formally if you would be prepared to marry me and form a couple in accordance with the Mars Cohabitation Act."

Jo smiled at his attempt to surround the question with some gravitas and replied,

"Yes, I am happy, very happy to accept your proposal," and kissed him warmly. She asked.

"Does that mean we can now go and see the president, I mean the AP, tomorrow and sort out the formalities?"

"Wow, hold on. It takes time to process the forms and get them accepted by the council committee and then there's my home Church and all that."

"Well, yes, but you're the chaplain so you can hardly

live in sin for too long," she taunted, "so you had better get going with the forms and things."

And this, he did.

Nobody seemed particularly surprised when the news leaked out a few days later in spite of the forms not being processed. The more observant villagers must have noticed already from the way they worked together and the president, who could be quite prudish as we saw, put no obstacles in their way. There was a slight complication owing to the international aspects but that was smoothed over eventually. The betrothal could not be formally announced owing to delays in sanction by Steve's home church, the good old Church of Scotland who decided it was a matter for the Presbytery of Edinburgh, that being the particular Presbytery allocated to cover the Mars community. They only met every two months and the Presbytery Clerk, being very proper, simply placed it on the normal business agenda. When the full Presbytery met, this item which was by far the most interesting on the Agenda, occupied most of the meeting. The Presbytery minutes subsequently recorded that, at the appointed sederunt, there was, inter alia, a deliverance regarding the betrothal, in post, of the Presbytery Regent for Mars, the Rev. Steve McKay, chaplain of the Mars village, requesting herewith accedence to his conjoining with a Dr Jo Thanawala, female, of Dharamshala, India. In accordance with Act MCIXVIII Anent IV, the aforesaid betrothal was sanctioned pro tem subject to a full report in due course to the General Assembly as it set a precedent. Although well-meaning, the Presbytery saw complete compliance with their ancient procedures as imperative. Once achieved it was passed with no further provisos except the report, the closest the Presbytery was going to get to awarding the betrothal their blessing.

Accordingly, the president, late one afternoon a few days after the church had intimated its acceptance, performed the so-called coupling ceremony in the presence of Captain Peter Reid and another member of the council, two being required to be present, together with a few friends of Jo and Steve. They met afterwards in the Mars Bar and various folk made supportive speeches including the president who after congratulating them, waxed eloquent on the advantageous effects of conjoining on room allocations within the domes. (Accommodation was still tight as some people were requiring isolation and continuing medical attention following the flu epidemic. In addition, the arrival of Drone 6 was due shortly and progress on the new Dome had been delayed owing to experimentation with new cement for the building blocks.) Steve and Jo then settled down to their combined role of running the chaplaincy and dealing with the never-ending flow of people with issues ranging from the effects of CD to family matters back on Earth.

It was one evening when they were chatting about their own families and in particular, Steve's parents that Jo asked him why he had become involved in the church in the first place; it must have been more than his association with his earlier church-going partner Mandy, she reasoned. Apart from all the things they had discussed before, there must have been something which sparked an awareness of an influence out there beyond the normal, otherwise, he would not have had the drive to come to Mars in the first place. Steve then recounted to her his experience of a few years before which had led to his own conviction on this matter.

"It was after a busy day when I was working at the rail office in Edinburgh. I was waiting on Waverley railway station for Mandy to return on the train from London where she had gone to visit a very ill aunt, her mum's sister. The plan was that we met at the station and caught the train on the branch to North Berwick together to pick up 5-year-old Bobby who was at a friend's house after a day at school. The London train was due to arrive a quarter of an hour before the North Berwick one was due to leave giving plenty of time for the transfer. However, the London train was late so the connection was going to be critical and I was becoming anxious. If the connection was not made, then Bobby could not be collected and Mandy, who was tired after a fraught day in London with her aunt would be upset. After the quarter of an hour was up, the North Berwick train was about to leave with no sight of the London train coming in although it was by now well overdue. I earnestly sent up a silent prayer: *Please God let the connection happen.* Then I had this strange peaceful assurance that my request had been heard. I knew, I just knew that my momentary prayer had been granted. I knew Mandy would catch that North Berwick train, I absolutely knew, quite how I don't know, but I was 100% sure.

"The station porter standing near me, to whom I had related the importance of the connection, eventually had to signal the North Berwick train off and it pulled out of Waverley station while I stood there but I still knew even as I watched it disappear into the tunnel at the end of the station. I stood there, transfixed and then, believe it or not, it came trundling back, back into the same platform and squeaked to a halt. I felt the power and knew that there is on occasion a real power in prayer. The station porter standing near me watching the train return said out of the blue:"I've never known that before, it must have been meant to be.' I was stunned. I felt I had experienced something beyond my understanding, I was somehow a bystander on a great stage of things happening that I could not control, far less comprehend, but knew the power was there, it was so real. Mandy arrived shortly after and we boarded the train and continued on our way. It took me about three days to lose the awareness that I had been privileged to peep into something beyond me and get back to normal life or at least as normal as it could be having had such an experience. I know others must have had similar experiences but this one was special for me, a scientist who had doubted many of the happenings in Palestine over 2000 years ago but had seen a 100-ton train reverse in its tracks and come back. I had felt the power of some mind out there way beyond our minds, some *mind of the universe*."

After a pause, he added, "That is why I know I'm at least not entirely wrong in pursuing the role I have on Mars but I cannot use this and other personal experiences of mine alone to convince others because I've no direct incontrovertible evidence for them. But I can assure those folk who say we are only the product of chemical inter-action and natural selection, that there is a reasonable doubt. The presence of a mind out there, that is a God, has to be shown to be equal to or more plausible than other possibilities to convince the modern human mind. That is why it is incumbent on us not just to simply say 'you must believe this because I do', but to show that it is the only explanation of the observations and facts before us."

Steve noticed Jo, while interested, was looking tired and said, "I've gone on too long, but you did ask."

"Not at all. You've provided me with another piece of the jigsaw in trying to work out what drives you to do this necessary but strange work in such a remote place. But there is still one piece missing. You've still got to

225

have a rationale for your 100-ton train reversing because we are surrounded by scientists and engineers here and that's the bit they'll stumble on, that's the very crux of the matter where they are concerned. How did your God stop the train?"

Steve suggested they continued later but she insisted he answered her now or the moment would be forever lost. So he carried on.

"Yes, I pondered that for some years until I stumbled upon the answer. You're correct, the train is composed of an infinitely great array of particles all obeying the rules of the universe so beautifully presented by Newton, Einstein, Hawking and all the other great scientists. God does not change these rules or make exceptions in the physical universe, it would be like him making one plus two equal four and, as we discussed before, that would be nonsensical. He works through the mind because He is the mind of the universe. This mind works through *our minds* because we are part of it, part of the same consciousness. In the case of the train, I believe it reversed in the tunnel because some train controller sitting at the station control panel realised that it would miss the passengers alighting from the late London train, set the signal to red and sent the message to go back into the station. It was an act of unrequited kindness and understanding by the controller. Kindness does not come from natural selection; it comes from elsewhere. It can reverse 100-ton trains and maybe it can move mountains it is so powerful. I could have called it love but that's become tainted with overuse in our language so I'll stick with kindness. God the mind of the universe operates through kindness. It was also an act of mild disobedience where the railway rules were concerned but that's one for later."

Jo understood but then asked about another aspect

which had occupied her thoughts. It was late but she wanted to clear these things in her mind once and for all before she retired to bed. Whether she entirely agreed with Steve or not, she needed to know the truth as he saw it, *this time not at a slant* but upfront.

"But tell me, how does the Christian part tie in with what you've told me; after all, the experience you had could have occurred if you were of any religion that believes there is a God or, what did you call it, a universal mind?'

Steve considered for a moment.

"That's true and had I been brought up elsewhere within another culture, I could have had the same revelation. I was schooled in the Christian culture and Jesus Christ, the basis of this Christian view, although He lived over 20 centuries ago, was the harbinger of a true understanding of God and thus a manifestation of God Himself. Jesus did not claim to be God but rather to point the way to God, but in doing so, Christians believe He became almost as one with God. (Almost, because He was also partly human.) They believe we are formed in the image of God. Most thinking Christians today realise this means our *minds* are in the image of God's mind, that is the mind of the universe we spoke about. (A few still say it applies to our bodies without considering at what bodily age or the fact there's no God with arms and legs out there in space, which is irresponsible of them because it spoils it for the rest of us.) It is our minds which are formed like the mind of God, a spiritual breath throughout the universe. That's why, through some mechanism we know not, we can tune in and communicate. Like our iPads can tune into the internet, our minds or souls can tune into the mind that permeates the universe, we can sometimes feel the breath and know it's there. Finally, when we dispense with the part of us which is mass, the molecules of our bodies, we are left with our minds alone, our thoughts past, present and future which become part of the great mind of the universe."

Steve paused so Jo came in with,

"But how does this correlate with the traditional Christian beliefs of the immaculate conception and the resurrection?"

"It doesn't correlate with it so much as encompass it. Christ is the greatest embodiment of God on Earth and throughout His teaching he emphasised that it is our minds and spirits that are part of the Spirit of God. This was beyond the comprehension of folk 2000 years ago so the message was embodied, literally, by the disciples and early church to include the immaculate *physical* conception and *physical* resurrection, that is they thought it meant the re-assembly of the molecules of His body after His death. The invitation to Timothy to feel the imprint of the nails in Jesus' hands was surely, even for them, figurative. It is not science and was never meant to be; it is a way of explaining the spiritual nature of the truth. As Emily Dickinson says;

'As lightning to the children eased
With explanation kind,
The truth must dazzle gradually
Or every man be blind.'"

"You know, during the Coronavirus pandemic of the early 20's most religious denominations avidly embraced electronics with public prayers and sermons on Zoom and the electronic cloud on which we all rely became saturated with it all. Yet many of them denied their God the same privilege, insisting that He still operated in an ancient physical world. The spatiality of God is not new, it's always been there and unchanged; it just seems to have been lost among all the pseudo-religious stuff floating around these days in current ideas, social media and not least in many churches. Some deep thinkers of old said this long ago before the science was better understood. Take, for example, Edwin Hatch, a deep-thinking, nineteenth-century Oxford academic who penned his deepest thoughts as hymns, as was the wont among theologians in Victorian days."

Steve flicked through his stack of hymns on his iPad, found it and read out three verses.

> *Breathe on me, breath of God,*
> *Fill me with life anew,*
> *That I may love what Thou dost love,*
> *And do what Thou wouldst do.*
>
> *Breathe on me, breath of God,*
> *Blend all my soul with Thine,*
> *Until this earthly part of me*
> *Glows with Thy fire divine.*
>
> *Breathe on me, breath of God,*
> *So shall I never die,*
> *But live with Thee the perfect life*
> *Of Thine eternity.*

"So, Edwin got there too. But hey, Jo, it's late and we've got a busy day ahead."

"And we've had the last hymn so we can say Amen and go," she added.

He laughed, "Sure, and tomorrow is Festival Day and I must be fit for the six-a-side game or the Dome D football captain may drop me from their team. That would do the chaplain irreparable damage and nobody would ever listen to him again."

"Never mind, I'll listen to you," said Jo, "Even if half the time you're away in a world of your own, way beyond the realms of what many find acceptable."

"Is that a polite way of saying you don't quite agree with all this?" responded Steve, but she had wandered off.

.

30

Going it Alone

THE FESTIVAL DAY was the brainchild of the assistant president. He felt that, following the flu epidemic and the power outage, the community needed a boost to raise their spirits. The plan was that, following several indoor sports sessions ranging from football and badminton to darts and bowls, there would be a market in the central area during the afternoon culminating in a new-rock concert in the evening. There were limitations on the range of sports available in the village partly due to the lack of space and partly due to the reduced gravity. Six-a-side football had become popular and Steve had become a star player for the Thursday Night Games Club that played on the confined pitch area in the central dome. The domes' mixed-gender teams had played each other and Domes A and D were in the Festival-Day final. Dome D football captain was John Abraham. He took his sporting role very seriously, much more so than his team members who just wanted some relaxation and exercise. So, sharp at 7 pm, they were limbering up for their match against Dome A. The winning side anticipated being entertained by the defeated team to pints of Patrick's Guinness in the Mars Bar. Patrick himself was the one and only referee. (As a result, he claimed the presidency of the Mars Interplanetary Football Federation, MIFF, and charged any challenger with being miffed.) The game itself, watched by most of the village, allowed half an hour each way with a 10-minute argument break in the middle. During the first half, Dome A scored twice and Steve got a yellow card for grounding Ben while the ball was out of play. In the second half, Dome D managed to score 3 while A scored a further once. As a drawn match could not be countenanced (as somebody had to buy the pints), they continued. Eventuality, A won and this cost the D team no less than 13 pints for the players and the referee.

A repeat of this exercise for badminton (where the shuttlecocks, aided by the lower gravity but with the same air resistance in the Dome, constantly travelled out of bounds) led to further drinks all round. This and the general air of congeniality encouraged by the party atmosphere meant that by late afternoon, virtually everybody was very happy. The AP returned fleetingly to his office to check on key operational items and was surprised to see an urgent communication from Earth as signalled by a red flashing light, on his screen. The Earth's UN Mars Committee Council were in colonial mistrust mode and were hardly enthusiastic about the concept of a Festival Day when the president had first raised it and had only agreed to it going ahead under certain conditions. The conditions had been drafted by some secretariat and were long and detailed. Essentially, they allowed restricted attendance to no more than 50% of the village in case of an emergency, only the minimum alcohol allowance of one pint per day, no outdoor activity in case it wore out the spacesuits and everything back to normal by midnight. The AP could be quite strict himself as we saw earlier but he was indignant about their patronising attitude and chose to carry on regardless. The trouble was that Earth could monitor everything that went on like some big-brother so he guessed they would react by the end of the day but surely not at this stage. The message was just a warning that there must be no extra alcohol and no extra village activity meaning no one going outside the domes. As it had only just arrived he decided not to acknowledge receipt of it so they would not know if he had seen it and to proceed with the late afternoon new-rock concert as planned. That action he knew was turning a blind eye and he had always been loyal before but he felt that lifting the spirits of his hard-working and loyal colleagues was more important than pandering to some self-important terrestrial committee which was, in any case, some 240 million miles away. He figured that sometimes kindness was more important than honesty at the end of the day.

The inclusion of a new rock concert at the end of the Festival had been conceived late one evening in the Mars Bar by a group of the younger engineers and scientists who felt they were losing out on the fun to be had by their terrestrial colleagues. The band music was called *new* rock because the music would have little resemblance to the rock music of the last century and strains of Bill Haley would not be heard, indeed it was largely folk songs and some traditional jazz emanating from the only three instruments that had found their way to Mars. These were one violin, one guitar and a flute that had been brought out by a resourceful scientist on the basis that he was studying musical sound propagation in the reduced atmosphere. There were also two home-made drums fashioned from redundant bits and pieces among the scientific equipment. The *rock* connection was merely the fact that. over a period, rocks large enough to sit on had been man-handled into the central Dome from outside and positioned around the edge of the open area as a decorative reminder of where they were. Being rather few windows and those only high in the Dome meant that once inside you could be anywhere on Earth let alone Mars. There was even a suggestion that the concert could be staged outside with folk in spacesuits before they remembered that sound does not travel in the almost non-existent Mars atmosphere.

The new rock concert was popular and almost everybody turned up. The first songs had been well-rehearsed and folk abandoned their inhibitions and joined in the somewhat mournful ballads about earthlings who had set off in spacecraft which became lost in space. The songs constituted the dying words of their occupants as they drifted off into infinite space. Steve thought these were reminiscent of the Portuguese Fados about sailors going off across the Atlantic never to return. As time wore on, the songs were less well-crafted but few noticed because the influence of Patrick's Guinness on generally abstemious folk was blurring their assessment. It was at this point that the band gave their rendering which became popular on Mars, of BYPO (Boring Your Pants Off). Some younger scientists took the message more literally than intended and started flinging garments at the band. The words referred unfavourably to the attempt of Earthlings to micro-control the new Martians as if they were puppets on strings rather than real entities occupying a new planet. One chorus went:

> Earth says we run and we run
> Earth says we're not here for fun
> They mucked up their planet
> In the way that they ran it
> Now they're mucking up this one.

Steve was beginning to feel uncomfortable, especially

when they assertively mispronounce *mucked* and *mucking* to express a much stronger feeling. He had joined in the festival fun as a sociable chaplain should, but it was when he joined the chorus that he started to worry about the whiff of anti-terrestrial sentiment pervading the merriment. Jo was enjoying herself which delighted him but he was tired and needed some space so he worked his way to the periphery away from the dancing couples and seated himself on one of the rocks. There was a large TV screen set up high in the Dome showing various live views of the festival revellers and he proceeded to watch this with a mild interest while wondering about the implications of the frustration with Earth or more precisely the controllers of the Mars venture based on Earth. Maybe it was inevitable; he remembered reading long ago about the same tendency among the early colonists in America.

As he continued to watch the screen in an absent-minded way, he realised, to his horror, that the view had switched to a camera outside the Dome and that he was seeing half a dozen people clad in their spacesuits dancing around in the open under a starlight Mars sky. Presumably, the AP had allowed this but surely there were restrictions; perhaps he had lifted these for a time. The outside revellers were dancing to music played by the band through their earphones but sure enough, they were doing so in the open on another planet under the infinite black space of the universe. What an experience, he was almost envious. After a while, they stopped and seemed to confer for a moment before building what looked like a stone man out of the rocks lying around on the regolith; a stone Earthling standing there in the remote rocky expanse of Mars. And then, they stood back, picked up small rocks and started stoning it again and again until the Earthling was no more than a pile of rocks with no form or likeness to any human being. He shuddered in horror and grief at the significance of this and shuddered again and again until he realised that Jo was shaking him.

"Steve, you're dozing off and the AP is looking for you."

Steve blinked and came to in an unbelieving way and was so relieved he gave Jo a kiss even although this was not allowed in public.

"Tell me, did any people go outside?"

"Yes, just for twenty minutes or so but the AP insisted they return, which they did."

"And did the overhead camera switch to them?"

"No, I don't think so but why do you ask?"

"Oh, I don't know, I had this odd dream but no matter, what does the AP want me for?"

She said, with a touch of pride, "He wants you to lead them all in a rendering of *Auld Lang Syne* to round things off but most people don't know the words other than the chorus."

Steve strode to the centre of the rock area, waited for them to gather round, scratched his beard for a moment and sung in a rich baritone voice the full rendering of Auld Lang Syne as they clasped hands and endeavoured to accompany him. Many reckoned later that that moment marked the true beginning of human beings becoming Martians, although Steve reckoned it just reinforced the point that Scotsmen turn up everywhere. Perhaps humans could go it alone on Mars after all, although they were still essentially Earthlings, and this was about to be reinforced.

31

Family Matters

THE NEXT MORNING, things were a little muted in the village. This was partly the morning-after effect of the party with quite a lot of clearing up being undertaken by embarrassed folk who were trying to redeem their excesses of the night before. The Earth committees were very unhappy and it was made clear to the assistant president that any thought of restoring his position to president was withdrawn, not that he was too concerned, and that Earth expected a full report on the occasion. The AP duly added this to the list of full reports on things he was due to submit to Earth and the village folk noticed that Earth had once again been patronising to their esteemed leader. The new head of the United Nations sub-committee for Mars Health and Safety was particularly incandescent that his authority had been undermined by the Mars council and had furious discussions with them. Unfortunately, the speed of light restriction on communication with Earth mitigated the effect; it's quite difficult to remain incandescent when there's a 25-minute delay after every sentence!

Steve continued to worry about this growing tension between Mars and Earth. The similarity to moves for independence long ago in the American colonies was still in his thoughts, although there were some essential differences. In the extreme situation of the folk in New

Hampshire some 250 years ago, they could survive a life without supplies from Europe but the humans on Mars were as yet far from self-sufficient. They could continue with the life-supporting equipment they had for now and perhaps a year or two into the future but when things broke down either mechanically, electrically or electronically there was only a limited ability on Mars to repair or replace defective parts. Some believed that Mars could trade with the Earth for the necessary parts using rare heavy elements that lay in abundance on the surface from the asteroids that had landed there over the millennia. Currently, many of these elements were only available in a few places and China had most of the mining rights, even those outside China. However, China now fully realised their value and had priced them accordingly leading to further tension with the West. While under ideal conditions this trade with Earth could be the basis for a long term economy, Mars would forever be subject to ransom by Earth restricting the flow of essential goods. For this reason and his firm belief in the Christian maxim that peacemakers are blessed, Steve felt he was obliged to act as an intermediary in bridging this widening gap with Earth. To this effect, he had several meetings with the AP and the Mars council members and even sent missives to the Church of Scotland encouraging them to do their part as the home church of the only chaplain on Mars. Unfortunately, none of this was to great effect.

However, an odd opportunity arose to progress bonding with the Earth when the first funerals were conducted a few weeks later. These funerals were for all the folk who had died owing to the Mars flu pandemic including our grumpy Australian sheep farmer who had passed away in the assurance of a boundless peace stretching way beyond the outer reaches of his beloved outback.

As predicted, the agreed form of committal caused no issues and communications with the families of the deceased folk had led to peaceful and meaningful services for all concerned. These funerals were widely followed in the world media and went some way to persuading those on Earth that Mars was acting professionally and respectfully in spite of being a very new and inexperienced community. Steve was beginning to feel at home on Mars more than anywhere he had been before and at peace with himself in his difficult role. But it proved to be the calm before the storm.

It was on a Sunday a few weeks later, one he would never forget, at about 12 noon after the normal morning gathering in the Chaplaincy Centre. The gathering was pretty well attended and things had gone well so he was enjoying a coffee in the quiet time after the service that ministers are allowed in their emotionally stressful lives. Jo came to join him after chatting to the attendees from the various cultures and creeds at the so-called multi-faith service. She poured herself a coffee too and sat down next to him and put her arm around his shoulder, there being nobody else present by then.

"There's something I should have told you a week or two ago," she said. "I joked about it long ago when you first interviewed me but this time it's for real."

Steve looked at her wondering what she was talking about.

"I'm pregnant," she announced matter of factly.

Steve looked at her wide-eyed and burst out,

"You can't be; why didn't you tell me? You know the rules here about abortion, we won't be allowed to have it, you know that—"

"Whow, Whow, let's hold on for a moment. Firstly, you should be pleased."

"OK, normally, had we been on Earth I would have been, of course, but here, it's just not allowed."

"And who says so?"

"The Mars council; they do have the ultimate say up here you know."

"Then we'll not tell them," she said, "because I've decided to have this baby and that's a decision."

Steve was beginning to get cross.

"There's no way you can have a baby on Mars. There may be health issues that we don't know about because nobody's done the research. What the hell are you thinking of; there's no midwives or medical equipment for babies, no baby milk or bloody cots or all the other things you need."

With rising panic, he added, "There are not even any fucking nappies here, it's just not possible."

Jo turned on him.

"Don't use that word," she said, "just remember, you're the chaplain and are meant to have standards. You should know better—the word is Diapers, not nappies, it's only in your stupid archaic Britain they call them that."

There was a lull and Jo started to cry.

Steve paused for a time but then put his arm around her, realising he had let himself down and not knowing what to say.

"I suppose crying is not allowed either but I'm doing that too," she said but then she composed herself a little and said, "And you might as well know that I'm also four months gone and there are only 6 weeks to go before the point where termination is forbidden according to the current regulations in most countries on Earth."

It was then that the fact dawned on Steve that Jo really meant it; she was going to go ahead come what may.

"You could have told me earlier," he muttered.

"Well, I wasn't sure myself what to do and you were stressed out with all the funerals here and I kept putting it off but now that I am more visibly pregnant, I realise the time has come to stop dithering."

Steve, recovering somewhat from his burst of temper, said, "You realise the council, on instruction from Earth, will try to persuade you that having a baby here is not possible. They may even insist that it is aborted using the UN legal mandate. That would be truly disastrous all round for relationships with Earth."

"That is why we are going to keep it to ourselves for the next six weeks."

Steve looked at her with a mixture of pride and foreboding. It was a brave decision on her part and of course, she correctly expected him to act jointly with her but he would, in doing that, be deceiving the authorities both on Mars and on Earth. It would truly pit them against the rest and would put his good colleagues and friends in an impossible position. There was no way out; she could not be shipped back to Earth unless there was a complete change to the spacecraft shuttle programme, an unlikely possibility. What had he done, how could he face his colleagues, how could he continue as chaplain? He sat and put his head in his hands in desperation.

Jo, on the other hand, was confident about the way forward and saw Steve's reluctance as a typical male posturing.

"Come on, Steve, it's not the end of the world, or even Mars, for that matter. OK, I'm having a baby, it's quite common you know, it's happened before, it'll be different here but we'll manage somehow and all these pig-headed authorities will just have to get used to it."

"But you're failing to appreciate the logistic and medical problems it creates let alone the effect on the space programme and all the plans made by the big committees. I tell you, it will start a war of attrition, they'll be on their moral high ground blaming one another. There may even be talk of infanticide among the extremists on the basis it can't be allowed to survive."

It was Jo's turn to be really cross; she wasn't very often but now she was and she blasted back.

"Now you're going too far, Steve. You're forgetting that you're the chaplain here, not some Buddhist Monk from my home town who's broken his chastity vows by screwing a local girl. You're losing your sense of proportion and your integrity because your own little plans have fallen apart. This is the universe, so get used to it."

Jo stormed off out of the chaplaincy to maximum effect except that the door would not slam because it was on one of those ridiculous buffer arms. She also realised belatedly she did not know where to go.

Patrick was just across from the chaplaincy tidying up in front of the Mars Bar. He had agreed not to open on Sunday mornings to avoid competing with the Chaplaincy Centre gathering.

"You look as if you've just seen the devil," he said cheerily and then from the look he got, realised he might have said the wrong thing so quickly added,

"So what about a quick half of Guinness on the house?"

"You're on, but make it one of your lime cocktails instead as I've decided to lay off alcohol for a few months— for, er, health reasons. In any case, you're not allowed to serve alcohol yet, it's too early."

"Sod the rules," he muttered as she followed him inside.

While preparing her lime cocktail, he sensed she was upset but not wanting to talk about it so, like any good bar attendant, he kept the conversation rolling along by a well-rehearsed monologue.

"You know, I hear rules have become an obsession on Earth. With the need to work for five days per week no longer the case and folk having more time for leisure pursuits, it's unfortunate that so many find enjoyment in telling others what they should do. Rules bestow power and control on those that devise them; it gives them a sense of importance and involvement. It also gives a structure and form to the lives of those who fall under their jurisdiction and provides the comfort of knowing that others have to be like them. So all in all, everybody wins by having rules."

Jo perked up a little and interjected.

"But I'm sure I heard you say, sod the rules," she responded.

"Yes, I did. While rules allow society to run smoothly and you sure need them, they also filter out all deeper thoughts and muffle the chance of any true understanding. Most of the religious folk who crowded into your chaplaincy this morning are just following rules laid down long ago by their parents and their religious orders—thou shalt do this or not do that. They are deemed to be good and loyal followers if they obey them. Yet, in the Christian case, for example, your leader broke the rules with alacrity and really upset the apple cart. Meanwhile, here's your lime cocktail—I trust you're going to save it until 2 pm, the official opening time today."

"Not if I have to hear any more of the publican's world view on rules,"

she said but gave him a smile as she needed the distraction.

She thought for a moment and said, "Actually, you're right about the obsession with largely unnecessary rules.

It started to become oppressive in the early 2020s following the Coronavirus pandemic when weak governments hid their ineffectiveness behind intolerably intrusive rules. Once they developed an appetite for this, they extended it to micromanaging the raising of children and inhibiting what we ate. Now, nearly twenty years later, we never have to think about anything as the rules cover every eventuality in life. Every aspect of everything we do seems to be proscribed in detail so we are losing the ability to think things through from basics. Indeed, it's become somewhat revolutionary to go back to first principles and anybody who does is pigeon-holed as a fundamentalist."

"That's so right," said Patrick, "unless you toe the line and unquestioningly obey, you are deemed a trouble-maker or even labelled a *denier*. I remember when at school we were all indoctrination into saving the planet by using wind power and anybody who questioned this was a climate denier. When the long still freeze of that winter in the early 2030s occurred and the wind stopped and the electricity stopped and some folk stopped living and froze to death, we were only saved because the nuclear power stations kept plodding along as they had for the previous 60 years. Now, of course, nuclear is considered a clean energy and gets its green badge of approval by all except the new deniers who conspire to question any type of energy. In many countries, if anybody questions things too publicly, they are accused of insubordination and end up with an incitement order placed on them which effectively prevents discussion of the big issues of the day."

"That's the Earth for you," he added, "not that it's much better here."

They were silent for a moment and then Jo said, "We do discuss these things and the big issues of life and death at our gatherings. I know you have reservations about the chaplaincy meetings, largely based on your childhood as we've discussed before, but that's all changed now so why don't you come join us sometime?"

"Maybe one day."

But then she thought; *you'll remember this conversation when you hear how I myself have broken these very rules big time.*

32

Thoughts among Foliage

STEVE WAS AWARE he had let himself down badly. While Jo and he had had many lively discussions on topics ranging from the universe to toothbrushes, Jo had never stomped off in a rage so it was a new experience for him. He decided that his allotment needed some attention and made his way through the far dome and the myriad of passages to a part of the thick polypropylene tunnel that was designated as his allotment. In a corner behind the foliage, he had installed a wee seat in his man cave and here he sat and thought for a while fuelled by the occasional chocolate lime. When the need arose, he had used this spot to think about things such as the green green grass of home on a planet far away and his parents, no longer young but kindly resigned to him being so distant. Fortunately, they were both well but what would happen if they became ill or worse. Oddly, although so far away he had felt integrally involved with them through their frequent communications, a sort of mind entanglement that overcame the distance (but more of that later).

Bobby was growing up and their correspondence was becoming less frequent as he became absorbed in things immediate to him. How would these and other folk feel about him becoming the father of the first human born on Mars? It would all depend on the stance taken by Earth folk on discovering that the rules had not been heeded, not even by the chaplain. He could not get his head around the implications of it all and, as sometimes the case when this happens, his mind slipped into protection mode and onto something more manageable. He found himself thinking about the humble plants around him in the horticultural tunnel; humble because they were not exotic but just ordinary plants that would attract no particular attention on Earth but were so special on Mars.

Steve had opted to oversee one of the vegetable patches, a mix of root crops and brassicas. He'd had first choice because after all, it was he who had first suggested to the AP the allocation of allotments to villagers and many of them had since discovered they had green fingers. Vegetables were the easiest and the most satisfying to grow. The wide range of healthy crops around him was amazing given the early disasters caused by the need to add vermiculite as well as fertilisers to the Martian regolith to prevent coagulation which had spoilt the first attempts at root vegetable growth. There had been much experimentation with the hydroponic growth of brassicas which would have obviated the need for any soil at all but it was found that growing plants in water solutions adversely affected the taste and was abandoned. The patch adjacent to Steve's contained barley and some hops and it was no surprise to discover that Patrick or Guinness man as some called him, was in charge of this area. He had discovered that it was possible to have two harvests over an Earth year (half a Mars year) which had surprised the analysts and delighted Patrick. It was against all odds that Guinness had become so popular as several large international drinks companies had undertaken research by sending seeds to the International Space Station and analysing their growth. The prestigious Scottish Whisky company of Ardbeg had even funded a small bottle going to the ISS in 2009 and later pronounced that the taste had deteriorated. He loosened the regolith around his plants with a hoe and planted some seedling lettuces as it was important that all the spare cultivated ground was used to good effect. After a little while, he sat down again feeling tired as in the horticultural areas the oxygen levels were set low and the carbon dioxide levels higher than usual on Earth to conserve the precious oxygen and assist plant growth.

The plants in the village were doing well and it had been one of the success stories of the colonisation. The previous time plants had been around on Mars was over 4 billion years ago if Fred's fossilised leaf structure was correctly dated. The bio-geologists on Earth had requested further forays into the Martian valleys where the early rocks were found in the hope of finding more plant life but the Mars council had insisted that this be undertaken as part of wider mapping activity owing to the considerable resources needed for these extra village activities. In any case, a considerable number of samples of fossilised organic microcells of various complexity had now been collected, analysed and accepted as evidence that organic life on Mars, like that on Earth, had been established within a short time after its formation.

That then begs the question, was life part of the Big Bang itself? They now knew microbiological life was there really early after cooling on at least two planets that were independent of one another.

One postulation, therefore, as we saw earlier is that the spark of life, that is the information, was there at the very start, at the time of the big bang inferno.

It's no less dramatic than postulating that this spark grew out of a primaeval sludge of chemicals washing around on the planets. The statistical chance of a life like ours developing from some mix of elements constituting a mere collection of photons and neutrons has been shown to be negligibly small both analytically and also experimentally. The statistical chance of the spark of life being somehow a consequence of the Big Bang may indeed be low but perhaps no lower that of it being a consequence of chemical interaction between the neutrons and photons on planets after the Big Bang.

Furthermore, if the very seed of life was there from the start, then why would it happen to be the Earth and Mars any more than other suitable planets out there encircling the stars? This then provides a case for life elsewhere in the universe. That is to say, if similar life evolves on other planets then it is most probably seeded by the same information source which was there from the beginning of time. That's quite a conclusion but it does follow from logical deduction. (At the risk of complicating things, if the seed of life or the information, was there at the beginning it is also here now as the Big Bang is continuing in our expanding universe. Time and the concepts of *before* and *after* are all man-made terms signifying a human concept of sequential progress which, as Stephen Hawkins explains so well, are physically meaningless in the great scheme of things.)

Steve being the chaplain and thus the religious leader on Mars, instinctively aligned his appreciation of these concepts with his deeply-held belief in a God or a mind within the universe. Some of the more thoughtful hymns condense the inner thoughts of those theologians who in times past considered these things in depth. In 1854, Father Frederick Faber penned *There's a Wideness in God's Mercy* with a verse in the middle that goes:

> *There is grace enough for thousands*
> *Of new worlds as great as this;*

There is room for fresh creations
In that upper home of bliss.

Bearing in mind the conservative nature of the times, it is astounding that he dares to contemplate thousands of new worlds like ours up there. Maybe those who never leave the green, green grass of home sometimes have an antenna for receiving the great truths that others labour so hard to attain. (Steve noted with disappointment that although his own Church of Scotland included this hymn in their hymnal they omitted this verse)

Steve's thoughts were drifting again but he had often found gardens, be they floral or edible, conducive to deeper clarification and he certainly needed some clarity now because he should be thinking about the fact that he had seeded more than the plants on his allotment. Steve and Jo avoided one another for the rest of the day after their morning's wee feud but finally met up in the chaplaincy mid-evening. While short-tempered annoyance had subsided, both were still wary and apprehensive about the way forward. Fortunately, Steve had spent much time thinking through the ramifications of their new situation. He was feeling embarrassed that he had even considered not welcoming the new infant into the world as any father should, (except that it wasn't the world of course) and he apologised to Jo for being less than immediately supportive. Jo said that she had had an interesting conversation on rules (without saying with whom) and that she appreciated why Steve, with his traditional western upbringing, would place so much emphasis on being correct and observing the rules, come what may.

They then had a long discussion about the practicalities of having a child on Mars at the colony's present state of development and how they would tell their colleagues.

They agreed to release the information after a few weeks when there could be no thought of termination. This would be difficult as Jo was already beginning to show a bulge so she volunteered to wear a particularly loose Gilet and to make a point of being seen eating fattening cakes on every possible occasion. As it happens, this was no hardship at all for Jo found that one of her prenatal food obsessions was doughnuts with jam centres which had been available from early on in the village owing to the American influence. It was more of a hardship for Steve who had to fund this expensive luxury on Mars from his chaplaincy salary. So they settled down to weathering the next six weeks but Steve felt very uncomfortable about hiding it from his colleagues and especially the AP whom he should really have told about it.

Fortunately, the arrival of the next spaceship, Drove 6, distracted the attention of the village over the next few weeks. It landed without incident on this occasion and the reception which had been much rehearsed went smoothly. Virtually, everybody was involved with welcoming and introducing the new villagers and ensuring they were installed in their new surroundings on Mars especially as their journey had been a particularly long one owing to the positions of Earth and Mars. Drove 6 was unusual in that it transported mainly freight, carrying large quantities of engineering equipment for manufacturing items on Mars so that the community could become more self-sustainable. It was also a REV (Return to Earth Vehicle) designed so that the return flight could cope with a reasonably large load of export items such as rare earth minerals. It crossed his mind that perhaps Jo could return to Earth when it left but he discarded any thought of this when he heard that, owing to the distance of Earth being near its maximum over the return time, she would have to be in weightless space for over a year. Solving body fluid issues for adults during space flights had been bad enough and he winced when he thought of dealing with baby poo and nappies, sorry diapers, in a weightless environment.

In the end the number of passengers on Drove 6 was reduced to 23 people, these being 7 crew, 8 new engineers, a medical doctor and 8 terminauts, more or less replacing those who had died. As before the 7 crew members had been selected with their ongoing employment as engineers in mind, so effectively there were 15 engineers. Some were construction experts employed to continue the building programme, some were space horticulture experts to further develop the food growing facilities and there was also a metallurgist to investigate metal extraction from the ore. The doctor was a specialist in gastro-enterology and added at a late stage owing to the growing concern about the many stomach complaints reported in the village. These new people were duly introduced to the chaplaincy and Steve and Jo spent much time dealing with the inevitable problems they had in acclimatising to their new environment.

The chaplaincy, following the pattern of the churches, mosques, temples and synagogues on the Earth over the last twenty years, had increasingly been accepted as a social and well-being hub. Indeed, on Earth, the local and central governments had moved towards relinquishing some of their responsibilities in this area in return for financial support of such institutions. It had developed this way following Coronavirus and the natural disasters in the late 2020s brought about by severe storms and tsunamis. Folk had flocked to such centres for community grieving and assistance and they became an acceptable place for the community to meet. One consequence of this for Steve was that the Sunday gatherings instigated by him when he arrived became acceptable to folk of all persuasions. It was at the end of one of these gatherings in the chaplaincy that Steve realised Sophie Brown was still seated at the back obviously upset after most folk had left. In the subsequent discussion with her, he had to decide how best to offer comfort here on Mars when the normal platitudes were insufficient.

33

Sophie's Entanglement

HER FULL NAME was Sophie Amanda Brown and she was the super-fit black woman who had become something of a heroine following her rescue of Ken and attempt to save Fred in Boulder Pit. Her background epitomised the highly motivated young American who achieved selection for the Mars programme. At school, she was precocious but intelligent and not at all phased by being black in a largely white middle-class suburb of Los Angeles. (When referred to as the black girl by her white compatriots, she loved to start an argument by assertively claiming she was *brown* from birth.) She had excelled at mathematics, obtaining a first degree and PhD from UCLA and had progressed to becoming a recognised international expert on string theory by the time she was 30. She also excelled at virtually any sport she tried and her dedication to her career and the gym made her somewhat scary to those around. She saw coming to Mars as her next career move and while much respected, especially after the Fred episode, she was seen as super-intelligent, slightly aloof and therefore not easily approachable by most of her colleagues.

She was deeply attached to her mother, her father having died some years before, and was shocked when she heard that her mother had been diagnosed with an aggressive bowel cancer. She sought the advice of the doctor on Mars and he had informed her that it was unlikely her mother would have long to live. She enquired about returning to Earth but there was no chance that she could go back in time to see her alive as Mars was at its farthest point from Earth and it would take nearly a year even if there had been a rocket scheduled to return. In despair, she visited the chaplaincy for the first time and felt decidedly out of place sitting at the back watching all the others chatting among themselves. She had briefly met Steve before at some meeting on pod allocations and once or twice in passing when he was with his circle of friends in the Mars Bar. As he came over to speak, she did not know what to expect.

"I don't think I've met you here before," he said, adding for good measure, "but you're very welcome, of course," as he sat down. Sophie looked up at him and decided to explain why she was there.

"No, not usually my scene but my mum is very ill and I'm the only child. I can't see her as she's 240 million miles away and I don't know what to do."

Steve expressed his concern about her mother and Sophie outlined some facts about her background in Los Angeles and how she had cared for them in difficult times, wearing herself out on their behalf.

"The trouble is, apart from a few neighbours, she does not really have friends there; my dad was the social one and when he died his friends never really took up with mum apart from the odd invite to gatherings where she felt she was representing him rather than being herself. She contacts me by text most days and I am probably her main confidante as well as her daughter. She's probably only got a few weeks left before the drugs turn her into a zombie so I share most things with her. We almost live each other's lives."

She stopped, not knowing what more she could say and feeling about to cry but Steve quickly picked up from the last phrase.

"That's wonderful, you really could not do more even if you were there, what a good way to put it; we almost live each other's lives."

She paused for a moment and said, "Thanks but aren't you meant to say that she'll soon be with Jesus and we'll all be joining her there one day and all that stuff I heard in Sunday school years ago?"

"Yes, Sunday schools are well-meant and had some positive effects but they have a downside because when the children grow up, they think religion is for children alone—like Father Christmas. Children are very perceptive and quickly simplify issues by pigeon-holing them into neat packages. I once heard a comedian joke that when he was young, he didn't like people but when he grew up, he realised it was just children. You're a top-notch mathematician who knows about space and time and string theory and all those other things Stephen Hawking explained many years ago. He came to the conclusion that there is no creator God in his posthumous book in 2018. I'm not going to now reinforce your concept of a typical Christian chaplain even if it's comforting."

She eyed him with interest. At least he was not going to patronise her.

"So how do you see it then?" she said with just a hint of challenge.

Steve was hardly ready for such a big question. Like a newly appointed government minister confronted by a persistent journalist, he had to say something so he bumbled on.

"Well, my current position is that since coming here

to Mars, I've realised more acutely that people are equally bundles of thought as well as atoms. OK, their bodies are seen and do all the practical things of life but the real them is their thoughts; it's about what goes on in their heads. If they are thinking and communicating then they are alive whatever the state of their body. Those thoughts, like the electronic messages we all use in our mobiles, are there in electromagnetic pulses which propagate the universe and are there forever—that's the part of us which persists. In thinking and communicating with your mum and living her life too, your thoughts become entangled in an inseparable way. When she dies, those thoughts continue as you mull over and revisit the happy times with her, they don't suddenly stop."

"Yes, I can see that," she said, "I feel entangled with my mum although she's so far away but what is this entanglement and how does it work?"

"I'm not sure I know what it is and how it works but I do know it's there. But, Sophie, you as a mathematician know more about entanglement than most. We know there're loads of particles everywhere but then there's also thoughts. You tell me what entanglement is in your terms."

Sophie said, "Well, you can find out all about it if you put *quantum entanglement* into Wikipedia." Steve looked at her and waited. After a moment, she added, "Sorry, that's ducking the question," and she gave the following short summary.

"Quantum entanglement is a feature of quantum mechanics that allows pairs of particles or groups of particles to transfer information instantaneously even when they are cosmic distances apart. It is sometimes called spooky because Einstein called it this when he and his colleagues isolated it in the early 1930s, well after his work on relativity. It is currently the subject of intense study by mathematicians working at the forefront of information transfer at the quantum level. Real physical experiments have confirmed its existence but scientists are divided on its exact nature and the extent to which it is instantaneous as the speed of light limitation applies to all systems. It has obvious implications for theories about the biological seed of life and the way life is propagated by pairing; *two it seems is the magic number of the universe.* I understand quantum entanglement has been around since the Big Bang and somehow links with the information bank of the universe. You, as chaplain, from what I've heard would no doubt call it the mind of the universe or God. It's not my speciality so beyond that you'll have to consult all those references you see in Wikipedia. It's currently one of the most exciting finds of particle mechanics."

Steve said, "Thanks, that's fascinating, so entanglement does exist for your thoughts and for particles and neither are understood."

"On that, we can agree," she said, "but how do you correlate entanglement in whatever form with the party line of your church and the Christian belief in Christ, surely the essence of Christianity?"

"Not easily," he admitted, "but also, not impossibly. Let me expand—but firstly, have you got time or are you due somewhere?"

"No, please carry on, I'm intrigued."

"Well, we've spoken about entanglement of thought and I've had similar discussions with others here on this. Essentially, we do not believe that all the creative things, the art and craft of humanity and the unrequited kindness everywhere among humans are simply the consequence of a purely cold and targeted natural selection process. Hawkins shows that interactions after the Big Bang follow proscribed laws of physics and lead to the universe that we know with its ever-expanding matter and black holes. With this, we agree but it does not preclude other influences in the universe. Physics has not yet accounted for the seed of life and indeed there is a body of thought that it was there at the start and emanated from the Bang itself. Wherever it came from, that life force is as assuredly there and it manifests itself in the ways we saw. We can be entangled or tuned in to this mind force as much as we are entangled with each other. The ancients called it God and gave it a decidedly male image. Perhaps we have a historical and cultural issue with the naming and the gender, but whatever it's called, It or He or She is most certainly there."

Sophie interrupted him, "Maybe that's true and maybe not, but if it is, it's still quite a long way from the beliefs of the religions."

"Not so far away as it looks if you forgive the ancient ways of expressing things. All the religions are based on the pursuit of kindness; that is the part which the laws of physics and natural cannot attain. In early times, when many of the key religions developed, there were limited ways of expressing things—nobody knew about electronic waves and tuning in; had they done it would have made explanations so much easier. If a caveman saw us talking on our mobiles, he would just assume we were praying! In the Christian religion, it was Jesus who showed the way to become entangled with God, the great mind. Indeed, the early Christians called it *The Way* and it was only later that churches developed and claimed it as their territory rather than being open to all. He epitomised kindness and became entangled and synonymous with it to the extent that Christians often pray to Jesus as a mediator rather than God deeming Him to be the Son of God?

"But is that a personal God?" asked Sophie.

"That's a needless question really," he replied, but then realised that was rather condescending and less than comforting when she was so entangled with her dying mother.

He quickly added, "What I mean is the sheer concept of entanglement is based on personal involvement so it cannot be otherwise. You just can't be entangled without it being a mutual love."

Sophie glanced at her timepiece; electronic watches had made a retro comeback after being outlawed long ago by the fashion kings.

"So what you're saying, in a nutshell, is that kindness can lead to entanglement not only with another person but also at the highest level with the mind of the universe, that's God to most folk, no matter whether it's now or even in the future."

"I think so," he said, beginning to wonder how he had arrived where he'd ended up, right at the limit of his comfort zone. He certainly would not have put it like that to many of his Christian friends but merely gone along with their acceptance of conventional and ancient beliefs. He knew they too can lead to an understanding in their own way and thus yield some consolation. Sometimes, the benevolent slant on the truth needed for comfort and kindness is preferable to being overwhelmed by the enormity of it all. Emily Dickinson was right:

the truth must dazzle gradually or every man be blind.

"Steve, I must be going," she said, "but thanks for spending the time consoling me on these things. Do you have parents worrying about you back home?"

"Yes, I do and I should communicate more often."

"Do they know about Jo—your own entanglement?" she said with a smile.

"Sure, I told them but they were a bit concerned about her being a Buddhist and how it would work out."

"Yes, we have all wondered about that too, but you seem to hit it off well," she said as she left.

He was left wondering what the Mars folk had actually said about him and Jo and the chaplaincy. They would surely have something more to say when they heard about the pending baby! No doubt he would be the butt of a few comments, but he had broad shoulders and he knew most of his colleagues would support him.

34

The Assistant
President Rules

A WEEK OR two later, when the AP received a request
from Steve and Jo to see him, he assumed at first it must
be something relating to the Chaplaincy Centre. He
had put a lot of issues their way and they seemed to be
coping well. He had never imagined there would be so
many people issues on Mars but in the overall scheme,
it was balanced out by there being relatively few unexpected technical problems. Of late, he had noticed that
while Jo looked especially fulsome and buoyant, Steve
looked somewhat fraught. He suspected that he had problems on the home front—perhaps the coupling with Jo
was not working out so well after all. Maybe the request
to see him was to discuss the procedures for decoupling
which he had had to enact for another pair a few months
before. (Divorce as they used to call it had become so
common that it could be done on the Internet on Earth
but owing to the social sensitivities on Mars it was a
requirement that this be undertaken by application to the
council.) With this possibility in mind, he allocated them
a mid-morning slot with the idea of putting the coffee on
for a break as he always enjoyed conversations with them
whatever the topic. He welcomed them in with a cheery,

"Grab a chair, guys, and we'll talk about whatever's on your minds; would you like a coffee?"

"Not at the moment, thanks," said Steve, wanting to get going.

Once settled, Jo took the lead.

"This is not about the chaplaincy where things are fine but rather about Steve and myself. You presided over us becoming a couple a few months ago but I have to tell you that I am now pregnant with Steve's baby which we know is not allowed on Mars."

Oh dear, thought the AP, *I seriously misjudged this one.* There was a long pause because Jo was not quite sure what to add and the AP had lapsed into a thoughtful stare. Eventually, the AP said,

"Yes, I should have realised. I did notice your infatuation with doughnuts and such things which was entirely out of keeping with your normal tastes, coming from North India where they only produce such sickly treats for Western tourists."

He moved his tablet in front of him and commenced a file search for the Mars rules covering such eventualities and gave away no sign of any personal feelings one way or the other which was disconcerting for Jo and Steve. He then said, picking his words carefully, "Now, you do realise that in the small print of your contract which you signed on agreeing to travel to Mars, there was an acceptance that should the need arise, abortion is necessary and I'm afraid mandatory owing to the unsuitability of Mars for childbirth. I have to advise you that you must register with Dr Wang immediately and take the course of special drugs developed for this contingency. I can tell you that you are not the first to approach me since my time on Mars and this was successful for them."

This latter point Steve did not know and was surprised

it had not been mentioned to him. However, before he could comment Jo came back with.

"That may be the case, Mr President (she called him that on more formal occasions), but Steve and I have decided we would like to have this baby and take the risk of childbirth here."

"Oh dear, I'm afraid that is really not allowable under the rules and would require me to implement the mandatory clause here in my instructions," said the AP indicating the script on his tablet.

Steve could sense the impending impasse and came in with, "It also says in our contract in Section 78a that a person on Mars is subject to the prevailing laws of their country on Earth. As Jo is twenty weeks through her pregnancy, abortion is not allowable unless it is a life-threatening emergency."

There was again pause of some time. The AP, although frustrated with many of the restrictions imposed by Earth, was not prepared to blatantly break the rules in such an important area, particularly when he felt there was a real risk and a danger to any of his staff involved. He also felt he had been slightly cornered. He latched on to the timing of the pregnancy, saying, "I will need to get a medical assessment of the current duration of your pregnancy to see if it is indeed outside the allowable period and then seek the advice of the medical advisors to the UN Mars Committee on Earth."

He turned towards Steve and added, "Steve, I am disappointed that you did not divulge this to me earlier when the timing would have been less critical."

Steve glanced at Jo who made no comment but the AP read the glance correctly and realised that Jo must have been totally determined and would have fought tooth and nail to keep the baby. He also realised in a flash that Steve had delayed for several weeks so that he was not put in the terrible position of enforcing an abortion on Jo. That might have caused a constitutional crisis between folk on Mars let alone the Earth.

He then contacted Dr Wang, a female medic and instructed that an examination be undertaken immediately to ascertain the facts and most importantly the estimated dates. Jo and Steve, sitting beyond his desk and observing this felt like schoolchildren in front of a senior teacher who knew he should be meting out some words of reprehension but saw no point because the decision lay outside his jurisdiction.

He looked up and said, "Please return at 2 pm this afternoon by which time, Dr Wang will have done the tests and have the results. This will also give me time to think about this turn of events and scrutinise the rules more closely."

Steve started to apologise for the trouble caused but they were waved away by the AP. Dr Wang duly subjected Jo to a medical examination later that morning.

On returning in the afternoon, they were ushered in to join three of their colleagues who had obviously been discussing the matter earnestly.

"I have asked our contracts specialist, Paul and also, Dr Wang herself to join me. I hope that's OK with you."

Jo and Steve nodded their approval but Steve wondered why Paul was there too. He had come to know him better since he first challenged him on some issues at an early gathering but he was still a stickler for the rules. The AP then went straight to the crux of the matter.

"I have to tell you that while there is always some tolerance in the dates involved, Dr Wang is of the opinion that there is a window of one week in which a legal abortion could be possible and has advised (in accordance with the regulations) that this potential birth should be terminated."

Jo's heart sunk and Steve's too now that he had accepted Jo's position of wishing to go ahead with the baby. The AP continued.

"However, being a major policy decision, I am obliged according to Paul, by my own terms of appointment to seek sanction from the UN Committee before proceeding with the abortion process. I have sent a request to the UN Mars Committee for urgent attention to this matter and expect a reply tomorrow."

Steve and Jo were totally crestfallen.

"Another issue is that we are at the Martian CDZ, but before I go into that, what about the coffee I offered earlier? I sure need one after this bombshell even if you don't."

The AP was trying to return to his normally affable self but Jo pointedly asked him to remind her what CDZ was and how it affected the situation. He did not answer immediately but instead, produced some coffee and sweet biscuits. He then settled down in his chair and adopted what Steve realised was his lecturing mode. Maybe the AP felt it was safer ground for him than all this emotion-wrought preoccupation with babies.

"Well, as you know, communication with Earth is much more problematic than first supposed. Everybody knows about the delay of up to 20 minutes and also the interference owing to dust storms which seem to affect the antenna. Much more serious is the Conjunction Dead Zone or CDZ which they knew about but didn't really plan for as it seldom occurs. When the Earth and Mars are on the opposite side of the Sun, in a conjunction position, not only can they not see one another due to the glare but the complete range of electronic waves are obscured. It can occur for some days until they are well in view of each other again. Don't forget the Mars synodic period (around the Sun) is about two years so the angle to the sun alters quite slowly. It was assumed that contact could be maintained over this period by bouncing the waves off Venus or even Mercury but sometimes they are not in the best positions either. It doesn't happen every year of course because the planetary circuits are in three dimensions, not two, so they are not opposite too often. We did have a partial dead zone of two and a half days a couple of years ago but we just did everything before or after and it was no particular issue. The one coming up now however is a full blanketing and is, therefore, more prolonged and serious. They are hoping to use Venus as a deflector although it is moving away at an acute angle so nobody's quite sure whether that will work."

Jo's mind was wandering away from the topic, not because it was more complicated than she'd thought but because she thought she felt a small kick inside her on the left-hand side. The AP realised she was preoccupied and assumed that he had lost his audience.

"A top-up of coffee perhaps," he enquired, but then added, remembering from long ago his wife's confinement as they called it then, "Maybe you have to be careful about having too much coffee, Jo, there was a scare about the caffeine levels during pregnancy many years ago."

She accordingly declined but Steve and Paul had another coffee and entered into a detailed discussion with the AP about the dead time zone.

Jo thought it was surreal and typical of males (although she could not say so with the politically correct restraints in force) that they were discussing unreal subjects such as the effects of conjunction in the solar system while the very real matter of the future of the baby inside her was put on hold.

Then something dawned on her. The AP had shown concern for her baby in recommending no further caffeine intake. Had he forgotten that he was officially meant to be insisting on a late abortion? Was it a mere slip through force of habit, or had he been steered by some primaeval instinct to protect the young of the species at all costs? She made no mention of this to Steve but pondered in her heart.

35

A Martian Miracle

WHEN THE UN Sub-Committee for Mars received notification that a member of the Scientific Staff on Mars was heavily pregnant and within a week of the abortion threshold, there was a considerable annoyance. Why did the Doctor on Mars not advise them earlier? Why did the AP not deal with it immediately? Why did the chaplain not advise them appropriately? Being informed that the doctor did not know about it earlier, that the rules insisted that the president (or presumably AP when acting for him) must obtain permission from Earth before instructing a mandatory termination and that the perpetrator was indeed the chaplain himself, did nothing to mollify their disapproval. They called an emergency meeting of the sub-committee and it decided to refer the matter upwards to the UN itself owing to different countries have slightly different abortion deadlines. Two days were lost before it was discussed in the main chamber and no decision was made until the third day because various delegates wanted to seek advice from their own governments. A vote was taken and by a narrow majority, it was decided to go ahead with granting permission for the mandatory abortion to proceed. In the end, it was swung by the argument that there were no maternity facilities on Mars and, even if the equipment was sent, it would take over 9 months to get there.

The news media loved the story. It had all the elements of human interest played out on an international stage not to mention the ethical debate on abortion. Being the chaplain himself involved as the paternal party gave it another layer of intrigue and it gained prominence among the various religious communities with strongly held views backed up by their ancient texts. In fact, the UN Public Relations department had never been so busy and if the truth were known they were revelling in the attention because the UN had become somewhat moribund in recent years, primarily dealing with matters of international law which were very boring. The official communique detailing the United Nation's approval was not sent off to Mars until the fourth day after receipt of the urgent request from the assistant president.

Those on Mars, where it was also a key news item, were very conscious of the delay and not least Jo and Steve who had been waiting on tenterhooks for the decision. Jo was threatening to go AWOL, don a spacesuit and wander off across the Martian desert rather than suffer the indignity of arrest and forced abortion. Steve said she was being melodramatic and reminded her that such a journey would be fatal for both her and the baby. Things were generally fraught and getting worse as the end of the week approached. On the fifth day, there was heightened activity around the domes because the electronic systems were starting to break down owing to the commencement of the CDZ and several folks reported that the Earth could no longer be seen from Mars as it gradually drifted behind the bright sun. Still, no communique had been received from the Earth although they understood it was being routed via Venus. On the sixth day, there was still no discernible signal as the Earth and

Mars were now at the peak of the conjunction position with Earth completely obliterated from Mars.

On the seventh day, the AP took an important decision. Having received no information from Earth, he announced that an Instant Referendum or IR of the Mars occupants would be held. Many countries across the Earth over the last few years had adopted the IR method of resolving difficult issues as it was ostensibly more democratic. (Cynics called it an IR-ony as it removed the need for politicians to make a decision.) Furthermore, in view of the urgency, it would be held that morning and all villagers were requested to respond on their tablets by immediately indicating their preference for A or B on the Mars voting form:

Instant Referendum Form

In the case of Dr J Thanawala who has been with child for nearly 20 weeks, do you support action as follows:

A) mandatory termination in view of the unsuitable environment for a child.

B) allowance of the birth and nurture of the child, the first on Mars, until transfer to Earth is possible.

[Please reply by 12 pm today indicating option A or B.]

The AP also announced an open meeting in the Central Dome at 12:30 pm when the result would be announced.

Nearly every occupant of the Village assembled in the great open space of the Central Dome to hear the result. Ken and an assistant had been asked to man the Earth communication receivers and transmitters in Dome B and so could not be there. The AP entered from his office at precisely 12:30 pm and seemed taken aback at the large number who had gathered. Previous announcements made in this way on decisions affecting them all such as alterations to the Drove timetable or the pending dust storms had never attracted so many. Any news would always appear on their tablets within a few hours so their presence at the announcement was largely a formality. He realised then that the whole community had taken a particular interest in this issue, talking about it in little groups by the watercooler or the Mars Bar. It had grown into a defining moment in the development of the Mars Colony. The AP had not drafted any statement and suddenly felt unprepared but there was no turning back so he launched forth into the unknown:

"Residents of Mars, whether you be astronauts, paranauts or terminauts. Today, you have decided, by democratic vote, to allow or disallow the birth of a child here on Mars. Our venture nearly 70 years ago to the Moon was deemed a giant step for mankind. When we first came to Mars, a further giant step was taken and the growth of our community is evidence of the success of that venture. Both of those steps were essentially visits into the unknown, a sojourn to a foreign land. Today, we make a momentous decision on whether we are prepared to inhabit another planet rather than just pay it a visit. That makes it a totally different occasion; as important to the extension of life as the time when the first amphibians lumbered out of the sea three billion years ago. This defining step is the propagation of our species beyond the Earth alone. This could mark the beginning of Life on Mars."

He was interrupted by Ken who had appeared from Dome B and said in a loud voice,

"Excuse me, President (Like Jo, Ken never referred to him as assistant), sorry to break in but we are at last reconnected with Earth and a backlog of urgent messages are coming through and one of them may concern this issue."

The AP, in turn, interrupted him,

"No doubt but Earthly matters can wait until the results of our IR are made known. There will be plenty of time to attend to them afterwards."

There was a general murmur of assent from the crowd and the AP continued, endeavouring to regain the sense of occasion he had developed to mark the official significance of the result. Ken looked agitated and slightly miffed.

"I therefore now, as assistant president on Mars and, in loco hominem, your returning officer, give the votes awarded as follows:

Option A, 9 Votes.

Option B, 175 Votes.

Non-Returns, 6.

I accordingly decline to sanction the mandatory abortion of the child carried by Dr J Thanawala and wish her and the baby all the best over the remaining weeks of her confinement."

A big cheer went up and everybody started talking to those around them but the AP quickly returned to his office, beckoning Ken to join him. Once there, he closed the door and said, "Ken, you were right to interrupt me so don't take it personally, but I do feel that weak messages, bounced to Earth from another planet after the period of intense electronic interference occasioned by CDZ, are too unreliable to form the basis of any important decision. Could you please log their safe receipt when they are properly confirmed?"

Ken looked into the eyes of the AP and needed no telepathic powers to read his message.

"I'll go back to the communication desk and log the time when they are *properly confirmed.* it may be many hours until things settle down properly."

Steve and Jo were, of course, overjoyed at the turn of events. A great milestone had been passed but as so often when that happens the full significance did not sink in until later. For the moment, they were celebrating with their friends the potential arrival of a child on Mars and the child himself (or herself) was neatly furled in a world of his own not knowing what a commotion he had caused, even before he was born.

The next day, clear communication with the Earth was properly established and messages sent up to three days before were logged and acted upon. One of these related to a formal instruction from the Mars Committee of the UN that the child should be aborted forthwith. The AP sent back a quick reply to say that it had been logged in too late and, as the allowable, abortion window was now passed, the Instruction could no longer be enacted. The administrators of the UN were furious but there was little they could do since it was they who, by prevaricating had caused the delay. The news media made much of this aspect and were sympathetic to the AP. The general consensus was that the occurrence of conjunction of Earth and Mars just when communication was so desperately needed was simply an Act of God. Indeed, it came to be known as a miracle that saved the life of an unborn infant and thereby led to life on Mars.

But to Ken, it was not a miracle. He had witnessed the AP pursuing his declaration of the voting result even though he had tried to inform him that Earth's communication was being reconnected. He felt the AP had guessed what the instruction would be and effectively turned a blind eye. It was he who had finally allowed the child to live so how could it be a miracle? When he met Steve later, he explained how it had been the expediency of a decision by the AP that had saved the day rather than a miracle of timing with the solar system. Steve though had no difficulty with this but still considered it to be a miracle. Over the years, he had expended much thought on the occurrence of miracles in a modern world, a world more knowledgeable than in the past. He attempted to allay Ken's concerns.

"Ken, there are several types of miracles. They may result from precise and expedient timing or from a dramatic change of mind or some think from a breaking of the rules of science. Examples in the Christian Bible of each might be the parting of the Red Sea, St Paul's conversion and turning water into wine. With a mind permeating the universe as we discussed before, then the first two are understandable as the manifestation of this mind. Indeed, the saving of our Mars baby was perhaps a combination of the first (the occurrence of the communication block) and the second (the AP being dilatory in processing the signal from Earth). There are not really degrees of miracles, it is either one or it is not and this in my book is as much a miracle as any other."

"OK, I see the logic of that but I have real difficulty with the last category, the breaking of the laws of science especially if they are part of the universal mind."

"Well, you are not alone," said Steve, "Indeed there may not be any in this category; I would certainly have trouble with this myself as an engineer. One of the most blatant violations of the scientific rules is the example I gave of turning water into wine, but maybe this miracle is actually categories one and two also."

"How do you mean?"

"Sorry, this is once again turning into one of my sermons, but essentially, it would be impossible to take the elements of water and turn some of them into the elements found in wine. The very atoms would have to be split and the story says nothing about a nuclear explosion.

"And why would the good Lord perform such a fundamental change when there were other ways of achieving the result. Could it not be that Jesus, a young lad at the time, saw the predicament of the wine running out and felt kindness and sympathy towards the guests among whom was his mother. He knew that the landlord would have his special mature wine stored safely away and he may have noticed it in the old earthen vessels in the cellar. Human nature being what it is, the landlord was not going to waste his best wine on these guests but Jesus disapproved of this ungenerous attitude and with the approval of his mother instructed the servants to use the good wine."Do whatever he asks you," she says with some authority. Once served, the guests are pleasantly surprised at the quality so the Landlord simply basks in the compliments. All win as a result of his unintended generosity. What a wonderful miracle illustrating the benefits and power of kindness and generosity of spirit; so much better and more profound than denigrating it to a conjuring trick with the elements.' At the end of the day, God is kindness; that is love. I should add that not all my Christian friends would see it that way."

"I see what you mean," said Ken. "Does that apply to all the scriptures?"

"I really don't know but I do know that the mind permeating the Universe that we spoke of, acts in all sorts of wonderful ways. If our new baby survives this first attempt to stem its life on Mars I'm sure it will survive others owing to this everlasting care."

Ken said nothing and after a pause, Steve said,

"Now since you have had the benefit of an unsolicited sermon and I've had a stressful day and Jo seems to have gone off somewhere with her girlie friends, I think you owe me a pint in the Mars Bar."

"You can only get half at a time," said Ken.

"I know what I said," replied Steve.

36

New Life on Mars

STEVE GOT UP early and went to the gym. Well, it was called the gym but actually, it was an annexe to the Central Dome and the equipment was one exercise bike brought from Earth. There were also improvised weights fashioned from rocks on the Martian surface and areas of the floor marked out for various exercises such as pilates and yoga. You had to be early in the morning to obtain the bike and you were only allowed half an hour which Steve found to be plenty. It was several months since Mars and the Earth had reluctantly accepted that a baby was going to be born on Mars and the child was now due in the next week or so. While Mars villagers had grown used to the idea, it being just another oddity in a strange environment, the ordinary folk on Earth were overawed with excitement at the prospect of the birth of a child in space. All the news media were reporting daily on developments and speculating on its future. The medical people were worrying about the childbirth itself and the effect of the lower gravity and high radiation levels on the child's growth. The paramedics were concerned about the oxygen levels and were devising emergency procedures in the event that they dropped as there were no space suits for babies. The psychologists were generally predicting doom and the nutritionists were warning about the lack of calcium, there being no cows on Mars.

Steve's trip to the gym was not entirely for exercise but partly because he was becoming tired of it all and needed to find some space. It seemed space was everywhere like the water around the ancient mariner but there was no space for him. He could have sought refuge at his allotment again but other aspiring horticulturalists were now assembling there more frequently. The constant questions, the interviews for Earth with their long responses and the burden of potential blame if it all went wrong were getting to him. His mum, in her last correspondence, had asked how he was really managing and, knowing he could not fool her, he tried to describe the constant pressure and the occasional regret that he had left the green, green grass of home. She had responded that it was his destiny and that all her friends simply thought he was very brave. He could imagine them chatting about it over coffee in her kitchen.

Partly, to achieve more space for himself and partly because he felt the chaplaincy centre was attracting an enthusiastic clique of folk rather than becoming a village-wide resource, he thought he should be taking the Christian message to the people rather than expecting them to come to him. After all, Jesus wandered the countryside and did not sit in the temple awaiting callers. So he spent a day or two in each of the work areas to get to know what happened and most importantly to get to know better the people making it all happen. He had spent time with the communication section and the horticultural team and today he was going to join the unit responsible for External Village Activity (EVA)

This involved him joining a team of Mars construction engineers who were building the next dome. The construction team included some of the new staff who had recently arrived on Drove 6 and also Chen, who had been stranded outside following the power breakdown incident. They seemed pleased to have him on board for a day and Steve was also pleased as it provided an opportunity to venture outside into the open and to see the vastness of space around him. A new and more efficient building block consolidator had been included with the new equipment from Earth and this allowed the breeze blocks to be automatically moulded from the sandy Mars regolith and silicon paste at a rate of about one every few minutes. Each slightly curved moulding was recessed to couple with the next which made building the domes straightforward. Small thick Perspex windows brought from Earth were included to give some natural light and a view but since there was nothing to see they were more decorative than useful. There was one electric lifting truck but much of the work had to be done by hand. As the blocks were only two-thirds of the weight on Earth, this was not as bad as it seems. As it never rained, water ingress was not an issue but the inside had to be gas-tight to keep in the atmosphere. This was done by spraying sealant on the inside when completed but even then there was some loss of precious air.

Steve was enjoying the involvement and the banter of the team as they chatted via their spacesuit intercoms. It was, in any case, good to get away from all the baby speculation and Jo had kindly suggested he had the day off as she had several days to go before D-day (deliverance day). He suspected she needed some space too and half a dozen of the caring ladies in the village had taken it upon themselves to be her guardian angels and were gathering together all the items required for birth and post-natal support. He began to appreciate that in the Indian culture babies and young children are seen as the responsibility of the wider community while in the West the nuclear family is more predominant.

He had been outside helping for over four hours when Chen came across to him and said, "Hey, Steve, they've been trying to get you on the Mars intranet for some time, they need you to return to the Central Dome as soon as possible. I'll run you back to the door in the Rover if you wish or if you are happy to wait ten minutes you can come back with us as our shift is about to finish."

"I can't imagine it's that urgent so I'll finish up here and come back with you."

By the time they had cleared up and driven back and he had divested himself of his spacesuit, an hour had elapsed. After a quick check over by the Doctor, a village requirement after an EVA, Steve made his way to the medical centre. On arrival, the duty nurse smiled and said, "Oh, we've been trying to contact you, I think you had better follow me."

For the first time, he began to wonder what was so urgent and to worry about whether Jo was well. But then, the nurse had smiled which she would not have done if there was anything amiss. He followed her to one of the two-bed units and she then stood aside.

Jo was sitting up in bed looking weary but radiantly happy. He realised to his surprise but also to his regret at having missed it all that she was nursing a very small baby. As he bent over to kiss her, she parted the shawl a little and there, peering blearily up at him was a little Indian face with dark eyes and a wisp of black hair. She answered his questioning look with, "She's a girl."

He hesitated just a nano-second before saying, "That's wonderful, I'm so—"

She interjected, "But you would have preferred a boy."

Something clicked into place in his mind like a press-stud being closed. He made a quick mental note to analyse it later and said, "No, I'm equally delighted either way as we discussed before and I'm so happy that you are fine too. You must be worn out. I'm so sorry I was not present at the birth, I was outside the village as you know."

"Yes, they said you'd turned your spacesuit link off, but whether you had or had not it doesn't matter because I'd have suggested you were not present any rate. Where I come from they still don't have the men around—too much false emotion and all that."

He would have felt miffed but she smiled so sweetly he forgot it and said, "This will go down in history, the first human born outside the Earth and a little Indian girl at that."

"Well," she said, "when you first saw me completely, you know, all of me, you said I was the most beautiful girl ever and that black folk were overdone, white folk were underdone but I was just right."

"Well, you've now got a baby that's just right too," she laughed.

He looked around quickly in case others were within earshot and was relieved to see they weren't. This being attributed to him by the media may not have gone down too well in some quarters!

He stayed around until one of the nurses (there seemed to be lots of auxiliary nurses suddenly) suggested she needed rest and then he gave Jo another kiss and left. As he walked away, he was met by a small crowd of his friends at the entrance who congratulated him with a cheer and steered him towards the Mars Bar where Patrick, never slow to seize a marketing opportunity, had already lined up a dozen half-pints of Guinness with the froth correctly scraped off. Everybody was overwhelmed with delight over the first real Martian as they insisted on calling his little Indian girl. So, he gave in to unadulterated celebration and just enjoyed the evening and slept like a zombie until gone eight the next morning. His good friends kept the stream of media interest from Earth at bay, judging that he needed a break before he faced the baying journalist pack.

37

Post-Natal Depression

ON RISING AND enquiring about Jo, he learnt that she was sleeping after a feed in the night and also that it had been a most effortless birth. The folk present had reasoned that it was because of everything being less weight, like a water birth but in the air but others thought it was just the relief after the particularly worrying gestation period. He made himself a coffee and started to work out the implications of his new situation for this new world of Mars and the old world of Earth. The media people were keen to interview him and he had to be clear on certain key things before then.

He had put on hold his emotion at finding he had indeed sired a wee Indian girl. Somehow, it was not quite his plan but what had clicked into place when Jo first told him was the realisation that his predilection in favour of a male, although totally inexcusable, was inevitable. Equality is a good aim but he thought it not always possible in practice for human beings reared on Earth. Thousands of years of social manipulation had embedded within them the lingering thought that the male is predominant. From the emperors of ancient civilisations to the rulers of today, men are in the majority. The religions are worse and there is no need to mention the hordes of bearded Priests, Imrans, Rabbis, Bishops and Ministers who by their very predominance propagate the myth. And worse still, the very mind of the universe, the godliness that permeates the whole firmament is endowed with a gender. The English language has no word for a single person devoid of gender except *it* which sounds disrespectful because it also applies to things. It was stated *All men are created equal* and although George Orwell added *but some are more equal than others* the *men* still remained. Admirable efforts to correct this can never entirely eradicate it, not while the great mind that is God, is anthropomorphised as a *male* human being. But maybe, on Mars with the expanse of space more immediate and challenging, this could be different. Maybe a little baby girl with light brown skin, dark brown eyes and a wisp of black hair could start the ball rolling in a different direction.

Also, to many on Earth, the fact that she was Indian would be foremost. Gone were the days when race was an issue, although it was only after the 2020s that real progress had been made partly due to increased inter-mixing and partly due to the terrible disease pandemics of the late 20s which had required a world-wide effort to eradicate. The Indians would, of course, be over the moon and maybe the resulting national pride would diminish the ills of the caste and culture which divides their country. The West would take the baby to heart, Indian or not, and go entirely gaga at the first wee Martian. She would be thoroughly westernised by the news media in the same way that the birth of Jesus has been in Europe and the USA. The little fair-headed baby of a beautiful light-skinned maiden portrayed in many nativity scenes in Christian Churches is evidence of the power of this westernisation. In the Middle East and the Far East the acceptance of an Indian girl as the first Martian could be uncomfortable for them.

Her name was important too; that would proba-bly be the first question many journalists would ask. He started rattling through possible names but then realised he must chat to Jo about this—she was after all an equal partner. On enquiring, he found she had now woken up so he went through to see her. After a prolonged cuddle, enquiring how she was and how the baby was doing and all that he launched into the matter of a name. (Once focussed on an issue, Steve had to get there with all speed!)

"I've been thinking about a name," he said, adding, "why ever with all the time we had, did we not decide on this before."

"Do we have to do this now?" she asked.

"Well, I've got an interview with the dreaded Earth (can't believe I said that) this morning and I cannot keep referring to her as The Baby. Any rate, it would look as if we had not thought about it."

"Speak for yourself, Mr Chaplain. I had one in mind months ago but didn't want to tell you as you seemed to assume it would be a little white boy, without actually saying so of course."

He was about to deny this but realised his case was weak, not even having thought of a name.

"OK, then, so what are you suggesting?"

"Maria."

"Maria McKay," he said slowly, emphasising the final 'ay' as in *my,*

"Yes, it fits. I first met that name as a child; somebody in my class was called Maria. What's your reason though?"

"Well, it sounds caring, it translates in one form or another into nearly every language and is formed from five letters of the seven in Martian."

"Very appropriate, OK, let's go with that. If you've been thinking about it for ages I doubt whether you'd be persuaded away from it in any case and since I've got no other suggestion I guess that finalises it."

Jo changed the subject (quit while you are winning she thought) and asked,

"So what do you think the media are going to ask?"

"Well, as before, they have submitted about 20 questions which somebody here will ask me and I'll respond and it'll be sent back as a single package arriving a quarter of an hour or so later. It's the only way they can do it and it makes for a rather stilted interview."

"So you don't know what the questions are?"

Steve looked slightly furtive and Jo knew she was onto something so she just waited.

"Actually, I'm not meant to, but I do know what they are. One of the junior news officers, an Arabic girl on the Mars desk at the UN, has become increasingly loyal to us here on Mars and so she accidentally leaked them to me."

"Accidentally?" said Jo, "but no matter, are there any interesting ones?"

Steve thought for a moment, "One of them is related to whether or not we should go back to Earth at the next opportunity, what with a baby and all that; I was planning to say,"it would not be our decision but we would have to if the authorities insisted'—which they probably will as you know."

Jo said pensively, "Maria was born here and this is technically her home. We should, of course, visit the grandparents and folk on Earth and show her to them, why would we not, then we should come back here. So I'm happy to *VISIT* Earth when we get the opportunity, perhaps on the next spacecraft in 9 months or so if there's room."

"Yes but that assumes they would want us to come back here to Mars. After all, Maria would have a decidedly odd childhood, no other children, no school, never out to play and so on apart from the possibility of long term effects on growth with the lower gravity. She could end up enormous."

"There could be other children before long I can assure you."

"Oh, I had not noticed, who is it?"

Jo put her finger to her lips so Steve decided he would just have to be more observant.

The nurse then indicated they were looking for him and Steve went off to deal with the questions from Earth. Since it was all recorded, he could at least have a second go at any answer he fluffed which was more than he could on Earth. Many of the questions showed little under-standing of life on Mars and others were about detailed issues on Earth which seemed distant and banal from the Mars viewpoint. It was difficult to work up much enthu-siasm for the latest interstate bickering or electric cars or clothing fashions when you only had utility vehicles and regulation coloured gilet or the increased rainfall in the tropics when you had none at all. He would like to have explained his view on inhabiting Mars and our future in the vastness of space, on life and death in a universe alive with electronic messages and strange particles and so on but there was no opportunity for this. Although he was the chaplain and had views on these things, all they seemed to want was instant answers. He left the Inter-view area feeling somewhat misunderstood and realised how remote Mars still was to the media on Earth.

While Mars folk had taken the arrival of a baby in their stride, the Earth had not and it was still the main news. The first pictures of baby Maria in her surround-ings in the Central Dome together with Steve's inter-view and all other things connected with the baby had viewing numbers not far short of the original landing on Mars. Those of all races, cultures and creeds had views on the allowance of the birth, the delivery, the place of a wee Indian girl in the future of humans in space and the creation of an international Martian state. The latter item became a very fertile mining area for political debate with some arguing Mars should remain the subject of an international agreement like Antarctica but allow those who wished to become residents while others considered they should retain the citizenship of their countries . This group felt that children born there should simply have the nationality of their parents. However, it would often be the case that the parents were multinational and some argued it should be the mother's nationality only.

Meanwhile, little baby Maria, who had started a great flutter of imaginative thinking, was blissfully unaware of it as she lay in her cosy cot which had been cobbled together from discarded packing and covered with blue Gilet material by Jo's maternal support group. She seemed very happy only crying when she was hungry and seemingly smiling at everybody although Jo and Steve knew it was mainly her preoccupation with the wind. Smells hung around in the confines of the Dome where air circulation was reduced to the minimum to conserve resources so folk were often reminded that there was a baby human being in their midst.

The Earth news media had some fun with headline articles ranging from:

Residents Produce their Own Life on Mars

above a picture of Baby Maria and her happy parents to:

Chaplaincy starts a Mars Crèche

with a photograph of the inside of the chaplaincy adorned with pink baby folia.

Beyond the headlines, though there was widespread support for the stand taken by the McKay's in having the baby and it had brought together opposing sides in some of the Earth's most contentious areas. Religions and casts in India submerged their traditional prejudices for the moment in the general rejoicing and viewed the comments of outsiders that Indians infiltrated everywhere including space as a compliment. The West and the Middle East were relieved that, being an Indian girl, neither the Muslims nor the Christians could claim divine rights for the first space baby. The Russians and the Americans could hardly claim the other had tampered with the outcome which saved a lot of political hassle for both and the Chinese just felt that the Mars authorities should have taken a tighter control of propagation planning like they had. Steve's own church in Scotland was hung up on the logistics of the pending baptism of the baby, the chaplain being the father, the assistant chaplain being the mother and there being no locum minister within 240 million miles to conduct the Service. The matter was deemed urgent and thus referred to the reconstituted Church without Walls Committee for reporting to the General Assembly the following May. There was, however, another matter of more weight that Steve wished to straighten out in his mind. As it happens, the matter was raised by an old friend of Steve's from his college days.

38

After-life on Mars

[A Chapter to omit if you're in a hurry to get to the end or find the after-life too daunting!]

AMONG THE PLETHORA of articles spawned by all this activity on Mars, there was one that particularly caught Steve's attention, firstly because of the author and secondly because of the content. The author was none other than Professor Green who had been Steve's tutor and latterly his unofficial mentor at New College. He had been a biologist before his entry into the Church of Scotland ministry and was delighted that the previous moderator (they only serve as such for a year) was also at one time a scientist. They had developed a friendship and it was partly this that paved the way for the church to appoint a chaplain for Mars. The content of the article was on the second big question that most people, including Steve, battle with at some point in their lives; what happens after we die? (The first question was, of course, where do we come from as considered earlier.) At different periods of his life, Steve would have answered this question in different ways but over the last few months of his time on Mars circumstances had conspired to steer him towards a different conclusion. He was, after all, the chaplain and was meant to have these key things sorted out for people when they asked and when necessary offer them comfort about the future. Professor Green's article had unwittingly provided a key piece in the puzzle for Steve and while there were still some missing parts of this puzzle, he could now begin to visualise the complete picture.

Socrates at his trial some two and a half thousand years ago (as recorded by Plato in *The Apology*) had said:

> *Let us reflect in this way, too, that there is good hope that death is a blessing, for it is one of two things: either the dead are nothing and have no perception of anything, or it is, as we are told, a change and a relocation of the soul from here to another place.*

The give-away phrase is, of course, the *as we are told* because the Athenian authorities were adamant that there should be adherence to their particular gods. Socrates was astute enough to avoid playing his hand too strongly; philosophising on death was one thing, experiencing it before necessary was another.

The human race is slow to learn and the matter of life hereafter is still monopolised by the beliefs of religions and, in the case of the many countries that have state religions, in effect by the government. Consequently, the greatest buildings over the centuries, from the pyramids to modern cathedrals, are edifices to an afterlife as portrayed by these bodies. An uncharitable position might be that the authorities, both church and state, have in the past exercised an undercurrent of control by propagating the need for adherence to accepted views regarding the afterlife, views that inevitably reward the good and damn the bad and hence contribute to maintaining a moral society. Today, that is less the case but there is still an ingrained assumption that acceptance of an afterlife can only arise from a religious stance. Steve, of course, was religious to the core but nevertheless, he had come to realise that this is a false assumption which was neither fair on religion nor science.

Steve knew that here he was on rocky ground because death is charged with emotion and grief owing to the perceived loss by those around. In no way would he seek to undermine this by even the smallest iota of analysis. If the required comfort needed earnest platitudes and the reinforcement of an eternal hug, then that is what he would provide. Eschatological religious beliefs are geared to enabling this care but are not essential, as evidenced by the superb care offered by, for example, the terminal cancer charities. But human beings are a resilient bunch and while they sometimes need exactly this reassurance at other times, even as they prepare to depart, they may look you in the eye and seek some rational answers as to where they are actually going. Then a less ethereal and much deeper response may be sought and to some, this may be more comforting than well-intentioned platitudes.

Sometime before, Professor Green had published a paper in an electronic theological journal with the heading *Immortality for All*. He was now retired and had more time to contemplate and follow the progress of his *protégé*, the Church's Man on Mars. Indeed, he had communicated with Steve on such topics from time to time. The paper was closely argued with carefully crafted allusions to his and other's previous work that human beings are immortal by virtue of their very existence in the universe and as such are part of the mind of the universe. Being couched in liturgical jargon and bespattered with obtuse references, it was less than accessible to the man in the street. However, a perceptive journalist had spotted it and written a short summary as follows:

Immortality for All

According to Professor Green of New College, Edinburgh, immortality is a state of mind and equally available to us all. In particular, he refutes the recent claim by some religious groups that those who visit other planets and die on them are denying themselves the prospect of an eternal life. He argues that an observer on Mars who peers up at Earth in the night sky does not see Earth as it is now but as it was say 20 minutes ago owing to the speed of light delay. So, for 20 minutes, Earthlings are going about their business the nature of which is unknown to our observer because it is in the future. While 20 minutes is not much compared to eternity, if our observer were transported to the edge of the Milky Way and viewed the Earthlings from there then Earthlings would be living 4 years in the future as it takes this time for light and thus knowledge to travel between the two. Maybe 4 years is not much compared to eternity either so perhaps our observer is at the edge of the universe in which case everything on Earth would be over 4 billion years in the future as this is the time it takes light and knowledge to get here. If our observer is a spirit or a mind occupying every corner of the universe including Earth and Mars, then the past, the present and the future are simply different viewpoints of the same thing. In other words, Professor Green believes;

*We actually live in an eternal **now** which can be re-enacted at anytime and anywhere.*

Professor Green develops this to show how it is corroborated by modern physics where the curvature of the space-time continuum means things do not always accord to what one would expect and how even time itself (as mathematicians have discovered) is merely a concept to help us through our everyday lives. He then equates this mind of the universe to the God of the ancients; 'a thousand years in your sight are but as yesterday when it is past, or as a watch in the night,' says the Psalmist. 'Did man emerge from non-being through his own devices; was he his own creator?' it says in the Quran. 'When you pray, say, Our Father which art in Heaven,' says Jesus in the Bible. Today, he argues as we approach the middle of the 21st Century and some of the vehemence between differing views has subsided we can, at last, see that leaving this Earth, whether to go to Mars or some other planet or, like all of us eventually, to become finally absorbed within the universal mind, we can at least say goodbye with the knowledge that we are all going on to some-where and in that sense are immortal. That is the ultimate kindness of the mind of the universe and, given that kindness is love, it is the love of God.

———————————

As we have seen, Steve, in his role as a chaplain, had to comfort the dying from every culture and creed. A good medical doctor in the days when they went out to visit their patients at home needed a doctor's bag stocked with the right items to deal with all contingencies. Similarly, he needed a bag full of different approaches ranging from pure comfort to explanation. Being Christian, he knew the Bible best, knowing it to be a most wonderful treasure trove of wisdom and comfort, but he had to be there for those of other cultures for whom this particular Holy Book was not the font of all wisdom. When challenged about the existence of anything beyond the cold particles, atoms, molecules of the micro-world or beyond the stars of the macro-world, he could draw on Professor Green's wise words of assurance.

Steve had reached the conclusion that true kindness is not part of natural selection; in religious terms, it is the love of God. The adjective true is added because kindness offered with a consequential benefit to the giver is not pure kindness. Here is meant unrequited kindness of no benefit to the giver. True kindness by human beings is a manifestation of the mind of the universe operating within them. It is evidence of something there beyond the particles of which they are formed. If this is not true then it's up to scientists to prove it's not the case because an enormous number of folk have found it to be so. Stephen Hawkins' theory of everything is brilliant but his *everything* may not be everything. That puts the boot on the other foot. Poor Fred, the ultimate analyst, could not stomach the thought that all was not as his text-book predicted and when he found life cells on Mars similar to the Earth's he realised that he had falsely based his understanding on the assumption that science and evolution explaining everything. This realisation and a touch of CD perhaps sent him over the top as we saw. If there is even an element of veracity in all this it leaves the door ajar for another influence in the universe way beyond what we have discovered so far. *So far* must always be added as a limitation on our deductions. If a Neanderthal man saw us using our mobiles he might assume we were praying, and in one sense we would be. As time progresses, we might discover more about the character of the universal mind, how it operates, how individuals can tune into it and pray, how prayer works and so on. In ancient times, it would have been expressed as God continuing to reveal more about his nature.

And finally, to return to immortality, Steve had been happy when on Earth to entrust himself to the terrestrial internet, all his writing, his learning, his medical records and even the money in his bank account (such as it was). All this was stored as electro-mechanical impulses in the ether. His bones and flesh, his physical molecules, might have walked the Earth for a period but the real *him*, his mind, his soul was up there in the ether as photons of thought. He realised now that whether his body left the Earth for Mars or whether his body disintegrated through death and left forever, the real him would still exist in these everlasting photons of thought. (As we noted earlier, scientists have indeed found that individual photons can positively bond and interact irrespective of distance as well as the time—try putting photon entanglement into Google). For some, this adds up to a comforting view of where we are going when we leave the planet. It is certainly an unknown realm but also weirdly exciting that even we become a little part of the universal mind and share its immortality.

Coming down to Earth after all this heady stuff, Steve realised there was a real difference between our body leaving the Earth for Mars and leaving for eternity in that one could return to Earth from Mars but not from eternity, except as ghosts. This set him thinking about whether he himself should be returning to Earth.

39

Marching Orders

AS PEOPLE CONTINUED to arrive in their droves, the Earth authorities began to become concerned about the increasingly independent stance taken by the Martian community. Growth of the colony was dependant on the flight timetables which were subject to the constantly varying distance of Mars from the Earth and the passenger capacity of the droves which varied with the freight payload transported. Flights to Mars had become relatively safe but the flights back still had their hazards although most of the departure technicalities had been overcome. All droves now had 5 legs rather than the original 3 because, while 3 were adequate to provide a stable arrangement, there were risks should one of the legs malfunction or land on a boulder as we saw earlier when Steve arrived. As there were expected to be around twice as many flights to Mars as there were returning, a store of droves would end up sitting on the regolith near the village. However, as the growth of commercial mining for rare elements on Mars expanded, this would use up this reserve, leading to a balance of Droves coming and going with perhaps just two or three Droves residing on Mars at any one time for an emergency. The people returning to Earth were expected to be scientists and engineers on contracts of two or three years but some terminauts had changed their minds and four who could afford to pay the exorbitant cost of the return flight had already left. The management consisting of the Mars council and some heads of sections were generally on 5-year contracts but some had opted to stay for longer periods. So, all in all, the village was a complex social structure with much coming and going like villages on Earth.

The terrestrial authorities and in particular the Mars committee of the UN had not foreseen the possibility of birth on Mars. As we saw, they deemed the house rules were sufficient to prevent this. Now that it had happened, they were in a quandary. Firstly, would it happen again? Secondly, the news media had gone completely gooey-eyed and were following the day to day life of Maria and her family at the chaplaincy like a soap opera. Baby Maria was the undoubted star; everybody loved her and she became the focus for humanity on the lifeless plains of Mars. Thirdly, it was anticipated that Maria would develop unknown growth peculiarities owing to the effect of the Mars environment and particularly the low gravity. It was one Monday morning after a two-day dust storm that the AP ushered Steve and Jo into his Office. Following some general chat and, of course, coffee, he raised the issue on his mind.

"The UN Committee has requested that I discuss with you both the plans for your future and the future of the Chaplaincy Centre. I should tell you that when Maria was born, they were of a mind to terminate your contract and order you both back. I prevailed on them to delay and hopefully achieve your agreement to a voluntarily return."

"Did they give reasons for my return before my contract expires?"

"Not explicitly," said the AP, "but their concerns over the last few months relate to the childhood experience of

Maria and the publicity afforded to the Mars chaplaincy. I can tell you though that the attention and preoccupation with your family by millions of folk who follow the day to day news bulletins is not always to the liking of the Earth authorities. They recognise that folk are fascinated by the novelty of life here and by the otherworldly aspects of existence it thrusts into the limelight. But the last thing they want is everybody re-examining their lives and the day to day things they have accepted for generations from some ethereal perspective. At its worst, it could lead to a breakdown of structured social norms in beliefs, politics and government. So they want to nip it in the bud and bring you back."

Steve said nothing. He was simply amazed at the influence he was having on so many folk back on Earth by simply going about his everyday business of being a chaplain and attending to the issues and concerns of his Mars parish. His mum and dad and friends had indeed told him in their correspondence but he just thought they were cheering him up as he was so far away. He could think of nothing to say (probably a first), but Jo came in with a practical question for the AP.

"When you said to Steve they want you to go back, did you mean him alone or the family?"

The AP had become a good friend of theirs but he started to look uncomfortable. He delayed answering by offering another round of coffee but finally eased himself back into his chair to face the inevitable.

"The authorities have a dilemma. They would like both of you and baby Maria to return. On the one hand, they are keen that the Mars village becomes primarily a commercial and mining outpost supplying the much-needed heavy elements rather than a colony where people want to live and die with all the consequent social interactions. Most of all, they want the chaplaincy, which in their view has become a distraction, to cease functioning now that its purpose is achieved. On the other hand, they have been advised by the astro-medical experts that a baby should not be subjected to a voyage of several months in a drove with its zero gravity and atmospheric variations because bone growth could be adversely affected. Baby Maria has become such a world star that should anything happen to her the authorities could be held responsible by several billion people. The only solution is that Jo and the Baby stay for much longer, some years I believe, while you, Steve, return alone." He paused and added, "I'm afraid that this is an instruction from them and they insist that I implement it in time for the next Drove departure which as you know is next month."

Jo looked really cross and was about to say something when Steve put a restraining hand on her arm, saying to the AP, "We'll need time to absorb all this. I assume I could resign my post and stay here in some other capacity."

"No, they insist that YOU return," he said firmly. "They would not entertain any other options. I'm sorry about that."

Jo was now looking angry and tearful and Steve gave the AP an almost defiant look as he quickly ushered her out and back to the chaplaincy.

40

Eastern Promise

STEVE AND JO hurried back to the chaplaincy to thrash out their take on this latest development. They needed their privacy but as they opened the door they were surprised to see their friends Chen, Mona and Patrick sitting around the central table waiting for them. The human mind is one of the fastest computers ever devised. Within a few nanoseconds and to their lasting credit, Steve and Jo refocused attention from their own devastating news and registered that others had problems too. There was obviously some issue of importance on their minds as even Patrick was looking surprisingly glum. Jo wiped away the remaining facial evidence of having been upset and started attending to the coffee machine while Steve settled himself down and asked them what was the matter.

Patrick kicked off by explaining that Chen and Mona had both been lonely, there being rather few Chinese folk in the village and so he had invited them to the Mars Bar. They had become regulars over the subsequent months and, although their Chinese taste buds had never developed to the point of liking his Guinness, they obviously enjoyed the ambience and each other's company. They often shared a corner seat and chatted away in their home language well into the evening. He had, therefore, got to know them quite well and they had often had interesting discussions on the world from a Chinese perspective. As a consequence, it was to him that they had turned in their current crisis and he had recommended that they speak with the chaplain. They had agreed to do this but asked him to accompany them, hence his presence there.

Patrick paused, waiting for Chen to take over but since he just sat there looking at the table, he continued and explained that the essence of the problem was that Mona was pregnant with their baby. They had delayed informing the Mars council as it would insist on abortion and this was the last thing they wanted. Also, they were in trepidation at informing their home Chinese authorities who they felt would react badly. Knowing that the chaplain and Jo had had this experience, they wanted to seek their advice in confidence on what to do. Jo who was now serving the coffee gave Steve an odd look which, once again, he was not quite sure how to interpret. Steve thanked Patrick for steering them towards the chaplaincy and asked him if he wanted to stay on. Chen looked up at last and said that Patrick had been very kind in keeping their secret and he would be happy for him to be there. Mona also agreed and it was then that Steve noticed she was obviously pregnant and by many months—why had he not noticed before he wondered. So that was why Jo had given him the odd look. He realised then that preoccupation with his own problems was already beginning to affect his role as an observant chaplain.

He knew both Chen and Mona from previous interactions although they had not been involved with the chaplaincy. It was Mona whom he knew best as she had been in the adjacent pod on his flight over from Earth (and developed a taste for his chocolate limes). They had chatted about their different backgrounds and hearing he was the chaplain she had opened discussions on the different beliefs in her country and the West. Chen was the young, bright electrical engineer who had been locked out of the Dome in the blackout with Captain Peter. It was well known in the village that it was his cool assessment and presence of mind that had saved the day. In some ways, the situation was similar to Jo's and his own and they were right to approach him. On the other hand, they were Chinese and the Mars council would need to confer with the Chinese government. Knowing what had happened on Steve's case and with their government's increasingly authoritarian stance, it was inevitable they would demand an abortion.

Steve explained the various options to them but received a quick response from Chen.

"We have decided to stay on Mars," he stated.

Mona was nodding her accent; they had obviously deliberated on the options themselves and agreed on their position.

Steve said, "But why? Your families and your people would surely welcome you back."

Mona was now shaking her head.

"Steve, as you know from our chats when we were leaving the Earth, the Eastern cultures and religions are different, it would not work out like that. We would be ostracised for disobeying the authorities and letting everybody down and we have promised each other that we will neither be separated nor go back."

There was a lull in the conversation as Steve, Jo and Ben absorbed the resolute nature of their decision. Mona reinforced their position by explaining, "We have made a promise that we shall wander off across the Martian desert in our spacesuits never to be heard of again and face whatever befalls in the next world rather than succumb to the indignity and shame of facing an unfor-giving Earth."

Steve realised once again, not that he needed remind-ing, that the sheer power of love could create a bond which was as strong as any physical interaction between the particles of the universe. But such strong bonding still had to reside within the restraints of the system. He said, "Thank you, Mona, for your clear explanation. I under-stand your reasons but the fact remains you are due to have a baby soon and I will have to inform the AP. I'll also explain your reasons as best I can. There are practical aspects of having another infant on board, more oxygen, more food etc. and he has a duty of care for the whole community."

"Yes, if you could see him over the next day or two, that would be great," said Chen, "because we really can't go back."

Patrick, who had been glum throughout the discourse, then came in as only he could with a thought of his own.

"I will have to place one of those notices about having no children nearer the Mars bar than 2 meters if we are going to have little ones all over the place."

There was laughter all round. Steve realised it had become a little fraught and his frivolous interjection was perfectly timed—thanks, Patrick.

Chen and Mona thanked Steve and left at that point but Patrick hung on and resumed his former sombre expression. Jo went to their private room, feeling slightly disappointed that events had conspired to thwart their own urgent discussion. Steve appraised his friend Patrick carefully for a moment and, noticed that he had lost some weight. He wondered if a health issue was worrying him but Patrick explained.

"I'm seriously homesick. It's not CD or any of these

funny psychological things, it's just that I need to get back to Earth and to Ireland and if I don't I'm afraid I'll go mad. Don't misunderstand me, I like the folk here and some aspects of life but I have to return home. I've got two years still to go on my contract but I will not make that in a sane condition. If I'm not on the Drove leaving in a couple of weeks I'll cling to the outside as it goes and float around the universe forever."

Steve was flabbergasted. Patrick had always seemed so happy and in control, clowning around with jesting banter and inane comments from the operational side of his part-time Bar. But then it was the clowns who were usually unhappy deep down. Steve knew there was no chance of him being allowed back early; they would probably feed him some strong drugs to submerge his true feelings, even from himself, that's the way it worked.

Steve said, "I'm so sorry to hear that, Patrick. How long have you felt this way?"

"I cannot really say," said Patrick, "It started so gradually—maybe three months ago. It's a matter of not seeing the family, missing the banter with the children, arguing with the guys down the pub, nobody ever buying ME a Guinness."

"The last one can be sorted right now," said Steve on cue.

"Thanks, Steve but I'm being really serious."

"So am I," said Steve, "So let's start by walking across the Dome and opening up your Bar and I'll serve YOU a half-pint (sorry about the half, but you know the rules)."

"Then I had better show you how to draw a decent glass of Mars Guinness, indeed, the best on the planet."

Steve then added mysteriously, "I do believe we can work something out to make your life worth living again."

Patrick looked at Steve questioningly for a moment, but then said, "Have you got some marks on you?"

"I didn't say I was paying too," Steve was heard to respond in the distance as they drifted off. But then they had a very serious conversation which was to have far-reaching consequences.

Meanwhile, Jo crept out of their room to clear the coffee cups away from the chaplaincy table. She had been crying in despair. Baby Maria sensed she was upset so she was crying too. Surely they, the authorities, however honourable and respectable and however much they knew best, did not have the right to separate their happy little family. She knew Steve fully agreed with her, at least now he did, but there was no way to circumnavigate the rules. The authorities had decreed that Steve should go and she should remain. Only another miracle, another real miracle could alter it now.

41

A Time to Give Up

TIME WAS ROLLING on and it was now only a few days before Steve departed Mars to return to Earth as instructed by the authorities. Jo seemed to be remarkably resigned to the fact that Steve was leaving. She had been promised that, as soon as Maria was old enough, they would be allowed to travel back but nobody would clarify when that was. She well remembered as a girl having the truth filtered by *when you are old enough* and knew it was the same again and there was no plan to return them in the near future or even at all. Everybody thought Steve seemed remarkably composed as the time approached, in fact almost unconcerned and wondered whether it was his only way of dealing with it. Indeed, he continued his chaplaincy duties as normal with little acknowledgement of his pending departure. When it came to his last Sunday morning, there was a larger number of folk attending than normal but oddly he did not allude to this being his last gathering and seemed to be at ease as if a great burden had been lifted from his shoulders. He spoke from an obscure book in the Old Testament of the Bible.

All ministers of religion, whatever their affiliation; hope to receive a text or a *message* on a topic from their Holy Book as a basis for their next sermon. On a good day, that happens; on a bad day, they may have to resurrect a sermon from the past. In Steve's case, it was the

313

Holy Bible which he considered the most wonderful book ever. Not a historical or scientific reference book, nor even a book for religious folk alone (although they often claimed it for themselves) but an ancient diamond mine with the precious stones buried deep in unexpected places among the myths and fables of the past. He had opened it around the middle to reveal the familiar passage in the Book of Ecclesiastics (NIV: Ch 3: Verse6) and stared at it. Buried there among the many things for which we should make time, a time for this and a time for that, he read,

There is a time to search and a time to give up.

He had found as chaplain that constant searching was very wearisome. It was a time to give up searching, to go with the flow and rely on grace. Perhaps it was a nudge to act on what he had found rather than forever seek. At best his searching could only take him a few steps towards a very distant goal; hopefully, those few steps had been in the right direction. The important thing it seemed was to act out of that part of love that is kindness. Kindness is the part of us that comes neither from physical matter nor the natural selection process but from the eternal information out there, from the universal mind, from God. This, he explained as best he could to this last gathering and he felt they now understood; the message had been received. Now, he had to act it out himself.

On the day of departure, the group of over twenty people due to return to Earth were assembled in a section of the Central Dome cordoned off as a departure terminus. This was the largest group to leave so far and consisted of those who had completed their contracts together with a few who had medical issues and a couple of the terminauts who had changed their minds and had enough marks to pay for the return trip. As it happened, he was returning on the refurbished Drone 5, the very one on which he had arrived but with many adaptions to the landing equipment. It was sitting atop the final rocket stage, also refurbished from an earlier flight and now charged up with precious fuel from the Mars storage cylinders. Ostensively, the passengers seemed happy enough but there was an undercurrent of apprehension because, although gravity on Mars is less than half that on Earth making it easier to leave, the fuel had been restricted to the absolute minimum. Furthermore, for the first time, some of the rocket propellant had been processed on Mars from the carbon, hydrogen and oxygen available on the planet. Also, for the first time, the people leaving were clad in a new design of very lightweight space suit which covered the whole body but gave more flexibility. It was difficult to see into the face masks from the outside so they had stitched little name tags on each suit for easy identification.

Several, including Steve, had asked to go to the toilet as late as possible owing to what they called their own propellant issues. Indeed, Steve was the last to return and they had sent out an urgent Tannoy message for him to join the departing travellers immediately. The management team responsible for departure assumed (and some hoped) that, being the chaplain, he must be praying for a safe journey. Furthermore, he was the only one having to say goodbye to his own Martian family so they tolerated the delay.

The silver-clad travellers with their black name tags and lightweight helmets then filed past the group of well-wishers, these being all the good friends and acquaintances they had made in their time on Mars. Virtually, everybody was there baring those involved with the engineering and control of the rocket itself. Among them was Jo holding baby Maria who had uttered her first word, 'Ma', only two days before. (Jo assumed it was Mama meaning mother but others wondered if it was her first attempt at Mars, the only world she had known and would know for some time.) Jo was not at the forefront of the group but keeping a low profile which seemed odd to some of those present but others wondered whether they felt the pang of parting in public would be too painful. Both Chen and Mona had been allowed to stay on Mars meanwhile in spite of the annoyance of NASA and the Chinese government and Jo was delighted at the prospect of another baby on Mars. The reprieve was actually more to do with their work, particularly Chen's as the electronic wiz-kid; he was just too valuable to release back to earth. As the travellers proceeded to walk down the long passage to the Drove, the village residents waved and cheered. It was impossible to tell from a distance who was who as they all looked the same in their silver spacesuits and dark helmets and the name tags were just too small to read. Finally, the five crew members, also in spacesuits but more bulky and substantial ones in yellow walked down the passage and the onlookers nervously hung around the Central Dome for the next hour until the lift-off procedure commenced. That would be the end of an era for Steve McKay and also for those remaining as they would no longer have a chaplaincy providing a retreat from the utilitarian coldness of their metal and concrete surroundings. How would they survive and how would the new babies develop, never having seen their motherland or the green green grass of home?

42

A Final Revelation

WHILE SEVERAL RESEARCH rockets, two unmanned Droves and two manned ones had left Mars for Earth before, it was still a risky flight. Some years earlier, one of the research rockets had missed the Earth and was drifting around space and the first of the manned Droves had crashed rather heavily on the Earth owing to parachute problems resulting in a fatality. While these issues had been successfully addressed, it still created a palpable tension among the villagers. People wandered around or clustered into small groups and chatted about inconsequential things while not mentioning the pending lift-off when their good friends would return to the Earth.

Half an hour before the 6:00 pm lift-off, Assistant President Leskovich felt somewhat lonely and drained, not desolate but bereft of anybody with whom he could chat in confidence at this important time. The stress of the last few weeks was beginning to tell. He had been circulating among the others offering words of support nearly all day and needed to sit down. At 56, he was older than many of them, indeed, practically, all of them except the terminauts who tended to cluster together as old folk often do. Some of the terminauts had fallen foul of the Mars pandemic but those remaining were remark-ably self- contained and seemed to be particularly happy considering they had come to Mars to die. He had noticed something odd about them recently and had been trying to put his finger on the reason. It was more than happy, it was as if they were regenerated; in fact, they were looking younger than they were, not older, that was it. Their faces seemed to bloom and their wrinkles had faded and they appeared more content. He wondered if this was just resignation to the final stage of their life or whether it was a physical effect of the low gravity and the consequent ease of body movement, giving them a new lease of life. If this was indeed the case, Mars would become saturated with terminauts seeking their nirvana in times to come and this would lead to the rapid growth of the colony.

Normally, he would chat with Steve about such things because he was receptive and would share his inner thoughts for better or worse. On earth, in earlier times, the AP would have steered clear of anybody with a reverend in front of their name but Steve was refreshingly different. Also, he suspected Steve enjoyed having an off-duty friend, even if he was the assistant president, who could tolerate his wicked sense of humour. Such a pity, he would no longer be around, he would really miss him, but there was always Patrick and his Irish banter. That's a point, where was Patrick; resting up no doubt in readiness for opening up for the evening? He knew Patrick had desperately wanted to go back to Earth but he had to decline his request; after all, he still had two years of his contract to run and he was doing useful work. He was also the proprietor of the Mars Bar and while this was technically a secondary activity of his, it had become a significant feature of the Mars community. Talking of which, he thought, that's just the place to sit quietly and relax for half an hour and, although he didn't admit it to anyone, worry a little about the immanent Drove lift-off.

318

Patrick did not open the Bar until 6:00 pm but being the boss, the AP had a master key so he would let himself in and sit there quietly; it would give Patrick a surprise when he came in and maybe he could console Patrick a little about not going back to Ireland. Immediately after the departure of the spaceship, the Bar would no doubt be crowded out. He made his way there, fiddled with his master key in the door lock for a moment and then successfully opened the door and crept in. But the pub was not empty.

Behind the bar, tidying the half-pint glasses was not Patrick, but Steve. For a moment, the AP was entirely disorientated by shock—had he had some sort of break-down, was he seeing things, had the strain been too much. He slumped down thinking he had lost control. But only for a moment; the human brain is definitely the fastest computer around and his mind refocused immediately as he stared at Steve who stared back, mesmerised by this early appearance of the AP himself in the Bar.

They continued to stare at each other until the AP broke the spell by saying, "So, you've remained and Patrick's taken your place on the Drove?"

Steve restrained himself from asking if that was a statement or a question, it was not the time for quibbling, so he explained slowly and carefully.

"He would have gone mad and wrecked the delicate balance of social life here being such a popular figure. It had to be done."

"And of course, you were only too pleased to stay here... er... in the interests of the community despite the ruling?"

"Something like that," admitted Steve.

"And Jo?"

"She's the only other person apart from my parents

who knows. They kindly said they understood but still look forward to seeing their lovely granddaughter on a future trip."

The AP now realised why Jo had appeared latterly so restrained and receptive of Steve's departure.

He said, "You realise that this will be viewed as an act of mutiny by the authorities on Earth and will lead to dire retribution. At the very least, you and I will both lose our positions, you for insurrection and me for lack of authority. The whole Mars council will be held responsible for lax governance."

Their eyes locked for a moment, then the AP seemed to relax a little and added, "Although I can tell you the Mars council is about to be denigrated for failing to operate Earth policies, in any case, and, as they say, if you're going to be hung for a lamb, it might as well be for a sheep."

Steve remembered when he had last had that quoted at him and was thinking it always seemed to lead to trouble. The AP was continuing.

"—and there won't be a bunch of roses for Patrick when he gets back."

"We discussed that at length and Patrick is prepared for the disgrace and the possibility of a custodial sentence but reckoned it was worth it if he was back on Earth and in God's country, as he called Ireland. He also reckoned he could survive afterwards by giving after-dinner speeches around the world and enjoying the associated entertainment."

"And what about the folk here on Mars when they discover that it was Patrick in the spacesuit instead of you?"

"Most realised that Patrick was unhappy behind his convivial veneer and will probably assume it was agreed by the Mars council and yourself; as you once said to me, sometimes it's best not to disabuse folk of their firmly held assumptions."

The AP wasn't sure he remembered saying that but went on to ask, "And you, what are you going to do?"

"Well, I'll have to give up being chaplain, at least for a time; I've obtained too many black marks on my priestly record. Also, I promised Patrick I'd cover for him at the Mars Bar until somebody else is found—he even showed me how to serve a decent half-pint of Guinness."

The AP was silent for a time and then said, "So, purely out of kindness for Patrick and love of Jo you determined to stay and let Patrick go in your place?"

"Not quite purely; there was an element of self-interest as I myself wanted to stay here longer too; if nothing else, it's conducive to deep thinking," said Steve, adding, "At the end of the day, you have to decide what you want to do and who you most care about and act accordingly. The inevitable trail of those whom you have upset may haunt you but it is better to have done some real good for some rather than appease the many."

There was an awkward silence, so Steve added, "And I've always wanted to run a Bar—I could be the new Mars barman."

"Actually, I'd like you to continue as chaplain and keep the chaplaincy operating for the foreseeable future. It has been a most successful feature of Mars life and as we become more independent of Earth we need a focal point for our broader thinking. I never thought I'd see it that way but there you are."

"Thank you," said Steve, "and the Mars Bar?"

"Are yes, the other successful institution," muttered the AP, but very absent-mindedly because he was suddenly absorbed with his iPad.

"Well, that's great. While we've been talking, the Drove made a successful lift-off so there'll be a lot of folk wanting to celebrate in the Mars Bar in a few moments."

During the intense conversation, they had almost forgotten the important events going on around them. They both looked greatly relieved and fell silent for a moment.

The AP then said, "It's just gone 6 pm. I thought the rules were that the Mars Bar opens sharp at 6 pm."

He looked up and met Steve's questioning look and added, with a wee twinkle in his eye, "And we would not want the new part-time barman falling foul of the rules on his first day, would we?"

———————————————